Sheri Murphy is a meditation instructor, Reiki master/teacher, and African Violet enthusiast. She received her B.A. in English and Book Arts at The University of Maine at Machias and went on to earn her M.A. in English Literature from Mercy College. She has traveled broadly, living in New Mexico, coastal Ireland, and Cape Breton Island. She presently lives and writes in a secluded village in coastal northern Maine with her writing partner, Baby Basil, a magnificent black and white Maine coon cat.

This work is dedicated with love to my sons:
Rob Galbraith, Matty Galbraith, and Joshua Luman.

Sheri Murphy

IN THE SERVICE OF THE KING

AUSTIN MACAULEY PUBLISHERS™

LONDON * CAMBRIDGE * NEW YORK * SHARJAH

Ordering Information:
Quantity sales: special discounts are available on quantity purchases by corporations, associations, and others. For details, contact the publisher at the address below.

Publisher's Cataloging-in-Publication data
Murphy, Sheri
In the Service of the King

ISBN 9781643783710 (Paperback)
ISBN 9781643783727 (Hardback)
ISBN 9781645367604 (ePub e-book)

Library of congress Control number: 2019907828

The main category of the book — Young Adult Fiction / Fantasy / Contemporary

www.austinmacauley.com/us

First Published (2019)
Austin Macauley Publishers LLC
40 Wall Street, 28th Floor
New York, NY 10005
USA

mail-usa@austinmacauley.com
+1 (646) 5125767

I would like to thank Joshua Luman and Steve Chambers for their constant help and encouragement; Angela Bast, my dear friend, who was always helpful throughout the writing process; and my sister, Kathy Austin, for always believing in me. I would also like to thank my amazing professors and friends, Heather Hepler and Bernie Vinzani, along with Dr. Marcus LiBrizzi, Erica Nadelhaft, and Dr. Gerard NeCastro for reading and encouraging me to go on after the first 150 pages. And finally, thank you to Austin Macauley Publishers for giving this first-time author a chance!

Table of Contents

Introduction

When the Tuatha de Danann departed the northern islands of the world, they traveled across the waters to Emerald Isle to train in the magical arts of Druidry, plants, knowledge, and prophecy. From the most powerful of the tribes of the Tuatha de Danann, the tribe of Dal gCais, dwellers on the River Shannon, two of the most skilled in the magical arts joined in holy union and gave birth to a son, Brian Boruma, who later became the High King of Ireland.

From infancy, Brian Boruma was discouraged from using his magical abilities, and this was his hardest challenge. His parents and grandparents knew that if he showed the slightest hint of his capability, he would get kidnapped and his magic used for evil purposes. In an apparent effort to subdue his powers, his family sent him away to a monastery to learn Christianity. However, in efforts to suppress his magical powers, he became ill. In the few times his skills got the best of him, he was punished and made to stay alone in a cold and damp area of the monastery. Finally, when he was 19 years old, taking only his harp, three golden coins, and a bag filled with bread, cheese, and wine, he ran away to the western shore of Emerald Isle.

Brian Boruma traveled for several days and finally found a remote cave near the ocean where he could rest. After building a campfire on the beach in front of the cave, he ate his meal and began to play his harp. There was no one near or far who could play the instrument as well or as beautifully as Brian Boruma. Magical harmony traveled in melodious sounds through the campfire, the earth, the air, the ocean's waters, and into the spirit realm, filling each of the five elements—earth, water, fire, air, and ether—with the young man's essence. His beautiful, sweet spirit filled every note with images of beauty, love, and courage.

Meanwhile, deep under the shimmering, emerald-green ocean waters, the daughter of Neptune stirred in her sleep. In her dreams, she saw a man lying on the beach, near a campfire, sleeping quietly with a harp under his arm. He carefully handed her a bundle wrapped in a blanket and told her to take it to her father's kingdom and protect it with her life. Suddenly, a different noise came into her dream, a stirring of activity outside her door which awakened her. She rose up out of her giant clamshell bed and floated to the ancient golden door. Looking out the aqua glass window in her door, she saw three of her handmaidens, sea nymphs, arguing with two enormous lobster guards. She opened the door to see what all the commotion was about and discovered that at least part of her dream was real. There was, in fact, a man lying on the beach near a campfire, sleeping with a harp under his arm. Knowing that she would never get past the lobster guards, she quickly grabbed her wand and ran to her secret back window, summoning her narwhale to take her to the beach as fast as possible!

Careful to avoid the guards, the narwhale transported her through ancient underwater caves, through deep crystalline cobalt and emerald waters, until they could see the reflection of The Pleiades rippling through the water, providing a marine compass to the beach where Brian Boruma slept peacefully. Forty feet from the shore, the King's daughter motioned for the narwhale to stop. After swimming the rest of the way to the wet, sandy shore, she focused her eyes on the fire and the young Prince lying nearby, while quietly making her way toward him. As she approached, she noticed a beautiful cloth lying close by, the same fabric that was in the bundle in her dream. Just as she was ready to reach for the material, Brian Boruma woke up!

From somewhere within them, they felt as if they had known each other their whole lives. They recognized one another as beings from a shared future. Both Neptune's daughter and Brian Boruma, having magical lineages, felt a kinship that they had never known in their lives. Beginning with the moment they looked into each other's eyes, they realized their destinies were intertwined, and they instantly fell magically in love.

After spending the night together and realizing that both of their parents would be sending out search parties, they decided to voyage together to the Slieve Mish Mountains, where they would remain safe. Holding hands and talking all the way, they walked on, stopping to rest and take their sustenance periodically. This account is the story of their lineage.

Chapter One
Solomon's Tower

Upon hearing the familiar early morning rooster's crow, Niamh woke up peacefully out of a deep and dream-filled sleep, a little chilled from the crisp autumn air. After wrapping her knitted, gray woolen shawl around her shoulders, she tiptoed to the window, as was her usual early morning habit, to look at the Owenglin River flowing peacefully by her father's property. The Owenglin was mighty and robust as it wound its way through Connemara but slowly relaxed as it passed her old homestead, nestled at the foothills of the Twelve Bens Mountains.

As she looked out the window, she took in the beautiful scenery; first noticing the cornstalks just turning golden beige from the crisp autumn air, waving so gently in the river's breeze. The mountains, with their lavender essence in the early morning, were lit by the golden sun, just barely peeking over the horizon, causing sparkling diamonds on the face of the river. The billowy cumulous clouds were white-tinged with deep rose and lilac, as the dawn manifested into the day. They floated gently by, guided by the soft morning winds coming off the mountains. Taking in all this beauty always made Niamh feel blessed beyond measure. Looking out her window in the early morning was her favorite part of the day.

After she cooked breakfast for her father, Liam O'Brien and her brother, Donal who was two years older; Niamh completed her chores and usually went walking. She loved to walk along the wildflower-laden riverbank. Her mother, Brigid, bless her soul, had been missing for almost two years and the responsibility of the household and cooking rested solely on Niamh. She missed her mother terribly but chose to be responsibly content, in spite of it all.

After washing up and serving the two men breakfast, she finally sat down with them to eat. Her brother, Donal, had a twinkle in his eye as he looked upon her and said, "*Go mbeire muid beo ar an am seo aris,*" (*may we be alive at this time next year*). Niamh smiled embarrassedly as his words reminded her that today was her twenty-first birthday.

"When you finish your meal, come along outside and see your present," her father urged.

"What do you think you are doing, getting me a present?" she responded with a shy smile.

"Oh, we thought you might be deserving of something special this year," Donal teased.

After Niamh cleared up the kitchen dishes and put the pans in the sink, Donal pulled a faded blue handkerchief out of his pocket and teasingly blindfolded Niamh and led her outside.

"Where will you be taking me off to, Donal? Are we going off to The Twelve Bens?" she asked him playfully.

"No, Sister, only to the field, and don't you go tearing at that handkerchief, understand?"

They walked for a minute or two more, across the field to the fenced-in area where their cows lazily ate the last of the summer grass. Suddenly, Donal removed the faded handkerchief from her eyes and there in front of her was the most beautiful horse she had ever seen. She was speechless and stood there staring for what seemed like an eternity.

The horse stood about 17 hands high, with a regal stature, head held high and proud. His coat and mane were pure white and glistened with the golden glow of the mid-morning Connemara sunlight. The horse appeared to be covered in sheer golden stardust. His eyes were a vibrant green with golden flecks, surrounded by black as if outlined in kohl like the ancient Egyptians.

"But how? Why? How can we afford this? How did you get him?" she stuttered, while a million scenarios raced through her mind. "I must be dreaming, Father," she said while quickly rubbing her eyes. Niamh was unaccustomed to receiving gifts, other than handmade clothing, shawls, or scarves and occasionally a book. In her wildest imagination she wouldn't have believed that she would receive anything as unique as a horse.

Niamh gently approached the horse, speaking to it in a soothingly low tone, making sure not to frighten him, and giving him time to get used to her presence. The horse acted as if it knew her for a very long time, allowing her to stand next to him while she smoothed his coat with her soft touch. There were two horses on the property, used for plowing and occasional errands, but they were not considered to be anything other than workhorses.

"Has he a name?" Niamh questioned, hoping in her heart that she could have the privilege of giving him a suitable name.

"He will when you come up with one. He has already been saddle-broken and he's all yours," Liam replied.

Niamh softly grabbed her brother's hand and walked toward her father so that she might embrace them both at once. Her heart felt as if it would burst with joy as she held them both close, thanking them for this blessed gift. Liam offered her the use of her mother's saddle but told her that it was still at the leatherworker's shop for repairs.

"That's fine, Father, I'll ride him without a saddle," Niamh said determinedly as she grabbed his mane and climbed on her horse.

"Let's go there, Fintan," she said as she clicked and gently brushed her heels into him. He started off with a slow walk, and as Niamh looked back at her father and brother, she said, "He is Fintan Wild Fire," as she urged him to gallop toward the river.

"Look at her ride. No one would ever suspect that she hasn't ridden since she was a wee lass," her father proclaimed proudly.

"She's a natural, and that's a fact, Papa," Donal said as he shaded his eyes from the sun, trying to get a focus on Niamh and Fintan racing along the river's edge.

Niamh couldn't believe the feeling of freedom she experienced while riding and how well Fintan handled the narrow trail along the riverbank. She looked like a vision with her long, pale, blond hair catching the sunlight and Fintan's white coat glistening with droplets of golden sun. She was amazed at how perceptive Fintan was and how she only had to think something and he would respond. As soon as she felt that she should turn around and race back to her brother and father, still standing in the corral watching her, Fintan turned and began running toward them. When she thought that she should slow down as she approached the men, Fintan slowed to a steady trot.

"Donal, he is perfection!" she cried out happily as Fintan walked toward them.

"You sure picked the right name out, Sister. He looked like a wild, white fire racing along the river."

"Papa, I'll start on my chores as soon as I brush him down," she said as she dismounted and headed to the barn, followed by Fintan.

Her father nodded to her, unable to smile from holding back tears as he remembered his wife, Brigid, who could ride like the wind. As Niamh grew in years, she reminded him more and more of her mother, who left walking one night to help a sick neighbor and never returned. A storm had come up suddenly out of the blue, and as night fell, the family assumed she was staying with the sick neighbor to avoid going into the storm and were sure she would return in the morning. The neighbors never saw her, and she never returned, her family believing she might have blown into the river, despite never finding her body.

She would have made her mother proud, Liam thought tearfully, remembering how Brigid doted on her children. She was unique and carried a special love for all people, but especially for her children. Brigid knew the ways of the sea and the ways of the plants and herbs and seemed to have a special knack for healing sick people and animals. She handled all of her patients with love and concern, never accepting a penny for her work. She referred to it as her 'job' or her 'work' and felt very blessed when called upon.

Niamh's short ride along the river was all it took to connect her heart to Fintan's. They both knew that destiny had arrived and their lives would be forever intertwined. She left Fintan standing outside the barn while she went inside to retrieve a brush when out of the corner of her eye she noticed a faint golden object glistening. Upon turning to see what it was, she found a worn brown leather satchel, one she had never seen before and thought it must be something that came along with Fintan. Picking it up, she realized that the glistening she saw out of the corner of her eye was a golden medallion embedded into the front of the leather. She would have to ask Donal about it later, but for now, she had to hurry to brush Fintan and get to her chores; before she left, she decided to wipe the tarnished part of the gold medallion to see the image.

Picking the handkerchief that Donal had blindfolded her with out of her pocket, she walked toward the old worn satchel that was sitting on an oaken barrel and picked it up. As she began to rub the medallion, an image became defined and more precise. An ancient symbol, one that Niamh recognized from her mother's journals, started vibrating. Niamh noticed that her heart began beating wildly with the same intensity as the medallion's, yet she continued to rub the emblem as there was one section that was still tarnished and unclear. Her heart felt like it was no longer her own, beating so loud in her ears that she felt as if her head would explode.

Suddenly, Fintan, who had been standing close to her, lowered his neck while pushing his muzzle into her shoulder. Without thinking, she climbed on his back and held on tightly to his mane with her right hand while clutching the leather bag's handle with her left. Upon leaving the barn, Fintan quickly picked up speed and ran with her in the direction of the Slieve Mish Mountains, which appeared magically in place of The Twelve Bens.

Racing along the trail, Niamh was calm and her heart was beating regularly once more, yet she was not herself. The intensity to reach an unknown destination had taken over her every thought, and she knew that whatever she was about to experience, Fintan would be there protecting and watching over her. She was deep in her thoughts as Fintan swam across the river with her on his back with no concern for the chilled water currents. Fintan lowered his head and moved it to the left so that Niamh could throw the leather satchel around his neck, freeing up her left hand so that she could have a better hold on his mane before reaching the roughest river current.

As soon as she grabbed his mane, a wind blew from the north, a dark wind called *Gaoth tuath-Dubh*. These winds were known to bring intensity and held sovereignty over all other winds. The sky suddenly became overcast and charcoal gray. The *Gaoth tuath* wind pulled her shawl from her shoulders and carried it away, yet Niamh held on tight to Fintan as they continued forth through the chilled autumn water and onto the other side.

Still racing, Fintan knew instinctively where the trail was that led up the east side the mountain. The path was rarely used and overgrown, yet it had been used in the old days by the kings of Ireland. A little more than halfway to the top, Fintan stopped. He smelled the air and seemed to recognize the area and then lowered to allow Niamh to dismount. He slowly walked away, leaving her standing alone. She began gathering twigs and moss from the nearby trees to build a fire, as she had become increasingly aware of her chilled, wet condition.

Fintan, knowing that Niamh was safe, quickly walked through the overgrown trail and climbed higher until he came upon a native standing stone, then turned left to go deeper into the brush and finally came to his destination. What appeared to be a grass-covered rock was a cave, and Fintan knew that the opening was on the other side. As he made his way around the massive outcrop, he stopped to smell the air. A faint hint of woodsmoke assured him that Niamh had been successful in starting the fire, so he continued forward until he reached the opening to the cave.

The cave didn't smell like other caves, dank and murky, but felt clean and sacred, with a slight hint of angelica root, which was quite familiar to Fintan. He walked inside, and when his eyes adjusted, he carefully pushed open the top of a hand-carved olive wood trunk and there, lying on top, was the gift he was about to give Niamh. Carefully grabbing it with his teeth, he worked his way out of the cave and back to the campfire. As the white horse approached Niamh, he noticed how she had carefully built a fire with the opening to the mountain to keep the winds from blowing it out.

She hasn't forgotten the ways, he thought to himself, and as soon as he had the thought, Niamh turned from the fire to look at him.

Aware of Fintan's thoughts, she asked, "What ways, Fintan?" then suddenly noticed what he had in his mouth. She got up from the fire and walked toward him, curious as to how and where he found anything on this remote mountain. As she took the gift from Fintan's mouth, she realized it was a beautiful, thick green woolen cape with ermine skins surrounding the opening and the hood. She was startled by the beauty of the wrap yet somehow recognized it. Fintan held the corner of the cloak in his teeth as Niamh put it on and pulled the hood up over her beautiful white-blond hair.

She is more beautiful than ever, thought Fintan as he gazed upon the beautiful Niamh, wearing the cape that had been her own in ancient times. There was not a mark or stain on the mantle and it smelled of angelica root and pine. Niamh hadn't noticed the symbol embroidered in a rose-colored thread on the front of it, the same symbol embedded in the gold medallion on the satchel that they brought with them from the barn.

Niamh had no words, only profoundly hidden emotions. She felt thankful to Fintan and hugged him tightly as a whirlwind of memories surrounded her, waiting for the right moment to enter her heart. She held on to Fintan's neck, hugging him, pouring love into him for what seemed like an eternity. The pain she felt from the loss of her mother began to surface, alongside an inner strength that had stayed buried deep inside her heart for the last two years. A skill used by many with the loss of a dear loved one is to shut down the emotions and bury them deep inside.

When Niamh recognized the pain in her father and brother's eyes at the wake and funeral of Brigid, an inner strength rose up inside her. She felt determined to take care of them and keep the household running as her mother had. As devastated as she was by the loss, she never cried. Instead, she continued to bring joy and strength to what was left of her family, holding on to the hope that her mother was not dead and would return with tales of being on an island somewhere, unable to return until the appointed time. To her, the empty pine casket at the funeral was a sign of hope that Brigid wasn't dead, yet to her father and brother, burying the empty coffin was final.

The hardest day Niamh had since losing her mother was when Breandon McKinney showed up and needed Brigid to help with an infection in his hand that occurred when a fishhook caught him. Breandon was a young man who was taking over his elderly father's fishing business. He had been out to sea and hadn't heard that Brigid was missing. He showed up with three sizeable, silvery codfish hanging from a line in exchange for Brigid's help. Niamh was at the sink, filling a washtub when Breandon knocked, so Donal answered the door.

"Donal, I brought fish to trade for your mother's healing touch," Breandon said smiling, while holding up his catch for Donal to admire.

"You are here too late, Brean, she's gone!" Needing air and unable to talk, Donal pushed past Breandon and walked away tearfully. Getting a glimpse of Niamh still standing at the sink, Breandon walked inside and, as he approached her, he collapsed into an old wooden kitchen chair and wept. It was Niamh who comforted him with soothing words and hot tea, rather than him reassuring her. She told herself that she had to be strong, every minute of every day.

As Breandon talked about how sweet and kind Brigid was, Niamh's sorrow was almost too hard to contain. When she thought she would break out in tears, she made a choice. Rather than allowing herself to cry, she excused herself and went to her mother's pantry, where Brigid kept her remedies and found the herbs to make a poultice for Breandon's swollen, red hand.

She boiled some water and arranged the herbs in a small muslin pack. After the water in the large cast-iron pot cooled down to a warm temperature, she held Breandon's hand as she carefully washed it out, draining the pus from the infection gently, then washed it again. She remembered seeing her mother do this many times, and as soon as the skin turned from red to dark pink, she knew that much of the infection had been taken out. The rest would be up to the herbs to pull out the virus that had gone deeper into his hand.

Niamh washed his hand one last time, then applied the poultice, wrapping his hand with a long clean strip of muslin to hold the dressing in place. She took boiled water out of the teakettle to make a cup of tea for Breandon that would break his fever and poured some hot water in a container for herself, this time adding different herbs.

As they sat at the table having their tea, they talked about Brigid and how beautiful and magical she was. They spoke about her knack for curing people, and Breandon mentioned that her 'gift' probably passed on to her daughter, recognizing that he was starting to feel better already.

"Breandon, can I share something with you?" Niamh carefully asked, letting her guard down a little. "I don't believe my mother is dead," she replied gravely, with a determined look in her eyes.

Breandon, thinking he was doing the right thing by helping her face the fact that her mother was dead and gone, grabbed her shoulders gently and said, "She's dead, Niamh. She's dead and gone and she's never coming back. You have to face the facts and realize it so that you can get on with your life."

Niamh sat frozen, staring into his eyes as in a trance. She struggled with his words and argued in her mind, not wanting to hear those words again. It was the hardest day she had experienced. She was kind to Breandon, and realized he was only trying to help her, but hearing those words felt like a stab wound. She recalled that memory of Breandon in her kitchen saying those words to her many times a day, and each time she remembered them, her mind kept saying, '*No, she is alive. I know she is alive.*'

Now, standing next to the warm, crackling fire, holding Fintan around his smooth white neck, her tears finally were allowed to fall. Fintan stood quietly, feeling her pain while it released through saltwater tears into his long, white, silky mane. He would treasure Niamh forever and protect her with his very life, carrying each of her precious tears in his heart as they journeyed together.

"Let's sit by the fire a while, Fintan. I need to rest before we carry on to the top," she said while drying her eyes on his mane.

"Fintan, I know Mother is alive. I can feel it. I can feel her presence with me all the time and I know she is somewhere watching over me, guiding me," she told him softly, with determination.

As she spoke, she took a random twig out of the fire, and with the red end that had been in the fire, traced the image that she saw on the satchel into the ground next to her. As she did so, the symbol lit up, as if made of fire. It pulsated with the same intensity that the medallion had, yet this time her heart did not race. She and Fintan watched it as it slowly vanished into the ground.

"Why do I know this symbol, Fintan? I recognize it and it is important but I don't know why," she questioned, still not realizing that the very same symbol was embroidered on her cape in rose-colored thread. "I know it has something to do with me and that it is important."

Fintan knew that it was time to go to the top of the mountain, and he began walking around the fire, making a circle. As he walked in a circle around it, he held the intention that the fire would remain contained within the ring and that Niamh's tears would be held in a sacred space so that healing might occur within her.

"I'm ready, Fintan, let's go to the top," she smiled softly.

Niamh walked on, sometimes taking the lead, and other times Fintan took the lead. Where the trail was brambles, she rode on Fintan's back until the path became soft grasses again. They worked their way to the top, winding along the trail on the east side, catching glimpses of a white raven, which appeared to be watching them or traveling with them. It was only quick glimpses, though, as the white raven was mysteriously trying to show Niamh that it was there; but it wasn't time to make its presence known yet. White ravens were very rare and hardly seen. If seen, it was in the spring. The white raven was a symbol of Branwen, the goddess of the spring and a daughter of the sea. She represented love and beauty. Perhaps it was because they were near the sea, on the eastern side of the mountain on this particular day, that the raven appeared to them. Maybe it was because today was Niamh's birthday and the day she received Fintan from her father and brother.

Finally, at the summit of the mountain, Niamh saw the ancient green stone tower once used by the kings of Ireland as they watched over the sea and air while making sacred pacts. As she ran her hand across the stones, she realized that the rocks were so close that there was not a single crack separating one from the other. The entire tower was made of green Connemara marble, native to her homeland, and stretched high off the mountain summit, reaching into the misty Irish sky. Upon touching the marble stones, Niamh decided to rest her forehead against the tower while she listened to the waves crashing against the shore far beneath her.

"Fintan, will you wait here or come with me to the top?" she asked.

I will be here waiting for you, he thought.

As she walked to the door, she noticed the same symbol engraved in metal and embedded in the plank. She pulled the old door open and saw a soft golden light emanating from somewhere within, so she quickly found the stairway leading to the top. The steps wound round and round the inside of the ancient tower and had a shiny yet worn handrail made of the same wood as the door. The same scent that she noticed when Fintan gave her the cape was in the tower, yet blended with other scents from the ocean. Salty air, combined with roses and mixed with angelica and frankincense, was a smell familiar to her but buried deep inside some long-hidden recesses of her memories.

Niamh felt that she wasn't alone in the tower, yet she had no fear. She brushed off the feeling and thought that because Fintan was waiting downstairs for her, she was mistaken, and continued her climb. She instinctively trusted Fintan, even if she didn't entirely trust her instincts yet.

She was finally on the top stair when she realized that her feelings were right. A man she recognized from her dreams was standing in the top of the tower, overlooking the sea to the west. She stood still, trying hard to remember what the dream was about before walking completely into the watchtower. She felt like she had been here before, standing near this man while he spoke to her, but she couldn't remember the words.

He was exactly as he was in her dreams, with his brown, wavy hair tied back with a thin, narrow strip of tanned leather to his long, dark crimson jacket and gray woolen pants. She even recognized his unusual dark-burgundy leather boots that reached to right below his knees. He had an intricately knitted, gray woolen scarf wound about his neck that reminded her of her shawl, the one she lost when crossing the river with Fintan. He was very tall, just as she remembered from her dream. Only seeing him from the back, she hoped that he had the same attractive face as the man from her dreams, and as he turned around, she realized that, yes, this in fact was the same man.

His eyes were a soft golden-brown, overshadowed by his somewhat thick black eyebrows. The scruff of his face was complementary to his appearance, giving him the look of a rugged explorer.

"Niamh, have some water," he said as he held out an engraved metal cup to her.

"How do you know my name, when I don't know yours?" she asked as she carefully took the cup from his hand.

"My name is Gabriel," he said as he reached out his hand to greet her. "Do you remember this place?" he asked.

"Yes, but I don't know how I remember it."

"Come over here with me and let's look out to the sea," he motioned to where he had been standing when she first saw him. The watchtower had four openings each facing one of the cardinal directions. The direction they faced now was due west. From this point, she could see the white-frothed waves creating large water mounds as they crashed against the granite rocks below, and looking out further, they could see miles and miles of ocean. While looking in the opposite direction, she could see the River Owenglin and small glimpses of burnished golden land.

Niamh was aware of Fintan's presence far below where she stood, but she couldn't see him.

"Fintan Wild Fire is a fine horse, Niamh. I've known him for a long time. He used to be mine. We have had some interesting adventures together over the years."

Upon hearing Fintan's name, she realized that, like Fintan, Gabriel could read her thoughts and wondered if she could read his, as she did with Fintan, although she hadn't tried up until this point. When Gabriel realized that she was trying to read his thoughts, he put an idea in his mind and held it there until she could see the image he created. The image he held in his mind was the mysterious symbol that had shown up on the satchel, the door, her drawing near the fire on the ground, and on her cape, which she still had not noticed.

"I know your name because I have walked with you in many lifetimes and many dreams," Gabriel explained. "You know me as well but haven't gotten your full memory back yet. I will help you with that, but for now let's watch through this window opening, as I know something is about to occur and am not sure exactly what it is yet."

"How do you know something is going to happen if you don't know what it is?" she asked curiously.

"I can feel it and have gotten glimpses of something but it's still unclear. I knew that you would be here seeing it with me when it happened though."

"Today is my birthday. Will this strange thing that we are going to see be some birthday wish?"

"No, not at all. But think about birthdays, Niamh. Your birthday is the ending of one year of your life and the beginning of a new year of your life. I feel that whatever we are about to see will be a precursor to leading you into the experiences of the next year of your life. I find it fascinating that we are here on your birthday, standing together in this tower, with Fintan below."

Gabriel and Niamh had been standing in the watchtower for almost an hour, exchanging ideas when suddenly the white raven flew in through the east opening and landed on the sill next to where they were standing. It was beautiful, as any raven is, but pure iridescent white, with pale green eyes. Although the raven was magnificent and entirely beautiful to look at, it carried a sense of mystical intensity. An ominous feeling prevailed. Niamh instinctively knew that the arrival of the white raven was a precursor to what they were soon to experience.

Suddenly, the sky turned to a pale lilac-gray, and the gray wind from the northwest, the *Gaoth an iar-thuath-Liath*, began blowing hard past the west window where they were standing and beyond the north window of the watchtower. Niamh knew that this wind could be exceptionally precarious. It was a wind of passage and change, taking influences from both the west and the north. The Irish believed that this wind brought discord and strife, great battles which might even lead to slaughter and bloodshed. Niamh couldn't tell if the wind held this much strength on the ground or if it only appeared to be, because they were so high up in the tower.

Niamh felt the ominous wind's chill, and while pulling her cape closer around her for warmth, her long, tan fingers happened across the embroidery for the first time. She pulled the embroidered part of the cape close to her face so that she could see what it was and immediately recognized the rose-colored embroidery that made up the same image as the mysterious symbol that kept cropping up since she acquired Fintan. She barely had enough time to recognize the symbol when the white raven cawed loudly three times, which led Gabriel to grab for Niamh's hand and pull her close as they peered out the west window... The sky turned from its lavender hue to dark gray, while the winds ceased, becoming perfect stillness.

Within seconds, Niamh, Gabriel, Fintan, and the white raven saw what they had all come to see. Three huge dragons, flying out from beneath the dark gray cover of the clouds, flew in from the west. They were dark in color, yet had a metallic outer covering, causing their scales to portray a shimmery movement similar to water. The dark green one was in the lead, flying in front of the other two. He was so close that they saw his large, dark, crimson nostrils flare as he flew over the tower. His talons were birdlike and razor sharp, stretching out in front and behind him as he flew, and his tail was spiked with onyx-tinted, triangular-shaped wedges beginning at his back and extending all the way to the tip of his tail. Flying so close, Niamh thought that this dragon appeared to be larger than any sailing vessel she had ever seen.

The next two voluminous dragons flew close behind the first. Their appearances were similar to the green dragon, but one was chestnut in color and the other was black. Immediately after flying past the tower, the black dragon turned to look into the tower, giving Gabriel and Niamh a chance to look straight into his eyes. His eyes looked murky, like a filmy dark-greenish-brown cesspool, and left a cold chill running through Niamh's bones.

They watched as the dragons gained speed and headed due east, causing Niamh to feel relieved that they had passed.

"Are there going to be more?" she asked Gabriel quietly, realizing that she had a firm grasp of the sleeve of his velvet overcoat.

"I think that is all, at least for now. You noticed that the winds were completely still just before their arrival and while they passed, yet have now resumed. I believe this is a sign that they have all passed through."

Niamh had so many questions but didn't know where to begin. She felt exhausted and needed to rest. Gabriel quietly led her down the stairs and outside, where Fintan was waiting for her. While Niamh spent time with Fintan, Gabriel built a warm fire, carefully tending it against the ocean winds. The sky was beginning to take on the dark, warm, golden tones of late afternoon as the sun slowly started making its way toward the western horizon.

As she sat by the campfire with Fintan and Gabriel, Niamh began to organize her thoughts, accepting yet questioning the surreal experiences of the last few hours. She wondered if she was dreaming all of this yet at the same time knew that it was a reality. It felt comfortable to her as if she had experienced situations similar to this in the past. She missed her dear mother and wondered if Brigid had ever experienced anything like this or knew these things existed.

Gabriel walked over to his pack, which had been lying on the ground under a nearby alder tree, and pulled out some pewter cups and a small pan. He poured some wine for both of them and handed Niamh some bread and cheese from his pack. He opened the bag again and found a small greenish-yellow apple that had orange streaks down its side for Fintan.

"Would you like one of these apples, Niamh? It's a Kerry Pippin, a little on the tangy side but crisp and delicious," he offered.

"Yes, please. I love those. They are from County Kerry, right?" she asked.

"Yes, they are, some of the best around," he replied. "Are you warm yet?"

"Yes, I'm quite comfortable! Thank you for the fire and the food. What is this place?" she asked.

"The kings called it the Tower of Solomon. It was used by the kings of Ireland and Jerusalem for many years as a sacred meeting place and a place where great decisions were made. They came here to see the truth. I know you have a lot of questions, Niamh. For now, though, try to get some rest after you eat. Fintan and I will watch the fire and be here when you wake up. I promise."

Niamh peacefully curled up tighter in her green woolen cape and fell asleep with her fingertips resting on the rose-colored embroidered symbol. She fell into a deep sleep and dreamed of her life in the future, in another place and time. In this dream, she recognized herself as a young woman who contained many of the same strengths that she possessed. In her dream, she became a future self: Trini O'Brien, who had also recently lost her mother. In her dream, John was Gabriel, Fintan was himself, and Old Sheniah, also a healer, resembled her mother.

As promised, Gabriel and Fintan watched over while she dreamed. Gabriel tended the fire and Fintan sniffed the air for any signs of intruders.

Chapter Two
Niamh's Dream

Trini sat cross-legged on the bed, slouching over her notebook, still wearing her long-time favorite faded pink threadbare flannel pajamas, occasionally picking up one of her many worn-out travel brochures and jotting down phone numbers in her notebook. Although she wasn't showered or dressed yet, her two new army-green suitcases, already packed and labeled, sat on the floor by the bedroom door. She still had a couple of hours before leaving her best friend Emily's house to go to the airport, where she would be taking a connecting flight from Hartford to New York, then boarding an Aer Lingus plane for a six-hour flight to Dublin. Deep in faraway thoughts, she didn't hear Emily's mother, Anne, yell for her to come downstairs for breakfast.

Anne was one of the kindest women that Trini had ever known. She looked after Trini just like she did her own daughter, with love and concern. Anne loved to cook and always put her special touch on everything she created, whether it was food or her crafts. She owned her business, The Twisted Grapevine, which was in a barn next door to her house. It was here that she sold all of her unique wooden animals, shelves, and trunks, along with potpourri made from the dried flowers on the property, grapevine wreaths, jams, jellies, and candy that she made herself. Each morning, Anne would wake up early and create a new treat to add to the already filled shelves of the store. During the long winter months, Anne would sit by the fireplace in their living room knitting scarves and hats out of sheep's wool to put in the store.

Trini was in the store late last night, helping Emily and Anne carry some new wooden cats from the shop and then making tiny little grapevine wreaths to put around their necks. Emily came up with the idea one morning to make collars for the cats out of grapevine and decorate each wreath collar with a tiny dried flower. They started off by making five cats with grapevine collars, which all sold in the first hour after the store opened, so Anne stayed up late for the next few nights making fifteen more. Anne made a special one for Trini: a tiny one that would fit in her suitcase. The second time Anne called, Trini heard her and told her she would be right down.

Trini showed up at the table still wearing her faded pink pajamas, carrying her travel brochures and notebook. Anne had made a special treat for Trini for breakfast, which was sitting in the middle of the table. When Trini saw it, she smiled the first smile she had been able to muster in over a month. It was a lime green cake made to look like a turtle, with kiwi slices for its shell and little arms with claws carved out of pieces of kiwi. Trini already knew that it wasn't a dessert cake and probably was made up of something nutritious inside because Anne prided herself on eating healthy foods. Trini saw that she had guessed right when Anne carved into it. Inside, there were layers of bananas, granola, and some heavy yogurt.

"Are you ready for your trip?"

"I suppose I am. My suitcases are packed," Trini answered quietly. "Thank you for the going-away turtle cake. I love it."

Just then, Trini looked outside to the store window they had decorated last night. "The window looks great, doesn't it? We did a good job," she said caringly, trying to change the subject.

She didn't want to talk about the trip, or why she was going. She tried to stay numb and not think, just get on the plane and go. She secretly wished she could always remain numb and was convinced that she would never experience happiness again. She went to that secret place within her heart; that place where people land for a while when they are trying to remain strong and not feel. If you feel nothing, no pain can reach you.

It was only a little over a month ago that she had a happy life with her mom. They were best friends and very close to Emily and Anne. They would all get together on holidays and during the week. Emily and Trini were in the same grade and had the same interests, while Anne and Trini's mother, Eve, were best friends and had everything in common. Both women were divorced, raising their daughters on their own, while each of their ex-husbands had remarried and moved away, never seeing their daughters. They had everything in common, until the boating accident that took Eve's life. Other than Emily, Anne, and a few distant relatives in Ireland, Trini was on her own and feeling numb. She traveled beyond the pain and hurt of losing her mom and into a strange numbness where she couldn't experience joy or happiness, yet neither could she feel pain or sorrow. She told Anne one morning that she felt like a robot, going through the motions of life without any feelings. She couldn't cry or laugh, yet somehow seeing the bright lime-green kiwi turtle cake brought a slight smile to her pale face.

Anne and Emily desperately wanted Trini to live with them forever. Anne even spoke to her about the possibility of adoption. Heaven knows she treated Trini the same as her daughter and had a special love for her. Trini knew that Anne and Emily were sincere and wanted her to stay, but at the same time she knew she had to go to Ireland; that's what her mom would have wanted her to do. Her mom was born in Connemara, Ireland, and moved to the United

States when she was a teenager. She used to tell Trini, "As much as I love my life here in the States, Ireland will always be my home." She wanted to wait until Trini graduated from high school before moving back, and the plan they made together was for Trini to graduate high school and then go to college in Ireland. After Trini's dad moved out, it was hard to get the money together for anything extra, so they never even visited Ireland, never mind move there.

Now that her mom was gone, she knew she had to go. After many conversations with Trini over the past month, Anne reluctantly contacted Sofia O'Brien, Trini's aunt, who agreed to take Trini in and let her go to school there. Trini had only met Sofia once when she visited the States and stayed for a week with Trini's mom. That was four years ago, though, and a lot can change in four years. Sofia was friendly and kind, however, a little reserved. She left Trini out of most of the conversations she had with Eve, which annoyed Trini. Neither her mother nor Anne had ever left her out; welcoming her contributions to all of their conversations. Feeling left out was something that Trini never wanted to grow accustomed to. She would have to make do while living with her aunt. After all, she would be in school during the days and her mom would have wanted her to make these arrangements work out. *Maybe after she gets to know me better, she will be friendlier,* Trini thought at first, but as the days went by, she didn't care if Sofia was that friendly to her or not. After Trini made her decision, there was no turning around.

Now that the day had arrived for her to leave, she knew she would miss Emily and Anne but was anxious to be on her way. She wanted to be away from the town, away from everything that reminded her of the life she had before the boating accident. She didn't want to go back to the same school in the fall and have everyone come up hugging her and telling her how sorry they were that she now had NO parent! Even though her father was still alive, she hadn't seen him since she was three years old and he never made any effort to contact her. No one, including Anne, knew where he was, so even if they wanted to reach him, they couldn't.

Anne, Emily, and Trini ate their kiwi turtle and tried to make light conversation until it was time for Trini to go and take her shower. Right before getting into the shower, Trini noticed a pair of long silver scissors glistening in sunlight from the bathroom window and without a second thought began cutting her beautiful, long hair off! She cut it straight, all the way around, a little longer than chin length. Everyone always told her how beautiful her hair was, and she was in no mood to hear anything like that in Ireland. She wanted to get away from everything, including compliments, where she would have to smile and say thank you and perhaps return the compliment.

She wanted to be left alone with her thoughts, and her numbness. When she looked in the mirror, she didn't recognize the girl looking back at her. It wasn't just the new hairstyle. There was something different about her eyes. They were no longer the eyes of a happy child, but the eyes of a young woman who could feel nothing through her numbness.

After her shower, she quickly swept up all the hair from the floor, tossed it in the trashcan, threw on her jeans and gray sweater, wrapped her handmade burgundy scarf around her neck, and ran a brush through her new hair. When she arrived at the bottom of the stairs, Anne asked her if she was cold. Trini was always cold lately and dressed as if it were autumn.

"I felt chilly," she said, "and it might be cold on the plane."

"Yes, it might be chilly when you get to Dublin, also. It will be dark when you arrive. By the way, I love your new hairstyle."

"Thank you. I'm tired of wearing it long."

Emily and Trini grabbed the suitcases and headed toward the car. It was about a forty-five-minute drive to Bradley Airport in Connecticut, where Trini would be taking a plane to New York then boarding an Aer Lingus plane for her six-hour flight. Emily got in the backseat and Trini sat in the front, with Anne driving.

"I can't wait to learn how to drive," Emily said while brushing some lint off the seat next to her.

What she wanted was to spend time with Trini, her best friend, without anyone else around. She was going to miss all their secret talks and all the fun they'd had together. She did a great job holding back tears, but inside her heart was breaking at the thoughts of having Trini move so far away. Trini told her that she doubted that her aunt would have Internet service, and it was costly to make calls from Ireland. It felt like a huge loss to think that she wouldn't be able to talk with her, never mind see her. After all, they grew up together and had so much in common. Trini knew all of her secrets and she knew Trini's. She thought that she would never be able to find a friend like Trini in the whole world. Their friendship had the quality of a once-in-a-lifetime friendship, one that was so rich and close that nothing could ever separate them from one another

Both girls, as well as Anne, tried to make small talk in the car on the way to the airport, but each of them knew that it was an effort to talk without crying. Before long, they arrived at the airport and said their goodbyes. Trini promised to let them know as soon as she arrived in Dublin and asked that she be able to wait by herself.

"There is no need for you to sit here for two hours, waiting for me to get on the plane," she told them. Anne knew that Trini just wanted to be alone and agreed to go on after she saw that Trini's suitcases were checked in, and she had spoken with the young woman at the check-in counter.

Trini sat by herself in the corner of the check-in area, not reading or talking to anyone, just alone in her thoughts, which was what she wanted. Time went by quickly, and Trini heard the announcement that it was time to board. "Goodbye Connecticut," she said as she got up to board the plane for her journey.

The plane ride from Connecticut to New York was only a little over an hour and went by quickly. The airport in New York, La Guardia was an international airport and much larger than the one in Connecticut. Anne had pre-arranged for someone to meet Trini to help her find her way to the Aer Lingus section of the airport. Once she was at the ticket counter, she stood in line for over an hour before going through the metal detectors to get to the seating area. Trini was thankful that she was so organized and remembered to put her passport in the front pocket of her carry-on backpack, making it easy to get. She took it out and gave it another look. There she was, smiling with her long, beautiful hair. She hated to look at the photo because it brought back too many memories of the days that she and her mom spent together and how happy they had both been.

On the plane, Trini's assigned seat was next to the window. She was one of the first to board, and after putting her carry-on in the storage unit above her, she slumped down, putting her knees up on the seat in front of her. She felt cold and tried to rewrap her scarf closer around her neck so that it would cover her ears and chin. She crossed her arms and closed her eyes, yet remaining aware that people were moving around, finding their seats, and opening and closing the storage above. Two seats were attached to hers, and she knew that the plane would be full soon and dreaded having to talk to anyone.

As she looked out the window, she wondered what it would be like to live in Ireland and whether she could find the reasons her mother had loved it so much. Each conversation that her mother had with her about Ireland began flooding her memory, so quickly that she didn't even notice when the other passengers sat down in the seats next to her and were startled when someone in the seat next to her spoke.

"How's it going?" she heard through the mists of her memories. It was a dark-haired boy who looked to be a couple of years older than she was. She just nodded her head and tried to ignore him.

"I'm John," he said, stretching out his hand to shake hers. Trini reluctantly put her hand forward to shake his and noticed that he had blue eyes and was wearing an army surplus jacket and jeans.

"Hi," she said without smiling and turned to look out the window.

"So," he said, smiling, "looks like a good day to go to Ireland."

She didn't respond, but turned away and closed her eyes, resting her head against the window. He took the hint, grabbed a book out of his carry-on, and began to read. After the plane was high in the sky, Trini fell fast asleep and deeply into a dream.

Chapter Three
Trini's Dream

She was in a museum, but not one that she recognized. There were books all around the displays on very high shelves. She identified many of the books as being the same ones that were in her house in Connecticut. When her father left, she was only three years old. He left quickly, and Trini's mother kept his study just as it was, never changing a thing. She would go in there perhaps once a week to dust and clean. Trini would help her mom dust and run the vacuum, then carefully look through some of the books. She couldn't read them because they were written in Irish Gaelic, all made of leather, and beautifully bound, but she loved to look at the sketches and symbols drawn in them.

Now, in her dream, she recognized some of the same books. Suddenly, she noticed a golden glow coming from one of the books on the top shelf. She tried to stretch to reach for the book, but it was much higher than she could reach. She went over to the librarian, an older woman with light brown hair and a very stern and stoic manner, and asked if someone could please get the glowing book down for her.

"Oh, no, Luv. This book will have to wait till you're older. You can't read this book yet," the librarian said in a stern Irish accent.

"But *why* can't I read it? I'm old enough now!" Trini demanded, "I have to see this glowing book. How can you say I'm not old enough to read it? Why are you telling me this?"

The librarian ignored her and went back to stamping the insides of a pile of books with an ink stamp, hitting the seal hard on the inkpad in between each stamp, until the noise became so loud that Trini walked back to the shelf where the glowing book was. It was still glowing!

After looking all around for a ladder, and not finding one, she began to jump, and as she jumped the library started shaking. The floors shook, and then the walls, and several books fell off the shelves but not the one she wanted. Suddenly, she noticed a tall boy who had been watching her. He had dark, curly hair and was wearing an army jacket and jeans.

"What are you doing?" he asked. Trini took a closer look and realized it was John, the young man sitting next to her on the plane.

"Please, help me," she pleaded. She might be able to reach the book if John hoisted her up.

"I will help you, only if you allow me to read the book with you," he said quite seriously.

As Trini pulled on the sleeve of his jacket, begging him to help her, she began talking quickly and knew that there was not a lot of time to get the book before it would stop glowing.

"Listen, I can't let you read the book with me because I need to be alone. I want to be alone. My mom died last month, and I'm sad. I just want to be by myself, but I *need* this book, and you can help me because you are tall. Please, help me!" she begged.

"I'm alone too, Trini, so I can help you," he said.

Suddenly, she stopped and stared into his eyes. "What do you mean? Did your mother die too?"

"I don't know because I have lived in an orphanage ever since I was a baby and no one seems to know who my parents are. I've run away, and I'm alone," he told her sincerely.

"Okay then, hurry and hoist me up there, and I will let you read it with me, but we have to hurry," she told him excitedly, as they were running out of time.

"Hurry, please, the glow is getting weaker."

John cupped his hands and Trini put one foot in his hands and held onto his shoulders, balancing herself as carefully as she could as he hoisted her toward the book.

Suddenly, a large, majestic white owl appeared out of nowhere. It began flying toward Trini, flapping its wings and making a loud shrill call, causing her to lose her balance while John steadied his grip on her ankle to help her not fall.

"I've got it," she whispered hurriedly to John as the white owl swooped quickly by her again, causing her to fall to the ground, knocking John down as she fell. They both shielded their faces as the owl flapped ferociously at them. This was no ordinary owl. There was something beyond dreamlike about it, something that felt sinister, and Trini's heart began racing wildly when she looked into its dark, blood-red eyes.

"Give me the book, quickly," John told Trini. She handed it to him and he put it inside the front of his army jacket with one hand while still shielding himself with his other hand from the owl's talons. The book felt hot and was burning against John's chest, but he kept it in his jacket even though the pain of the heat was starting to hurt him.

"Trini, watch out," he yelled while he pulled her closer to him, protecting her from the owl, which made one final swoop in a circle around them. This time, the owl came in so tightly that it scratched its razor-sharp talons into

John's exposed hand, and then it went around again and scratched Trini on her hand.

"It wants the book," Trini said.

"Well, it is not going to get it," John said as he grabbed Trini's hand and ran with her out of the library.

Quite suddenly, when they got outside of the library, they found themselves running in a lush green forest with the owl still flying frantically after them.

"It's getting closer, John," Trini realized when she looked back, still running.

"I know! This book must be exceptional, or it wouldn't want it so badly," he said as he tightened his grip on Trini's hand, pulling her to run even faster.

"I'm getting out of breath. We have to hide or something."

As soon as she said this, she noticed a horse, standing under a tree in the near distance, beside a stream. It was very sleek and shiny, and at first appearance, it looked silver, with a very long white mane.

"Come on, this way!" she pulled John in the direction of the horse. As they approached, she realized it was not precisely silver, but more of a pearly white color. As soon as the horse saw the two running toward him, with the owl close behind, he bolted and ran toward them to help them. Trini knew how to ride but John didn't, so she quickly jumped on the horse and motioned for John to climb on behind her.

"Hold on to my waist," she told him as she grabbed the horse's long, silky white mane and wrapped her right hand carefully around it. She made a soft clicking sound, causing the horse to take off running. The owl was gaining speed and flew close to them with its outstretched talons pointing right at John's head, when the horse suddenly made a quick turn, almost causing Trini and John to fall off, but then quickly turned in the opposite direction, allowing the two to balance themselves.

"John, duck!" Trini yelled as she saw that the horse was racing quickly toward some trees whose branches hung low. She now had no control over the horse and realized that it was leading them rather than her leading it. It seemed to know where it was going. They had to duck very low to get through these branches without being thrown off, and the owl was too big to fly through these thick woods without flying closer to the ground. Now that it had to fly low, it was unable to reach its talons into Trini or John.

Suddenly, Trini saw an ancient, massive stone wall ahead and realized they were trapped. She expected the horse to slow down as the wall came closer, but instead of slowing down, it increased its speed. Trini quickly realized that the horse was going to try to make the jump over the wall.

"Reach your arms around me and try to grab its mane. Stay low!" she shouted back to John just in the nick of time as the horse took to the air and began gliding over the wall. It felt as if they were suspended in mid-air as the horse cleared the wall before landing on soft sand on the other side. They were now next to the ocean, where the horse began walking rather than running. Trini started to be concerned as she looked over at the wall that they had just leaped over and realized that it appeared to be around twelve feet high, at least from where they were on the beach.

She looked as far as she could along the top edge of the wall and didn't see the owl anywhere, but she still felt threatened, as if the owl could suddenly appear over the wall. No matter how hard she tried to get the horse to move faster, it had a mind of its own and seemed to be in control. It walked briskly through the sand until it came to the hard, wet sand where the ocean gently lapped against the shore and suddenly stopped. Trini and John took this as a sign to climb down from off its back and stretch their legs.

"Do you still have the book?"

John didn't need to reach inside his jacket to know that the book was still there, as it had been burning against his chest since he put it in his jacket.

"I do!" he said as he heaved a great sigh and shook his head a little.

"I think we should take cover or at least be close to that wall. If the owl comes back and looks over the wall, it might not see us if we're close to it," suggested Trini.

They started to walk away from the horse, but it blocked their path, not allowing them to pass. As John and Trini moved toward the right, the horse prevented them again. Each time they tried to move, the horse got in front of them, not letting them pass until they realized that the horse was only going to allow them to walk on the beach, following the shoreline toward the left, so they continued forward.

"It wants us to stay on the beach!" said John, and Trini nodded her head in agreement.

"Do you think we are in Ireland?" she asked after walking some distance and realizing that she had never been here before; but this place did have a feeling of familiarity to her.

"I think so. It feels like Ireland, in a way."

The horse continued to walk alongside them, keeping them walking at a pretty steady pace until they saw a curl of pale, gray smoke above the tree line, where it stopped and lifted its head, sniffing at the air. It looked over at both of them and nodded its head up and down as if to say, 'This is right!'

For the first time, Trini got to look in the horse's eyes and realized they were the most beautiful shade of green, almost the same color as grass, but glowing, like grass when the afternoon sun is upon it, with golden flecks of light. She had never seen a horse with eyes like these, never mind a horse that could jump a wall as this one had. She realized she was thirsty and wondered if the horse was, too; and just as she thought that, the horse started nudging her, almost pushing her toward the wall again.

At the same time, she and John noticed an opening in the wall that they might be able to fit through, but the horse was too large. They all walked up to the opening, being prodded by the horse closer and closer until they realized that the horse was trying to get them to go through. Both Trini and John were hesitant, but the horse kept nudging them, letting them know that this was what they were supposed to do. Finally, John grabbed Trini's hand and said, "It wants us to go through, come on! It hasn't steered us wrong yet."

He went through first, and then reached his hand back through and grabbed hers, leading her. Both of them were very hesitant to be on the other side of the stone wall, especially since the owl might be over there; and without the horse leading them, they were on their own.

"Here is a path, Trini. I think we should follow it and see where it leads. This is the same direction as the smoke that we saw over the tree line when we were on the beach," John told her as they carefully made their way over some brambles to get onto the narrow dirt path.

The path was very narrow and led higher and higher through the thick woods, while periodically allowing glimpses of the ocean. Trini looked down to the shore to see if the horse was anywhere in sight but never got another glimpse of it. Whenever she would pause to listen, John would grab her hand and walk faster up the winding path toward the location where they saw the smoke. They could smell the smoke now, in short spurts. It seemed to be carried on the soft breezes, showing them that they were getting close to something.

"I hope there is water wherever we are going. I am so thirsty!"

"I wish that horse had been able to come with us through the wall," she replied.

"Trini, look! Steps!" John pointed out while leading her toward them. The stone steps looked very worn and had little violet and bright pink flowers on either side, which looked as if they were always there and had not been placed or planted.

"Wait here," he told her, "I'm going up there and see what is at the top."

"Not without me you aren't!" she said as she kept up with each of his steps, close behind him.

Trini and John climbed the stone stairs, not being able to see what was at the top, but as the steps continued higher, they realized that they had a good view at one point of the shoreline. As they looked down upon it, they realized that the horse that had helped them was walking down below. When the horse saw them, it reared up, standing up on its two hind legs with one front leg high in the air.

"What do you think it did that for?" asked John.

"I think it wants us to go on!" she said intuitively.

So go on they did, until they reached the top where the land flattened out into a bright green yard with the lushest grass they had ever seen. Sitting at the end of the yard was a white cottage with a thatched roof and a small gray curl of smoke coming out of the chimney. Trini and John stood still for a moment, not knowing whether to yell to see if someone was inside or continue forth to knock at the door. The door was dark green, and fragrant pink roses were growing up white wooden trellises on either side.

"Ready?" asked John, and without giving her time to respond, he grabbed her hand again and led her to the door. John gently tapped at the door and waited. He knocked again. Still no answer.

"Try tapping louder. Maybe someone lives here who can't hear well."

"Someone must live here, judging from the smoke coming from the chimney," he said to Trini questioningly. Trini began to call out quietly at first and then became louder, "Hello. Is anyone here?" she kept up. No answer.

"John, you try!"

"Let's go around the back of the house and see if someone is outside. Maybe they are in their garden," John suggested.

"I have a better idea, I'll go around back, and check, and you stay here in the front in case someone comes to the door."

Trini backed up from the front of the house to see what the best way to get to the back would be. There were a lot of bushes and vines, growing on both sides of the house, so she decided to walk toward the left where she saw, on the other side of the bushes, an arbor with a small picket gate. After opening the gate and going through, she saw the most beautiful gardens in the back that she had ever seen. She would have loved to look more closely at them but forced her mind to concentrate on finding out where the owner of the cottage was, so she focused on the task at hand and did a quick survey of the area closest to the back of the house. After seeing no one in the backyard, she decided to try to find the back door and knock on it.

As she walked around the side of some beautiful flowering purple plant, she saw that the back door was open and decided to yell inside to see if someone would answer her. No one answered! Trini saw a large pitcher sitting on the table filled with something that appeared to be lemonade and two clear crystal glasses, along with a note. Suddenly, her thirst got the best of her and she went inside. She didn't know whether or not to drink the lemonade or let John in first, and she noticed the note on the table, which surprisingly had 'Trini and John' written on it.

She ran to the door and let John in and ushered him toward the table. "Look at this," she said quietly. "There is a note to us. How could anyone know we were coming here, and where could the owner be?" she asked John while handing him the note and pouring the drink into the two glasses.

"What does it say?" she asked while hurriedly gulping her drink.

"I can't tell, Trini. I think it's in Gaelic," he answered while straining to see.

They both stood there trying to decipher the writing, when suddenly they saw that they had left the back door open and heard a whooshing sound outside. A very large black-and-white, long-haired cat climbed down from his window seat and ran to the door, stood up on two legs, and quickly slammed the door shut with his two front paws.

"Lock it quickly!" the cat said.

Without being shocked that the cat had stood on two legs, slammed the door, and spoken to them, Trini quickly ran over and bolted the door while John ran to the front door to make sure it was secure. Then suddenly, it occurred to her that even though she was in a dream, there was a talking cat.

"Can you speak?" she asked the cat, who had the same emerald green eyes as the horse, complete with flecks of gold, exactly like the horse.

"Of course I can," the cat replied. "Can you?"

"Yes, of course, you heard me speaking to John."

"And you heard me speaking to both of you to lock the door!" the cat said matter-of-factly. "I speak Gaelic and English!" it added proudly.

"Can you tell us what this note says?" asked Trini while holding the note up for the cat to read.

"No, sorry. I can't read," he said.

"What is your name?" asked Trini while looking into its beautiful eyes, which reminded her of the pearly white horse with the silky white mane who had helped her and John.

"I'm Basil. I'm a magical cat. I can walk on two legs, speak in two languages, and know my ABCs but can't read yet," he said proudly.

"I wish I knew what this note says," said John seriously.

"It says, *Dear Trini and John. Please help yourselves to my house and my food. The white owl is dangerous to you. Don't let him in, and don't let him have the book. The book is a book of magic and will help you. You will find more information in the bookshelves here. My horse, Fintan, who helped you earlier, will help you again. I'm sorry I can't be with you now, but one of the whales was injured and I have gone to help her heal,*" said Basil carefully.

39

"I thought you said you couldn't read," said Trini tauntingly.

"I didn't read it, Old Sheniah said it to me in Gaelic before she left, and since you cannot understand Gaelic, I said it to you in English," Basil told them.

"And who might Old Sheniah be?" asked John.

"Well," said Basil as he squinted up his hairy face and looked up for a moment while he tried to figure out a way to explain to them who she was. "She is sort of like a person, but filled with a lot more magic than people use. Old Sheniah grows plants and heals things like whales, seals, and birds, and lives here with me. She's my best friend in the whole world, and my other two best friends live here as well. They are the horse you saw earlier, his name is Fintan Wild Fire, and a girl named Dillis. "

"When will Old Sheniah be back?" John asked.

"Whenever she finishes her business. She's out on the rocks now, healing a whale that was caught in a net."

"What does she look like?" asked Trini curiously. She had images in her mind of an old witch-type crone with a long nose and a wart at the tip. Perhaps wearing long, black clothing and a shawl with very old, beat-up, worn-out leather shoes, and handmade knitted stockings with holes in them. She imagined Old Sheniah to have black, beady eyes and smell like a mixture of oils and herbs.

"Ah, there is a photo of her in my room. I'll show you, just follow me," Basil said as he walked on four legs to a room in the back of the house that was sunny and nicely decorated.

"There she is!" He pointed to a photo of a young woman, lovely with long, flowing white hair. She had an intense but pleasant look in her eyes and a very soft smile on her attractive face.

"This must have been taken a long time ago, when she was young?" asked John.

"Two weeks ago, when her son came for a visit," said Basil.

"But this woman looks very young, I thought you said her name was Old Sheniah?" asked John curiously.

"Oh, she is old. Two hundred years old!" said Basil informatively.

"Then how does she look so young and beautiful?" asked Trini.

"She's magic, just like me, and just like Fintan. What can I say?" said Basil as he headed out of the room and into the parlor, leaving John and Trini in his room gazing at the beautiful young woman in the photo.

"Look at her eyes, John. She has the same color eyes as Fintan Wild Fire and Basil. That rich emerald green with gold flecks! She looks so familiar to me."

"We need to get into that book and find out what all this mystery is about," said Trini. Just as she said this, the white owl came screeching and plowing into the windowpane, almost breaking the glass.

"Please come in this room. It is quieter in here. The Old Hoot won't be able to aggravate us in here," said Basil.

As Trini and John left Basil's room, they shut the door behind them, just in case 'The Old Hoot,' as Basil called him, might be able to break the window. At least this way it couldn't get past the bedroom door and into the rest of the cottage.

Chapter Four
The Golden Glows

Trini and John came into the parlor, where there was an old stone fireplace glowing with a yellow-red fire. Trini looked around the room and was amazed at how beautiful it was. There were two matching rocking chairs painted pale green and had hand-painted pink roses on the backs. They had cushioned seats in a beautiful fabric with roses on them that matched the curtains. There was also a couch, upholstered with a material similar to the other fabrics but with bigger roses. There was a beautiful hand-looped rug on the floor, which also had roses and vines on it.

Trini thought that this room, along with the other places she saw in the cottage, did not in any way match the image of an old crone's house. She thought that old crones should have rickety old wooden handmade furniture, right? Everything should be dark and gloomy, with tinctures and dried herbs sitting about, instead of such beautiful, bright, and cheery rooms like these. But, at least these rooms matched the house of the photo of the beautiful woman with emerald eyes that she saw in Basil's room.

"Tell me more about Old Sheniah," Trini asked Basil as she sat down on the beautiful rug next to the fireplace.

"What else do you want to know?"

"Where did she come by all these beautiful things?" John asked.

"We made them!" announced Basil. "We made the curtains, the rugs, the paintings on the walls, the stained glass in the windows, and almost everything in here."

"Do you help her make all this?" Trini asked.

"Well, she helps me more than I help her."

"I think I will just let this go for now," said John, shaking his head in amazement. "I have some other more important things I would like to know. First of all, is it safe to open the book here?"

"Yes, by all means!" said Basil, "You can open it here, but you will need Dillis to translate it for you. I'll go and find her. She's around here somewhere."

Basil left the two sitting in the parlor, staring at each other in wonderment. Finally, John took out the book and Trini sat up on the couch next to him. They both wondered who Dillis might be and why they hadn't seen her anywhere since they came into the cottage. They doubted that Dillis would be outside since the Old Hoot was still out there trying to get in, and also wondered what strange place they had come upon. This was unlike anything they had ever known and there was a sense of feeling like Hansel and Gretel, although this house and its grounds were much more beautiful than any candy cottage could be.

"I'll wait to open it until Basil gets back with Dillis, whoever that is!" said John quietly. He was still wondering if he should open it at all when Basil came back with a beautiful little dark-haired girl following behind him.

"Trini and John, I'd like you to meet Dillis. Old Sheniah found her on the beach a couple of years ago, and she lives here with us," said Basil as he sidled up next to Dillis. Dillis was the most beautiful little girl they had ever seen. She had dark, curly hair, tan skin, and aqua eyes. She had on a short green dress that looked like it was made on a loom, out of natural but soft fabric. She was barefoot but had a tiny gold ring on one of her toes.

"Dillis, can you sit up there on the couch between Trini and John and help them read the book they brought with them?" Basil asked her sweetly. She looked so small that neither of them could believe that she could read; never mind a book written in Gaelic.

"It is a magic book," Basil explained as Dillis touched it. "It is one of the Golden Glows," he said softly, translating Dillis's thoughts.

Dillis gently motioned for John to hand her the book, and as he did, she held it up to her forehead without even opening it and closed her eyes. She had one little finger, her right index finger, pushing into the book, which is how she was holding it up to her head. Trini and John watched while she seemed to be focusing on understanding something. Her eyes, although closed, at times would squeeze further shut and she would let out deep sighs. John and Trini sat in wide-eyed wonder while Dillis continued her process of holding the book to her forehead. John started to ask a question, but as soon as he opened his mouth to speak, Basil waved a paw, motioning for him to be still.

After a ten-minute timespan, Dillis set the book back on John's lap and got up from the couch and walked over to the table where Basil had poured a drink for her into a little metal mug. After taking several slow sips, she walked over and sat in the rocking chair next to the fireplace.

For several minutes, no one spoke a word. Trini and John sat quietly, waiting for Dillis to reveal to them whatever she knew about the book, while Basil sat close to Dillis, as peaceful as could be. It was hard to believe that this beautiful little girl was bilingual, and Trini began doubting that she could translate the book. As soon as she had that thought, Basil stared straight into her eyes with a disapproving look. She knew he was reading her thoughts and felt as if she was being reprimanded for doubting Dillis's abilities. It was so quiet you could hear a pin drop, when suddenly Dillis cocked her head to the side and scrunched her eyes a little, like someone who suddenly understands something.

"We can go outside now!" Basil said happily.

"But how can we go outside, when Old Hoot is out there ready to get us?" asked Trini.

"We will be safe now. Fintan is back!" Basil said calmly as he was being picked up by Dillis and carried toward the door. Dillis reached up and unlocked the door while balancing Basil in her arms. Basil was very large and fluffy, and almost as big as Dillis, but somehow she was carrying him through the open door while he was motioning for Trini and John to follow along.

When they went outside, they saw that Fintan was standing in the beautiful garden with sunlight rippling across his beautiful coat and mane. As the small group approached him, John noticed Fintan's beautiful golden-speckled, green eyes glowing softly in the soft yellow sunlight.

After looking around carefully to make sure Old Hoot was nowhere in sight, Trini and John sat down in the grass next to where Fintan was standing in the sunlight, and Dillis sat down close by, setting Basil down right next to her. Fintan lowered himself down directly behind where Trini and John were seated and allowed them to rest their backs on him. They were very comfortable leaning on Fintan like this as if they had known him forever.

"Old Sheniah sent me back to let you know that she is spending the night in the cave. She wants me to stay up here for the night and make sure Old Hoot doesn't come back," Fintan announced in a soft voice through his special way of communicating through thought.

"You came back just in time. Dillis is about to translate the book," said John in hopes that his comment would speed up the process, being anxious to hear the translation.

Basil and Dillis looked at each other and rolled their eyes. They had learned many lessons from Old Sheniah over the last couple of years about the downside of being impatient.

"How is the whale doing?" asked Basil.

"She is doing much better, but her baby was also caught in the net. Thankfully, some dolphins finally gnawed through the ropes and got the baby to the cave where its mother and Old Sheniah were waiting. She is spending the night in order to help the baby feel more comfortable. The baby whale was so scared without its mom and so hungry by the time the dolphins got the net loose and helped it find its mom."

Trini could feel her restlessness fading away along with her impatience as they sat in the sun listening to Fintan talk in his special way about the whale and her baby. She picked a piece of the soft grass and began shredding it little by little, pulling each dark green strand, peeling it like one might peel a banana. The garden was exquisite in the sunshine with its amazing scents permeating the air. There were flowers of every kind and color, reaching with their blooms toward the sun. In one area there were vegetables, and at the edge were luscious violet-colored grapes spilling prolifically across a wooden arbor.

The garden was teeming with life: colorful birds were singing sweetly in the trees, butterflies were happily gliding from one area to the next, stopping in front of the newcomers from time to time before drifting away, and little lime-green grasshoppers were gingerly bopping up and down through the grass. At one point, John motioned for Trini to look to the right where two small olive-green frogs were gaily hopping together, heading toward the shade of the giant, buttery yellow sunflowers.

It was so peaceful and tranquil here that Trini and John allowed themselves to relax for the first time since the owl attacked them in the library. As they sat in the comforting warmth of the sun, the stinging wounds from Old Hoot's talons searing into their skin began to heal up until the sting was nothing more than a memory. The quiet peacefulness of the garden, along with the salty ocean air flowing softly and gently through the pine trees on the edge of the property, was like magic to their souls and healing to their lonely hearts.

John and Trini gradually began losing their anxiousness, taking on confident yet calm appearances. It was a much-needed time in their lives after all the loss that both of them had lived through. A feeling of soft familiarity came upon them, causing them to feel as if this was their home, a home that they both craved; a home with a heart.

Suddenly, it struck Trini that Dillis must have lost her parents also, and as soon as she had this thought, she turned to look at Dillis, who smiled at her as if she understood what Trini was thinking.

"Can you read minds?" Trini asked her carefully.

"She doesn't exactly read minds the way you are thinking," Basil answered for the little girl.

"I know she can tell what I'm thinking," Trini responded, looking right at her. "She responds whenever I think something, whether it is about her or not."

"She is very intuitive by nature, but ever since she moved here, Old Sheniah helped her realize that it is a beautiful gift to be able to understand

46

thoughts and encouraged her to honor her gift and not hide it, so her gift has become stronger. I think where she came from, people were discouraging her about it," Fintan explained kindly.

"But why would someone discourage what you call hearing thoughts? What harm could come of it?" John asked.

"People sometimes don't accept things that they cannot understand. It is a form of fear, and some call it human nature. I don't believe it is human nature to have a fear, though. I think human nature is brave and kind," said Dillis in her sweet Irish accent, finally speaking aloud for the first time since Trini and John had arrived.

"You can talk!" they both said at the same time, surprised.

"She only talks after she determines whether she trusts someone," explained Basil. "We aren't entirely sure what happened to her before Old Sheniah found her. She was wandering alone on the beach. After we saw her, we set up a tent on the beach and built a campfire, staying on the beach day and night, all week, thinking that someone might come to find her. She wasn't talking at all then, nothing all week, so we had no way to know where she came from or if she had any family out there looking for her. At that time, Fintan had been away, carrying some supplies up into the Slieve Mish Mountains for a friend of ours, and we wanted to wait on the beach until he got back to help us carry everything back up here."

"By the time Fintan came back, at the end of the week, we still hadn't found anyone to claim Dillis. She hadn't seen Fintan yet, but when he returned and she saw him, they were immediately drawn to each other, and that is when Fintan was able to connect to her thoughts and understand what happened to her. She didn't trust people, and where she comes from, little girls were not significant. They were used as workers, and parents were disappointed to have daughters and considered them as something to get rid of. So, of course she didn't feel safe sharing with Old Sheniah, or me. Cats were also unimportant. They were treated like rats, something to get rid of. Once she saw Fintan, though, she felt instant love and opened her thoughts to allow him to understand her."

As Basil spoke about Dillis, she got up and walked over to Fintan, petting his soft mane and kissing him on his forehead.

"It is quite obvious that she loves you!" said John to Fintan.

"She is a special one, for sure, and the feeling is mutual," he replied.

"So, I have an important question," began Trini, "how is it that you both can talk? Where we come from, cats and horses don't talk."

"They do talk, Trini, but you don't know how to listen. All cats and horses can talk and do talk all the time. Well, let me put it this way, all cats and horses are capable of talking, some choose not to, of course."

"Do all animals talk?" she asked.

"They do!" Basil replied. "When they feel like they can trust someone, but it is then up to the person to hear them, and most people are not taught how to listen very well to people, never mind animals. When I came here, I could already talk, but where I came from, there was no one who knew how to listen. I was so happy to find Old Sheniah, who could listen and understand me."

"Can she listen and understand all animals?" asked John.

"She does. She told us that she has always known, ever since she was a baby, about two-hundred years ago. Sometimes, she has to change something in her mind to understand some animals, but she has learned how to do it and has been teaching all of us."

"Have people always had the ability to talk with animals?" Trini asked seriously.

"Yes," answered Fintan, quite seriously, "people began believing that the Bible and other sacred books meant to teach that animals were supposed to be underneath humans. It was a misinterpretation of these scriptures that caused so much change. Before these misunderstandings happened, people shared a good relationship with animals and almost everyone could communicate with them."

"Old Sheniah told us that in the country where you and Trini are from, a long time ago, the Native American Indians thought very highly of animals and even called them their 'brothers' and 'sisters.' She said that those people even respected trees and mountains, rivers and streams, and all animals, whether or not they walked, flew, swam, or crawled, were special and sacred to them, the same as people."

"It's too bad about the misunderstanding," said Trini sadly. "I never knew any of this. I thought that animals and people had no way of communicating, and that cats and dogs were pets to be loved, horses were pets to be ridden, fish were pets to be fed and admired, and birds were to be kept in cages and hopefully would entertain us by singing."

"Yes, it is too bad. That is how most people think of animals," said Fintan thoughtfully. "We are so fortunate to have found each other and be here at the same time, where it is safe and comfortable to be who we are!"

"What about Old Hoot? Can he talk?" asked John reluctantly; thinking that he probably wouldn't like anything Old Hoot had to say.

"Oh, yes, he can talk, but a person controls him. The person who controls him is very mean and abusive, causing Old Hoot to act so mean. Often, when people or animals are abused or mistreated, they project negativity at others. That's why it is important to learn to see through the outer personalities of people and animals and look into their hearts. There is always a reason why people or animals act up," said Fintan pensively.

While Fintan had been talking, Dillis was busy carefully placing some small stones in the form of a circle. She had finished making her ring and got up and ran over to a beautiful, tall fir tree and seemed to be looking for something.

"What do you think Dillis is looking for?" asked Trini curiously.

"She's gathering up some things to help you to see what the book means," Basil replied.

Dillis apparently found what she was looking for and walked back to her stone circle. All eyes were upon her, observing her as she ran her little fingers across the stick that she brought back with her, careful not to hurt herself on the jagged point at the end. After looking at the stick, and then down at the circle for a minute, she sat down next to her ring and closed her eyes. She looked so peaceful and wise sitting there on the ground. Trini decided to count the stones and realized there were twelve stones altogether. Suddenly, Dillis opened her eyes and gently tossed the stick into the middle of the circle, not disturbing any of the rocks.

"Do you know what this means?" Dillis asked in her Irish accent, but without waiting for an answer, she began to explain. "This is a wheel. A Medicine Wheel. It is a sacred symbol to some people. Everyone's life is a circle, and we all go round and round it. These stones are directions, and the stick that I threw in the center is to show which direction you are headed in now. Each direction has a meaning. When you have a lesson to learn, the lesson is born in the top of the circle; the top is like your mind or heart, where ideas come from in the North. Then, you go around the wheel to the right, where your ideas become inspired by creativity in the East. After your ideas collect the energy of creativity, they travel to the bottom, to the South, where your innocence and your purity gather up your ideas to carry them up to the top to be born. When you are negative, or if there is negativity around you, the South loses its strength and cannot carry your idea back up to the top to be born. After the creative thought takes on its highest form of purity, it travels further along the wheel to the west, to the place of the introspection, where you meditate on it, allowing it to rest in your mind, before it completes its journey. It is important to stay calm and peaceful, so that your ideas can be light enough to get carried to the top to be born," she told the group seriously.

"Is this what the glowing book is about?" asked John.

"It does contain this, but this is not all it has. There is a lot more, but you won't ever understand the book until you understand the Sacred Circle and how to stay peaceful," Dillis said as she stared into each of the group's eyes, one at a time. "Lesson Number One in the glowing magic book begins with this. When any lesson or new time comes up in your life, whether it is a hard lesson or an easy one, staying peaceful is the most important thing you can ever do. Every time you get all riled up, you add so much weight to your lesson that it makes it too hard to get through, to make it to the top where it is born, so you get stuck in one spot. Haven't you ever felt stuck, especially after you were angry or impatient? You get stuck, right here," Dillis said as she picked up the stick and stuck its sharp pointed end into the bottom of the stone wheel. "You won't move any further. You won't get anything accomplished, and you won't grow up."

"I get what she's talking about, Trini," said John as he stared into the wheel.

"I think I do too," Trini said to John. She seems to be right about this. Every time I get impatient, nothing seems to go right. When I get mad, things get a lot worse. Right before my mom died, I was so upset because I wanted to go with my best friend to the movies but Mom said that I couldn't go out because I hadn't finished my homework. I got so angry and decided I would try to make a deal with her that if I finished my homework, she would drop me off at the movies. I was so impatient that I rushed through all my math problems and rushed downstairs to tell her that I was finished. I hurried her out of the door, complaining the whole way. Well, I guess I made her pretty nervous because when she backed up out of the driveway, she ran into our neighbor's trashcans and dented up the back of our van. Then, by the time she dropped me off at the movies, I realized that I had forgotten to bring my money and phone with me and my best friend wasn't anywhere to be found. I had to wait two hours, alone, before my mom came back to get me. It was horrible sitting in the waiting room at the theatre, smelling all the popcorn and candy, not having anyone with me for those two hours, and missing the movie."

Everyone in the group listened intently, but Dillis was thoroughly engaged and her eyes were focused entirely on Trini.

"One good thing about it was that it gave me time to think about how rude I was to my mom and how, if I had only done what I was supposed to do, I wouldn't have found myself alone with no money. As soon as I got picked up, I apologized to her and she informed me that she went straight to the mechanic to get an estimate on her fender. It was going to cost us $600! I felt horrible because we don't ever have very much extra money. The next day, when I went to school, I had even more of a lesson when the paper that I rushed through came back with an 'F' marked across the top. I had never gotten an 'F' on anything. I was always on the honor roll. If I didn't get good grades, I would be removed from playing any sports at school."

"Oh, that's a good story," said Dillis.

"Why is it so good?" Trini asked seriously.

"It's good because you had many bad things happen that brought you back to being good!"

Everyone in the group laughed at how adorable Dillis was in her interpretation. Dillis was so little and cute, and her accent made her even sweeter. She could go from zero to charming in a very short time. From serious to funny so quickly that you would never expect it, which made her even more entertaining.

"And did your mom love you after this?" she asked quite seriously.

"Yes, she always loved me. No matter what I did wrong, she was always there for me. When I came home from school, she had made my favorite meal for our supper. I was so embarrassed about my 'F' and didn't want to tell her, but it blurted right out of my mouth at the dinner table. I was sitting there listening to her talk about how excited she was that she finally found a strawberry saxifraga houseplant that she had been trying to get for months, and suddenly all the words just poured out, 'I got an F in math!' I shouted and started crying. And do you know what she did? Instead of telling me I was grounded, especially after all the trouble I caused with her car getting wrecked, she came over and hugged me and told me she loved me."

Dillis's beautiful green eyes became misty as she heard Trini's story. She could barely remember her mom, but something in Trini's story touched her heart and caused her to have a quick glimpse of being held by her mom. She remembered that they were on a large boat, in the middle of a vast sea, and an angry man was tugging at her mom. Her mom was trying to hold on to her and push the man's arm aside. There was yelling, and the only words that Dillis remembered were her mom's, saying, "Get away from us, you monster!"

And the man's snarling words, "You'll be sorry, you and that little heathen baby." Suddenly, she and her mother were in the air, falling...falling...she remembered hanging on to her mother, and water, water everywhere, so much water. That is all she remembered, but that was enough to create tears.

Fintan moved his head over closer to Dillis and nuzzled her, causing her to remember where she was and regain her composure.

"I'm sorry that you don't have a mom. I don't either, but now I have Old Sheniah," she said softly. "I don't mind sharing her with you if you would like."

Trini smiled at the little girl, suddenly feeling a kinship with her as she realized how hard her life must have been, being so young.

"You don't need to feel bad for me!" Dillis said as soon as she realized what Trini was thinking. "I have a great life!"

"I was feeling bad for you, John, and myself!" she said seriously, "None of us have our parents."

"But we all have each other, *plus* Old Sheniah!" Basil interjected. "I don't have my mom either, or a dad, and no one here does, including Fintan. We have all been through a lot and left to our own devices, but thankfully we all have each other; and when you are determined to make it in life, there is always a way made! Yes, there have been adjustments to all of our lifestyles, and yes, we have gone through some rough spots, but the secret to having a good life is to make it your own. Own your life and make it happy! All of us here have discussed this so many times with each other, and with Old Sheniah, and we have all thought at one time or another that how we live our lives is only up to us. If you take responsibility for your own life and happiness, then you never have anyone else to blame for it. Blame is a hard lesson, you know."

"What do you mean by this?" asked John.

"As long as there is someone to blame, you never get to really grow up," Basil began explaining. "It is a childish thing to blame your parents, your teachers, your brothers and sisters, or worse yet, blame life. Once you make up your whole mind that your life is yours and that you are going to be happy and good, no matter what, and decide that you will never blame anyone, including yourself, you have Lesson Number Two."

"Both Lesson Number One, which Dillis shared, and now Lesson Number Two are significant, according to the book. You can't get any further along in your understanding until you understand those two. They are essential. Isn't this right, Dillis? Isn't this what Lesson Number Two in the book is about?" asked Basil as a backup to what he was saying.

"Ah yes, this is so important, every bit as important as Lesson Number One. Hardly anyone ever gets past those two lessons. They are so important, yet, because they are so simple, people don't pay them much mind. Then, people go on trying to understand the other lessons, but they can't. The other ones don't make any sense without the first two. We all want to be grown-ups, just like Old Sheniah. We don't want to be 'bad' or 'grouchy' old grown-ups, though, but 'happy' and 'smart' grown-ups. We want to be grown-ups who can take care of ourselves and be responsible for ourselves. We can make it easy, or we can make it hard on ourselves. By making a decision, a 'whole' decision that, no matter what happens, we will stay calm, like we learned in Lesson One, and not blame anyone, including ourselves, as we learned in Lesson Two, we make it easier on ourselves in the long run."

"Did you say not even to blame ourselves?" asked John.

"I did. It is important to blame no one, and that includes yourself," replied Basil.

"Then who will we blame, if we can't blame someone else and we can't blame ourselves?" asked Trini curiously.

"Is it necessary to blame anyone at all?" asked Fintan.

"Of course it is. Problems have to be someone's fault. If we can't blame another person, can't blame ourselves, and can't blame life, then what is left? Blame God?" asked John.

"No, you can't even blame God," replied Basil.

"Then *who or what* is left?" asked Trini, trying to think hard to see if they had left anyone or anything out.

"The secret is no blame, in Lesson Number Two. Give up on the idea of blame. Blame is a horrible pit that people all over the world fall into and then find that it is too deep to crawl out of. It is an old way of thinking. Now is a new time, and you have the chance to start right now on a fresh path. Can you live your life without blaming something or someone?" Basil asked.

"I'm not sure because it makes so much sense that someone or something is responsible for problems," said Trini matter-of-factly.

"What if you chose not to blame and just looked at each problem like you would look at a math problem. A problem that is in need of a solution. Keep it simple, and keep it fun. And another part to this is, what if we didn't even call them 'problems,' but call them 'challenges' or 'assignments' like you do in math. By changing your ideas and perceptions of what you are experiencing, you can change your attitude toward it."

"I love this idea. Give up on blame entirely. Cross it off the books! Throw 'blame' in the ocean. It serves no purpose, so get rid of it. Before moving here, I cut off my long hair; it no longer served a purpose, so I cut it off and threw it in the trash. I could do the same thing with blame. Throw it away because it doesn't help anyone," Trini spoke very excitedly.

The five of them: Fintan, Dillis, Basil, John, and Trini sat in the sunny yard for a long time, discussing what life would be like if the two 'Lessons' were followed at all times. They each cited times where their anger got the best of them, how badly it turned out, and what it would have been like if they had remained peaceful and not blamed anyone. As they shared their stories, a remarkable thing began to happen: John and Trini started to feel the closeness of family that they had craved and desired for their whole lives now fulfilled. They felt at home at Old Sheniah's cabin and her magical yard.

The 'Lessons' had already begun doing their magical work in them, changing them, causing their hearts to open up, preparing them for the next phase of their lives. As the magic of the golden glow book began its work in each of them in the group, butterflies and birds flew around them, landing closer and sometimes on them. The sun sent its golden rays through the violet grapes in the arbor, leaving patterns on the soft grass, while soft, salty ocean breezes blew gently across their faces. Trini suddenly realized that this was the first time she felt warm, not chilled, since her mom passed away. She took her scarf off and wrapped it lovingly around Fintan's neck.

Chapter Five
Dublin

"Excuse me, Miss," said the flight attendant as she gently tapped Trini on the arm, "excuse me," she repeated.

Trini sat up and realized that she was no longer in the dream, but in the plane, and they were getting ready to land in Dublin.

"Please, if you don't mind, fasten your seatbelt now, as we are getting ready to land soon," said the flight attendant kindly in an Irish accent.

Trini fastened her seatbelt while looking out the window at the outline of the buildings below and a very dark river snaking through the city. Many lights lit up the airport and runway, and Trini gradually awakened to realize once again that John from her dream was the same person who was sitting next to her on the plane. He caught her looking at him and smiled.

"Where will you be staying in Dublin?"

This time, she wasn't afraid or feeling too distant to talk to him. He felt like someone she had been friends with since her dream and responded with a soft smile.

"I'm staying at The Drumchonndrah," she informed him. "But just for two days, then I'm heading off to live with my aunt."

"I am also staying at The Drumchonndrah," John told her with surprise. "Want to share a taxi after we go through customs?"

"Sure, why not? After all, we are going to the same place. How about if we drop our bags off, then try to find some food? I'm starving!"

"What do you like to eat?" John asked her. He was surprised that she finally seemed a little friendlier. *Sometimes sleep will do wonders for a person's personality,* he thought.

"I don't know," she said thoughtfully. She had been so out of touch with herself since her mother's death that she never really thought about food. She wasn't sure if she had been thinking about anything at all, other than what her mom would have wanted her to do. She remembered thinking quite often about Ireland and how her mother always promised that they would go there together after Trini graduated from high school. Now that she was off on her own, starting a new life in a new country, she might like different foods, things that she hadn't tried before. *Now that I have short hair, maybe I should re-design myself entirely,* she thought to herself.

"I like Indian food," she said suddenly, surprising herself as she heard those words come out of her mouth. She had never even tried Indian food.

"I do too," said John, surprised. "Anything in particular?"

"All Indian food. Everything they make," she said determinedly.

"I'm not sure if there are Indian restaurants in Dublin, but if there is one, we will find it," he promised.

Trini sat back as the plane began circling the Dublin airspace, preparing for landing. She remembered her dream, how John was so helpful and serious; she remembered Fintan, Dillis, and Basil as well. She wished the flight attendant hadn't awakened her and felt like the dream was more real than anything she had felt in a very long time. She wondered what it would have been like to meet Old Sheniah and felt sad when she considered that it was just a dream, that Old Sheniah and the rest of them weren't real. They felt so real to her, but now she had to force herself to deal with landing in Dublin and starting a new life alone in Ireland. A million thoughts tried to flood into her mind, but the thoughts came without the feelings.

"I just realized I should have asked you if anyone was meeting you at the airport," John said to her.

"Nobody. Anyone meeting you?" she asked.

"Not a soul," he said, somewhat sadly.

"My aunt is visiting one of her friends and won't be back to her house for a couple of days, so I am staying in Dublin for that time then taking a bus on the third day. It is a six-hour ride from Dublin," she told him. "Right before I left Connecticut, she called and told my friend's mom that someone was sick and she had to leave, but it was too late to change my flight," she admitted.

"I've read that there is a lot to do in Dublin. I was thinking about going to the museum," he told her.

"The National Museum?" Trini asked, once again remembering her dream.

"Yes, it has been around since 1887 and has free admittance. I can't wait to see the Irish collections of books," he told her.

With her dream feeling so real, she was startled when he mentioned the museum, and again when he mentioned the books. She wanted to tell him about the dream, but she had only just met him. Already she had agreed to take a taxi with him since they would be staying at the same bed and breakfast, and also decided to find an Indian restaurant and have dinner with him.

After they went through customs and collected their luggage, they went outside the airport and hailed a taxi.

"Do you know where The Drumchonndrah Bed and Breakfast is?" John asked the taxi driver.

"Yes, as a matter of fact, I do. My aunt owns it," he responded in a strong Irish accent. "Have you been here before?"

"First time for me," said Trini quietly. "How far is it?"

"I'll have you there in a flash," the driver told her.

"Tell Mairi, the owner, that her nephew Padraic sends his love," he said as he pulled up in front of the bed and breakfast. "Hold on, Lass. I'll get that door for you," he said as he rushed out to get her door. "Will the lad be taking your cases or would you like for me to get those for you?"

"I'll take mine," said Trini.

"Independent, right?" Padraic said teasingly.

"Would you happen to know where we might find an Indian restaurant?" John asked as he paid the taxi fare.

"There's about three of them close by here. The best one is in town, and I can stay and drive you if you are interested," Padraic offered.

"Thanks, but we'll take our chances on something close," John decided.

Chapter Six
Halley Torrington

The early morning sun warms the earth and the solid ground defrosts, becoming flexible, pliable, warm, and wet, and prepares to receive. Earthworms begin to aerate the ground. Light, warmth, air, and fertilizer from the birds above and the animals beneath decompose in order to provide the soil with nourishment. Rain causes trunks, stems, and branches to relax and lose rigidity. In preparation, Mother Earth awakens from her sweet repose. Winds are summoned to exercise and cleanse. Cleansing rain, cleansing winds, cleansing sun...all speaking to Mother Earth and her children to prepare and receive.

A whispered hush, a gentle prompting, a great spirit, a holy spirit, speaks softly to humanity, "You are designed and created as one with this plan. You are not separate from nature, you are part of it. Does the tree know that the gentle pushing of the winds is exercising it, preparing it for strength and endurance, or that the soil is being warmed and cleansed by the sun and the rains?"

The beasts and the fowl disseminate nutrients into the ground, and leaves and plants shed unused portions. All combined, these add together and become decomposed and become nourishment for the earth, which is so sacred and giving; this same ground contains the nourishment to sustain humanity. Nature speaks, "Is the ground offended by the excrement or by being trodden upon, or by being walked upon? Does it blame someone, or does it realize it is being nourished?"

"Is the tree offended by the winds that test its strength and exercise from it to become stronger winds?"

"Is Mother Earth offended when it is awakened by the heat and the light of the sun?"

The spring sunshine emitted a warm golden glow onto the forest floor through the pine trees, giving the forest a feeling of surreal magic. You could almost envision the Prince and Princess of the fairies leading a troupe of elves, gnomes, and fairies home after a night of dance and celebration, through the golden dewdrops and the still moist ferns, under the canopy of majestic balsams, pines, and firs. *Yes, it is indeed a day of golden magic,* Trini thought as she slowly walked on the earthen pathway. To Trini, all days were filled with the wonder of life but today was blissful. She had eager anticipation as if some pleasant surprise were about to occur.

Each day, for the past two weeks, Trini had followed a pathway through the forest, leading past a frog pond on the right, then headed left, up to an old, unused logging trail. At the top of the logging trail was a ridge where she sat each day to write in her journal and eat her lunch. She usually wrote and ate simultaneously, occasionally stopping to watch a hawk or observe the squirrels playing in the trees on the ridge.

Trini had just finished her second year at college, studying forest conservation, and decided to spend the end of spring in the forest, observing and contemplating. She had spent some time during school in the woods and found it to be magical—another world, separate, and distinct from the stuffy classrooms at school. Here, she could learn and experience this magical world first-hand; without the lectures, diagrams, and distractions. She loved the smells of the forest and the element of surprise from sudden sightings of one of the birds or animals she had studied in her textbooks or seen in the films that she saw every Friday. Most of all, she loved the patterns the light made on her path as she passed under the freshly scented pine boughs. She loved the way the wind wound its way through the branches, picking up scents and delivering them to her, like a friend bringing her a present.

The ridge was an extraordinary place because it was here that she saw her first elk. It was standing at the top of the ridge one morning, looking out onto the valley, and suddenly realized that Trini was standing a mere ten feet away. It looked at her with complete trust, unafraid of her presence. Trini stood awestruck by the beauty and grandeur of this regal creature as it stared straight into her eyes. She felt as if her whole life up to this point was designed to bring her to this ridge to have this encounter with this glorious being. It felt like they were communicating. She felt as if her life would never be the same again, and that some significant teaching had entered into her through the eyes of the elk—straight into her soul. The experience brought tears to her eyes. While the elk sensed this, he slowly turned and walked into the trees and out of sight.

Usually, when one has such a moving experience as this, the thoughts of the experience become obsessive for a time. In Trini's experience, this was not the case. However, a change occurred in her thoughts and feelings about life, which ushered in a new determination and commitment that until now hadn't been present. What she was determined and committed to was unexplainable, but it brought her great peace and a sense of freedom that she had never experienced in her life, and especially had not experienced since she lost her mother. From the time the elk looked into her eyes, her soul began a new journey.

Trini took off her backpack and opened her thermos. The tea mixture that she made this morning felt refreshing to her throat. She had brewed some sassafras and sarsaparilla tea and added some lemon and honey, hoping that it would help the roughness in her throat that had been there, nagging away, for the past few days. One of her college professors studied herbal remedies and suggested that Trini take one of her books to read. Trini thought that the idea of nature's pharmaceuticals was interesting, to say the least, and decided to give this remedy a try. Her professor, Halley Torrington, was such a vibrant being, with the most intense, sparkling blue eyes. She always had a particularly healthy, peacefully happy glow about her, which awakened Trini's curiosity. Halley's interest in teaching plant life to her students went beyond the textbooks. She had brought in several unusual plants during the year and told the most interesting stories as she displayed them. She talked about them as if they were people, beings with feelings. Most of the class listened intently as Halley gave her discussions, but few asked questions, so Trini often stayed after class to talk with Halley and examine the plants more carefully.

One day, after class, Trini picked up a plant with strangely shaped, wispy leaves and scraggly-edged yellow flowers on the stem. It wasn't a particularly beautiful plant and was a little limp from sitting out in the classroom. As she gathered the plant into her hands, an incredible peace came over her, which she felt was coming from the plant.

"How odd. When I picked up this plant, I felt so peaceful all of a sudden. The peaceful feeling began in my hand and moved through my body and mind," Trini told her.

"How sensitive you are, Trini. This plant's name is chamomile. Its purpose is to help people relax and enjoy their time. It's fascinating that you so quickly felt the peace that chamomile brings. People brew tea from this plant's flowers, and after drinking it, usually decide to feel peaceful," Halley explained.

"What do you mean, 'decide' to feel peaceful?" Trini asked, feeling puzzled by this unusual remark.

To this, Halley responded, "Feelings are a choice, Trini."

Trini wanted to stay and explore this new way of thinking but needed to get to her next class to take an exam. *Are feelings a choice? How can this be?* she wondered.

A red-tailed hawk screeched overhead, which brought Trini back to the here and now. She was so lost in her thoughts about the elk, the chamomile, and feelings being a 'choice' that she had eaten her entire sandwich without even realizing it. She looked up into the sky to see the hawk gliding gracefully in the air. *I wish I could fly with him,* she thought pensively as she watched him for several minutes more as he went back and forth from the treetops on the ridge to the air, finally sighting his prey beneath and diving with perfect timing to claim his lunch.

The bright noonday sun felt warm on her skin, so she took her sweater off, mussing her hair in the process. Instead of brushing it, she just tied it back and took off her hiking boots, allowing her feet to feel the sun's warmth. "Spring is terrific in the woods," she said aloud.

"It certainly is," said a man's voice coming from behind her, startling her.

She looked behind to see a tall man with long, chestnut-brown hair tied back like hers. He was wearing jeans and a white t-shirt, similar to her own, and had a sweatshirt and a camera strapped to his shoulder. He was wearing dark-tinted sunglasses and a gray woolen scarf.

"I hope I didn't startle you. My name's John."

"Hi, I'm Trini," she smiled as she stood up and reached for his hand to shake.

"Well, Trini, you have a fever, you know," he said in a very concerned way.

"How do you know?" she asked, puzzled.

"The vibration in your hand," he smiled.

"My hand isn't shaking."

"No, by vibration I mean on the inside of your hand," John tried to explain.

"How can you feel the inside of my hand?"

"I'll explain all of that in a minute, but first let me build a small fire over here and we will make you some tea to get rid of that fever. I'll be right back."

He started quickly down the trail, and within a couple of minutes, came back with a limber, pale-green branch. After peeling some of the bark, he placed a couple of pieces into a pan that he had pulled out of his backpack. He set some small twigs on the ground and began to build a fire. Trini had a million questions, but as was her nature, she sat quietly, waiting for the appropriate time to ask them.

The fire took off quite readily. Trini watched as John poured some clear water into the pan with the bark already in it. *How peaceful he seems, and how confident,* she thought.

She noticed a strange acidic smell permeating the air around the pan; not at all unpleasant, but unusual. It blended nicely into the forest smells that she had now grown accustomed to. John carefully removed the pan from the small fire and sat it on a nearby flat, gray rock in the yellow sun to steep.

Finally, John sat down and smiled at Trini and told her that the tea would soon be ready to drink.

"What was the bark that you put into the water?" she finally asked.

"It is willow bark. I pulled a branch off a willow tree down by the frog pond," he explained. "Willow bark can be used the same way as aspirin, you know, except without any side effects, like stomach aches or nausea," he explained.

Nature's pharmaceuticals, she thought. "I've been learning a little bit about it in college," she told him.

"What are you studying, Trini?"

"I've been studying forest conservation for two years, but I've just recently begun to learn about using plants as medicine."

"Here, your tea is ready," John said as he handed her one of the two pewter cups he had in his pack. *Two pewter cups. This feels familiar to me, as if it has happened before. This must be a déjà vu experience,* Trini pondered.

She sat quietly, sipping the warm tea as she gazed out over the ridge, watching fluffy white clouds slowly drifting by. She forgot about her questions for the time being and was pulled into the moment, savoring the life of the forest. The air smelled sweet from the sun-warmed earth, and the magical feeling that was with Trini since the early morning was lingering softly beside her. Now and then, she looked over at John, still wearing his sunglasses and poking a charred stick into the small fire. His thick, dark eyebrows were a little furrowed, she noticed, as if he were trying to figure something out.

"A penny for your thoughts?" Trini chided.

"If you gave me a penny for each thought, I would be quite wealthy," he laughed. "First of all, I was thinking about how to explain inner vibration to you, and secondly, I was wondering if you noticed your elk over there, watching you."

"Where?" Trini asked enthusiastically.

"He is about twenty feet to your right, behind that cluster of balsams," John moved his head in the direction of the elk. Trini very cautiously turned her body around to face the direction that John had nodded toward.

"Why do you call him *my* elk?"

"Because he has been close to you for the two weeks that you've been coming here," John explained.

"I never saw you, and I've only seen the elk one time, on my first day," she whispered.

"We have both been in plain sight many times, but you didn't notice," John teased.

"Why do you think he has been watching me?" she asked.

"It is his 'medicine,' a sort of animal magic, to watch and protect. It's just what he does. It comes naturally to him as breathing does to us," he explained.

Trini slowly stood up and took a couple of small steps in the direction of the elk. He didn't move. She stood quietly watching as the elk turned and softly walked out into the woods.

"What is elk's medicine?" she turned to face John with her question. "And what is an inner vibration?"

John smiled and motioned for her to come and sit on the ridge with him while he readied himself to begin teaching her.

"Where would you like to begin, Trini?" John asked as he stilled his thoughts and readied himself for her questions.

"I had so many questions in my mind before today, but now I feel empty like I don't know anything. I feel as if I've entered a whole new world, filled with beauty and life," Trini tried to explain and half-smiled sheepishly. She rarely talked to strangers, and even with classmates or friends, she was not considered outgoing or open. Today felt different. Here she was, sharing her feelings with a stranger and feeling completely comfortable. He felt familiar to her, as if she knew him well.

"Let's begin with inner vibration then," John spoke as he carefully studied her expression. "Each person's body has its own harmony. Within the DNA resides a program. Each thing that goes into our body, either through our ears or eyes, or even our mouths and noses, has a vibration or harmony. When the vibratory rate of whatever we have been in contact with, such as music, enters into our body, it relates to the harmonics within our DNA. When we intake something that is at a higher vibratory rate, it feeds life into us. Truth, understanding, peace, wisdom, and ideas that are pure, without a motive, actually raise our vibratory rate to that of the higher elements. We are then in alignment with those ideas that are 'of the light.' You have heard, 'like attracts like?' In this way, light attracts light; questions attract more questions, peace attracts more peace. This is why it is essential to spend time in meditation and prayer. It helps to maintain inner order, which will draw more inner peace, which in turn creates good health and vitality, or good energy."

Although these concepts were difficult to understand, Trini accepted them readily. Upon hearing John's explanation, she felt as if she somehow had known this and that he was just helping her to 'recall' this information. She listened intently as he continued to explain to her how everything, whether it be a plant, animal, rock, person, or air, has an appointed vibratory rate, and when we are open to learning about purity, we are taught the higher ways of life and nature. We are taught to accept nature and to become one with creation.

John spoke confidently and calmly to Trini and didn't in any way make her feel intimidated by his profound understanding. She listened enthusiastically and became so engrossed in what he was telling her that nothing else existed.

"Did you know that scientists have recorded music from the DNA of people and some animals and that it sounds like a song?" he asked.

"No, I didn't know that, but I would sure love to hear the music. What does it sound like?" she asked, eagerly awaiting his response.

"What I heard sounded like a symphony, like many instruments playing many notes. You can hear the heart beating like a drum, and the sounds of blood moving are similar to bells. It all fits together quite nicely with an underlying melody. Each person has their melody, although I do not know the person whose DNA I heard."

"I wonder what the elk's DNA sounds like," Trini said.

John reached over and touched the palm of Trini's hand. "Your fever is gone. How does your throat feel?" he asked.

"Much better, thank you, but how did you know about my throat?" she asked.

"Have you ever heard of chakras?" he questioned.

"I've heard of chakras but know very little about the subject. Why, can you see chakras?"

"Yes, I saw a haziness around your throat chakra and that is how I knew you were having an issue with your throat. The throat chakra is normally blue, but when you see a haze or discoloration in any chakra, you would know to focus your healing energy on that spot," he told her.

"I'm feeling well, thanks for your help," she smiled.

"I have an appointment in town later today, so I guess I should be heading back down the ridge," John said as he threw his camera bag over his shoulder.

"But wait, I would like to learn more. Will I see you again?" Trini asked.

"I'm sure we will meet again soon. Trini, it has been a pleasure," he said as he playfully bowed and walked away.

Trini sat quietly for a moment, watching the woods and thinking about the day. She knew earlier that there was a magical feeling in the air, but today was incredibly magical. Seeing the elk, having her throat healed, hearing all the new information from John, all added to the magic. *I knew that I wanted to grow and understand things, but if you don't know what you want to know, how can you find answers?*

She took her notebook and pen out of her backpack and excitedly wrote notes about John, DNA, elks, chakras, and red-tailed hawks. At the end of the page, she wrote, 'The woods are truly magical.'

After packing up her things, she took one last look at the hawk, which was still flying over the ridge, and headed back down the trail. As she passed the frog pond, she noticed for the first time the willow tree from which John had taken a branch to pull the bark to make her tea. She stopped and looked at the other trees that surrounded the pond and wondered if they too contained medicine. She made a mental note of the black birch tree and decided to ask John, if they ever meet again, if it had medicine and what it was used for. She was particularly drawn to the black birch tree. It seemed as if the sun was shining so brightly on it that it glowed.

Trini left the woods feeling more determined than ever to discover all she could learn about life. She wished that she could talk to Halley and tell her about her day and all the discoveries she had come upon. She thought that Halley and John had the same type of calm serenity and the same softness in their voices. John seemed so familiar to her, but she just couldn't place him. *I wish I knew what color his eyes are. He never took off his sunglasses.*

Rather than go directly back to the campground where she had been staying for the past two weeks, Trini drove straight into town to the library, hoping to find some books about DNA, chakras, and the plants that she had become familiar with earlier. When she pulled her car into the parking space in front of the library, rather than get out right away, she sat quietly, feeling thankful for the events that transpired during the day. She felt whole and healthy, full, and yet at the same time, empty. Before going in, she quickly looked at herself in the car mirror. Being in the woods and sleeping outside in the lean-to had done wonders for her health and strength. Her eyes were bright with excitement for life, and her skin glowed radiantly. The sore throat that had been bothering her was utterly non-existent. She quickly ran a hairbrush through her hair and applied some tinted lip-gloss.

Trini usually loved the musky smell of libraries, but today it smelled reasonably offensive to her after spending so much time in the fresh air of the woods. After wandering around for a few minutes, gathering up several books, she found a table near a window and laid the books out in front of herself. The first of the books that caught her eye was about the seven chakras. She glanced through it quickly and decided to put it in the 'keep' pile. She picked up another book about increasing one's intuition and chose not to take that one for the time being. There wasn't anything available on spiritual vibrations or animal medicines, but she did find one about DNA. She finally decided on the DNA book and the seven chakras book and carried them to the desk to check out.

Rather than building a fire and cooking her supper in the evening as she had been doing, she decided to stop in at one of the local restaurants and get something to bring back to the campground for her supper. That way, she could begin reading her new books while there was still light. After ordering some soup and a sandwich, she asked, "Could I also have a cup of tea while I'm waiting?"

Trini sat, drinking her tea, daydreaming, when she heard a familiar voice. "May I join you?"

"Halley. What are you doing here? I've been thinking about you today. Please, sit down."

"Trini, I'm so happy to see you," Halley said while giving Trini a warm hug.

"I made reservations at the campground, but something happened and they couldn't find my reservation and now they are full," she explained.

"I'm staying at the campground in a lean-to. You are welcome to stay with me if you like," Trini offered.

"What a blessing!" Halley smiled. "This is great. I had a feeling that something terrific was going to happen on this trip. Have you eaten? Let me buy you dinner," she offered.

"Oh, actually I just ordered something to take back with me. I went to the library and found some information on a couple of things I wanted to learn more about; rather than taking the time to cook and clean up, I decided to bring something back with me," she explained.

"My, you are anxious to hit those books! I'll order something and follow you back. Are you sure you would like some company? I don't want to intrude on your study time," she laughed.

"I would LOVE for you to stay with me. I've been pretty much alone here for two weeks, Halley. I've loved the solitude, but more than that, I'd love to spend some time with you."

"How much longer will you be staying at the campground, Trini?"

"Well, I'm not sure yet, but at least another week," she answered.

The waitress brought the bag containing Trini's dinner and set it on the table with the bill. "Since I haven't even ordered yet, you go on, Trini. I'll meet you back at the campground," Halley told her.

"The name of my lean-to is Balsam. It is the fourth lean-to on the same side as the river. I'll let the park ranger know to expect you," Trini offered.

After a short talk with the park ranger, Trini drove into her parking space beside the lean-to. She felt incredibly lucky to have gotten Balsam. It sat facing the river and had more privacy than the other sites in the campground. She checked around to make sure that everything was in order and began to build a fire. She was so excited about Halley being there that she hadn't even thought about her books, so she grabbed her backpack and unloaded them onto the picnic table just as Halley was driving in.

"This place is so beautiful, Trini. I've only stayed in tents, never in a lean-to. How wonderful that it faces the river."

The two women unpacked their supper and sat at the table to eat. Halley noticed the books sitting out and picked up the one about the seven chakras. "This one is excellent, Trini," she told her.

"You've read it?" Trini asked, puzzled.

"Yes, I've read several books on the subject and have attended a few seminars as well. Learning about the seven chakras is an essential step in spiritual growth," Halley told her.

"This is the first book that I was drawn to in the library today, Halley. Will you tell me something about it?"

"Sure, what would you like to know?"

Trini laughed and replied, "EVERYTHING. I know NOTHING. I don't even know what a chakra is."

Halley laughed at Trini's innocence and eagerness to learn and said, "Then let's start at the beginning, Trini. Before I begin, I need to tell you something. When I am outside of college and I'm talking or sharing, I often refer to sacred texts. I just wanted to make you aware of that. A lot of people become offended when you mention any sacred or religious references. None of the professors are allowed to speak about anything of a 'religious nature' in the classroom," she tried to explain.

"I don't think that I would be offended at all, Halley, I didn't know that there were rules like that at the college," Trini admitted.

"Oh, yes, at most schools they have a law now that is called The Separation of Church and State. Many people are up in arms about it, particularly in public elementary schools, and have chosen to teach their children at home."

"So, shall we begin?" Halley said, mimicking her 'professor' voice. "First, I will show you a chart. There is one in this book. This guide can be used for our reference, take a look."

Chakra Chart:

Number	Color	Name of Spirit	Location
One	Red	Understanding	Pelvic Area
Two	Orange	Counsel	Under Navel/Reproductive Area
Three	Yellow	Wisdom	Navel/Solar Plexus

Four	Green	Knowledge	Heart
Five	Blue	Might	Throat
Six	Purple	Reverence	Forehead
Seven	White	Righteousness	Top of the Head/Crown

"As you can see, Trini, these are numbered one through seven. Number one is actually at the base of your body, and they move up to number seven, which is at the top of your head," she explained.

"A lot of this seems self-explanatory, but where do you get the names of the seven spirits, Halley?" Trini asked.

"In brief, they are from some of the holy books and teachings, Trini, and are referred to as the seven spirits that stand before the Creator and praise Him continually. We will get into that more deeply, but first, let me explain that your body is considered to be the temple and everything is inside of you. I know that this may sound odd to you right now, but you will see it much more clearly as we go on."

"Somehow, I know that you are right, Halley, but I know that I've never heard this anywhere. Isn't that odd?" she questioned.

"Well, actually, it isn't that odd. I'm going to help you remember a lot more," she promised. "The overview of chakras is like this, Trini. They are energy centers of the body and their vibratory rate is the same as the colors they correspond to. When these energy centers are not working properly, we say that you are in a state of dis-ease (disease). When the energy centers are clear, you are well. Modern medicine does not deal with this because their training is for the physical body, and the chakras, although they are within the physical body, are within the spiritual body. The body is made up of four distinct units: body, mind, soul, and spirit. Although there are four, in wellness they operate well together as one unit."

"In western medicine, as I said before, only the physical body is addressed. It is unfortunate that the other three components are left out. Logically thinking, doesn't it make sense that the mind tells the body how to function? And yet, the mind isn't addressed. It is treated separately, by psychologists and psychiatrists. In holistic medicine, all four aspects are treated—body, mind, soul, and spirit—along with the chakras and many other inner body workings. Holistic should be called whole-istic because it addresses the whole being."

"Halley, I find all of this so fascinating but after a whole lifetime of thinking in the ways of western medicine, it must take many years to learn to think differently and learn holistic medicine."

"It isn't very hard at all, Trini. You have to learn to trust yourself and trust the process. I believe that we were made in the image of the Creator. Think about it, Trini. If a cow had a baby, what would it be?"

Trini giggled, "A baby cow, a calf."

"And if a monkey had a baby, what would it be?"

"Well, a baby monkey," she replied.

"And if a snake had a baby, what would it be?"

"A baby snake." Trini still was puzzled as to where Halley was taking this.

"So, if the Creator had a baby, what would it be? If it were made in the Creator's likeness and image, it would have to be a baby creator, correct?" Halley asked.

"Well, yes, I suppose," Trini said.

"Here, we have a Being who is gifted and brilliant enough to create a whole universe, the earth inhabited by people, and an ocean inhabited by sea life, trees, forests, air, all of this. Wouldn't you think that some of that creativity would filter through to the children?"

Trini thought quietly for a moment, and all sorts of possibilities entered her mind. "Ah, and if we can create illnesses, we can also create wellness!"

"Exactly, Trini," Halley responded excitedly as she reached over and hugged her. "We can be co-creators to create our lives to be in harmony with abundant life."

"What do you mean by 'abundant life'?" Trini questioned.

"Abundant health, abundant wealth, abundant happiness. Most abundance would fit into these categories. Who wouldn't want to live an abundant life?"

"Most people don't believe that is possible for them," Trini added.

"Exactly, Trini, but as children of a creator, this is our inheritance, once we live in harmony with creation's plan. Think about this: if you had a child, you would love that child and want to give it everything that was good for it, wouldn't you?"

"Of course I would," Trini exclaimed.

"And of course, the Creator would want everything that is good for His children. He would want all of His children to have abundant life because they are loved. It's all about love, Trini. But not the kind of love that has been portrayed for so long," Halley said with a faraway look in her eyes. She was thinking about how much pain people experience in relationships, and in her own life, before she had this knowledge.

The amber sun was now sinking low in the amethyst sky, spreading its golden blanket across the campground, embracing the pines with its glowing aura. The river sparkled with a million gemstones of light. Halley got up from the picnic bench and walked closer to the river. "This place is magic!"

I would call this an abundant life, Trini thought as she soaked in her surroundings.

The two women watched as the sky turned from amethyst to electric blue, while the amber sun said its farewells as it glowed over the horizon.

"This shade of blue is like the light from the throat chakra, Trini," Halley said quietly. "Can you visualize this color as being inside you, inside of your throat?"

Trini stared into the evening sky for a moment and then closed her eyes, visualizing the color she saw and then tried to imagine it as being in her throat and down her neck. Halley walked back to the fire and Trini opened her eyes and followed.

"Visualization is a very powerful tool, Trini, and so is meditation. As you learn more and more, you will find that you have more need for quiet downtime. The body, mind, soul, and spirit need time to process this new information. It is processed within you when you are still and quiet, when the thoughts are at rest. The colors of the rainbow correlate with the colors of the chakras. Kind of like a promise that everything is going to be good."

"Halley, do you visualize a rainbow inside of yourself?" Trini asked.

"That visualization is perfect to do, Trini. It is also good to break it down into each color, to focus on each one individually."

"What is the purpose or work of the throat chakra?" Trini questioned. She had a particular interest in this one since she had just been healed of her fever and sore throat.

"The throat chakra is the energy center that you use for talking, Trini. Sometimes, it clouds up from not saying what is on your mind. It is the center of communication. It works closely with the heart chakra, and one usually affects the other. If you grew up in a home where children were to be seen and not heard, or if you were punished for speaking up, after a while, your throat chakra would cloud and wouldn't operate in wellness. Or, if you have been hurt by saying how you feel and having someone misunderstand you, this can also affect the throat chakra. Often, people who are very quiet have a multitude of thoughts floating around and would love to speak or comment on what they are thinking, but because their throat chakra has been affected, they remain quiet. This sometimes creates symptoms in the throat or neck area."

"I was just healed today of a sore throat and a fever," Trini told her. "Was that because of my throat chakra not functioning properly?"

"It very well could be, Trini. What method of healing did you use?" she asked.

Trini explained how she had met John in the woods earlier and how he made tea for her fever. She also told her about using sarsaparilla and sassafras earlier.

"I do believe that there are plants and remedies from nature that can help the four bodies establish themselves in wellness," Halley responded. "Sarsaparilla and sassafras are excellent for the throat chakra, and willow bark is great for pain or fevers."

"As I was walking back down the trail, after meeting John, I passed the frog pond and noticed a black birch tree. It seemed to be drawing me. Do you know what its medicinal properties are?" Trini asked.

"Any time you are so drawn to anything, it is always for a reason, whether it be a book, a plant, an animal, or a person. There is always something to be gained. The black birch tree bark has many useful properties. It strengthens the immune system by adding iron to your blood. You could make a tea out of the bark and take a cup a day for a couple of weeks, and it would not only build up your immune system but enhance your creativity as well. Your body won't work overtime to build up its blood supply and would get the help it needs to do so. It would put you in a more restful condition, therefore allowing you to become peaceful enough for your creativity to blossom. I believe that there are other benefits, as well. Perhaps there may be something in the book I loaned to you."

"I want to learn everything," Trini smiled.

"It is essential to be very patient with yourself and not push too hard to learn. Try to relax and take it one step at a time, as it comes, and you'll enjoy your new world immensely."

Halley knew full well that Trini was not about to let any grass grow under her feet. She wasn't the type of person who would sit back and wait for experience or knowledge. She would seek it out, making it a priority. She knew, not only from having her in her classroom as a student but from the look of enthusiasm in her eyes. It seemed as if a lifeline had been thrown to her, a lifeline to becoming a healer. Not only from that look in Trini's eyes but because Halley had insight into people, partially from experiencing so much in her life and partially because she had done extensive work within herself, and was very attuned to the energies and vibrations in others, as well as herself.

"You'll learn a lot and experience a lot in your lifetime, Trini. Healers always seem to experience things on so many levels because they are being trained. The man you met, John, is giving a lecture at the library tomorrow. I'm going, and I would love for you to come with me."

"I would love to," Trini said, thinking that she would love to see him again. "I feel as if I've met John before. He looks so familiar."

Chapter Seven
Prince of the Power of the Air

Niamh slept dreamily by the fire, still dreaming about Trini and John, Fintan, Dillis, Basil, and Old Sheniah, with Fintan watching over her while Gabriel climbed up the long winding stairway to the top of Solomon's Tower. Finally, at the top, he opened the satchel that Fintan had carried on his neck across the Owenglin River's currents. Inside, Gabriel found what he had suspected to be there: Brigid's most current journal, bound in leather and tied with rawhide strips. After carefully untying it, he skimmed through the worn pages, noting that Brigid had dated each entry. She began writing the journal only three days before her 'accident,' yet journal entries continued forward until two weeks before today. All entries were written in Brigid's handwriting.

On the last page, there was a symbol unlike the symbols on the satchel, the tower, and Niamh's cloak. It held an ominous appearance, and underneath it was written, 'If you do not run your subconscious mind yourself, someone else will.' Gabriel understood this to mean that either Brigid was being attacked by the Prince of the Power of the Air or was dealing with someone who was. After reading more of her journal, he realized it was time for Niamh to wake up, and after carefully tying the journal with its laces, he placed it back in the leather satchel and headed back down the stairs.

"How was your sleep, Niamh?" he asked as he tended the fire.

"I had a dream that felt so much like reality, and Fintan was in my dream," she said quietly. "In the dream, my name was Trini O'Brien and my mother had died. There was a woman who looked like my mother, named Old Sheniah. She was a healer, like my mother, and although I never got to meet her, I saw a photo of her."

"Niamh, we need to get you back home soon. It will be dark, and I'm sure your father is worried about you. I have a boat that we can cross the river in, and Fintan can swim alongside us."

"I can't go back yet. I have to have some way of understanding all this. If I go back now without understanding the symbols or this experience, and especially those dragons, I will go crazy with worry. After my dream, I feel more strongly than ever that my mother is still alive somewhere. I need answers, Gabriel."

Gabriel knew that she would have a tough time without answers, but at the same time, he knew that he had to be careful about the way he explained things to her, or she wouldn't go back. If he told her that he knew her mother was alive, she would insist on having him help her find Brigid.

"Niamh, the dragons that you saw were heading toward your village. They are signs that darkness will be unleashed there. You will need to go back; otherwise, Fintan will be blamed for your disappearance," he tried to explain.

"Fintan, why would anyone blame poor Fintan?"

"If you are missing, after having only received Fintan today, they will say that he wouldn't let you control him and that he must have caused some dreadful accident. If you don't go back soon, Fintan might be taken from you."

"Niamh, the dragons that you saw are images of the Prince of the Power of the Air. There are four crown princes in each realm: four in the dark realm and four in the light realm. In the light realm, the four crown princes are Michael, Gabriel, Uriel, and Raphael; we call them archangels. In the dark realm, the one whom we call the Prince of the Power of the Air can control the mind. There is also one who tries to control the body, one who tries to control the spirit, and one who tries to control the soul or the emotions. Solomon's Tower and this surrounding property are protected magically from any of the crowned princes' influences. This is why the ancient kings of Ireland and Jerusalem came here; to see the truth clearly and to sign sacred pacts."

"I will go back. I couldn't bear to have Fintan taken from me or placed in danger," she promised.

"When you go back, I want you to remember something that is very, very important: 'If you do not run your subconscious mind yourself, someone else will.'"

"I will remember it, but what does it mean exactly?"

"It means that you have to stay strong and walk in the light. No matter what darkness or evil you hear about, stay true to who you are. Guard over your thoughts carefully and wisely. You will hear things that won't make sense at first. Don't react! Stay quiet within your being and watch things play out. You are of your mother's lineage, a healer with a pure heart. You will be called upon to make important decisions, life-changing decisions. Stay true to who you are and everything will work out. The Prince of the Power of the Air will have influences working with people by the time you get back. Handle things the way your mother would: with strong love and peace," he warned.

"Is the Prince of the Power of the Air a real being? One that I will see?" she asked.

"He is quite real, but he will only reveal himself through people, through their actions, and words. When people are not in the correct frame of mind, when they are in any negative thought patterns, the Prince of the Power of the Air uses that as an opportunity to begin working on their minds. He can use a small thought to blow up into a huge situation, causing people to think differently than they would normally think."

"I will stay strong. I am strong. Even since my mother went missing, I have stayed strong."

"Yes, you are very strong, and you have made wise decisions in taking care of your brother and father. Your brother has been having a tough time, harder than you might expect. He is a good man but made some wrong choices because of his pain. He will need your love and support when you get back," Gabriel warned.

"Will Fintan be fine if I leave now?"

"Yes, he will be fine, but we need to leave here soon."

Niamh stood up from the fire and took her beautiful cape off, then handed it to Gabriel.

"Fintan, run this back to the cave for now, and we will meet you on the shore," he said while throwing the cape around Fintan's neck. By the time Gabriel and Niamh traveled down the wooded trail to the shore, Fintan was there waiting for them. As promised, Gabriel's boat was tied nearby. After carefully helping Niamh into the small boat, he took an oar from inside the boat and hurried it gently into the current. Fintan walked into the water and then began swimming close behind them. Upon reaching the shore, Gabriel stood up and jumped toward the land, pulling the boat in closer so that Niamh wouldn't have to walk in the water. Fintan stepped onto the dry land and shook himself to release water from his coat and mane.

Niamh reached over and put her arms around Gabriel's neck and thanked him for being there. Gabriel promised that they would see each other soon.

"You take care of her, Fintan Wild Fire," he smiled as he patted Fintan on the shoulder.

"Well, Fintan, what do you make of all this?" she asked as they walked side by side on the Ridge Road, going back to her homestead.

Remember the advice that Gabriel gave you, he thought.

As the two travelers approached the farm, Niamh had a cold chill run up her spine. She saw Deliah, her best friend, standing in the yard talking to Liam. Suddenly, Deliah looked over to where Fintan and Niamh were and ran over to them.

"Where have you been?" she asked. "We have needed you here. Donal is sick."

"What happened? I'm sorry I wasn't here. It was my birthday, Donal and Dad gave me Fintan and I was out riding him."

Deliah was crying and holding Niamh's hand very hard. "It's my fault. Everything is my fault," she cried.

"Is Donal here?" Niamh inquired.

"Yes, he's in his room. We didn't know what to do, so I sent my brother to get the doctor. You weren't here to help. The doctor is with him now. He asked that we wait outside while he examines him."

"Wait here with Dad, Deliah. I'm going in to check on him," Niamh said as she loosened Deliah's grip on her hand while motioning for Fintan to go to the barn.

As Niamh came into the kitchen, she noticed a strong smell of alcohol and followed the scent to the spare room where Donal and the doctor were. When the doctor saw her, he motioned for her to come in.

"Doctor Mahoney. Thank you for coming. Is my brother alright?"

"He's going to be down for a while, Niamh. His body is very toxic from alcohol. He has been drinking a lot, and it has affected his organs. He will need water every hour for the next twenty-four hours and no food. It does seem as if there is something else going on with your brother as well. I don't think all of this is just from drinking."

"I didn't even know he had been drinking. Do you mean just today, drinking?" Niamh asked.

"No, according to the shape he's in, he's been drinking for at least a couple of years. Probably, from what I hear from Deliah, quite frequently since your dear mother was gone," he explained gently.

"I can't believe this. I see Donal almost every day. We aren't a drinking family. He works here on the farm. How could I not have known about this?"

"People who drink in excess can often hide it well, especially if they know their families won't approve of it, which I'm sure Liam doesn't."

"But today, during the day, he was drinking?" she asked.

"Oh, yes, he's been drinking a *lot*. He was in town with Deliah and she brought him back here."

"What else can you tell me, Doctor? What else can I do for him? Will he have permanent damage? Will he recover?"

"Niamh, if you can find a way to keep him away from alcohol, he will live. If he keeps on drinking, he will die," he told her sincerely. "There is something else going on here, something I am unsure about also."

"So, water only for twenty-four hours and no food. Is there anything else?"

"No, not really anything at this point. Watch him. He shouldn't be up trying to walk around or anything. I gave him something for the pain, so make sure he stays in bed. I'll be back to check on him tomorrow night, but as I said, I feel that there is something else going on as well."

"Pain?"

"From the liver damage."

"What do we owe you, Doctor?"

"You don't owe me a bit. I owed your mother for helping me with my patients," he explained.

"Thank you, Doctor. I'm going in to check on him now," she said as she walked into Donal's room.

"Donal, dear Donal. Are you alright, Brother?" she asked while feeling his forehead. "I'm so sorry I wasn't here to care for you. Can I do anything to make you more comfortable?"

"Don't let them take Fintan from you. I got him fair and square. He's yours. Hide him if you have to, but don't let them take him," he said as he fell off to sleep.

She rubbed his arm and tried to wake him, but then she remembered that the doctor had given him something to make him sleep so that he wouldn't try to walk around in his condition. The room smelled like stale smoke and alcohol, and Donal looked a mess. She opened the window to let some fresh air in and went into the kitchen to heat up some water to clean Donal's face and hands when Deliah came in.

"This is all my fault, Niamh," she said, crying.

"I'm sure it isn't your fault. How could it possibly be your fault?"

"Oh, believe me, it is," she said as she held her head in her hands, like one who is ashamed and worried.

Deliah and Niamh had been best friends since they were old enough to walk. Niamh thought of her as a family member, as the sister that she never had. She couldn't imagine Deliah doing anything that would hurt Donal. Although they hadn't spent much time together since the disappearance of Brigid, Niamh still thought of her as a sister.

"I told your father, and now I'm going to tell you, Niamh. I'm pregnant with Donal's baby. I told Donal recently and he's been drinking ever since," she confessed tearfully. "Well, he's been drinking on a somewhat regular basis since your mom passed, but since I told him about the pregnancy, he has been drinking non-stop."

Niamh was angry, not because of the pregnancy, but because Deliah never even told her that she had been seeing Donal. She couldn't believe that Deliah would keep something like this from her after they had been closer than sisters for their whole lives. She still couldn't understand why Deliah believed that Donal's illness which, according to the doctor, was caused by a drinking problem, could be Deliah's fault. Something deep inside her told her that this story was not real, and she wondered why.

"You aren't saying anything. You hate me, right?" Deliah asked, still crying.

"How long have you been close to him?" Niamh asked.

"As a close friend, almost two years. He came to me after your mother went missing and needed comfort," she explained. "As more than that, it has only been a couple of months."

"Why wouldn't you tell me? We have shared everything since we were little girls. I had no idea. Do you love him?" Niamh asked hopefully. At least it would give her some comfort to know that Donal was loved.

"Of course I do. I couldn't tell you because, well, you are his sister and we haven't seen much of each other since you have been busy here at the homestead after your mother passed away."

"But why didn't you tell me that he was drinking so much? I could have stopped him. I could have told my father, and he would have stopped him. Why didn't *you* stop him?" Niamh asked angrily.

"I tried to stop him. He would lie to me about it. He would sneak out of your house at night, after you and your father would be asleep, and go into town to drink and gamble. Lately, he ended up at my house many a night in rough shape, unable to get back home. Then, he would wake up before dawn and head back home to work at the farm all day, hoping no one would know," she said quietly.

"That reason isn't good enough. Now, Donal is in a rough condition with ruined organs and we might not be able to correct the damages," Niamh said while removing the hot water from the stove. Something about Deliah's story didn't ring true in Niamh's spirit, and she wanted to say that to Deliah but remembered what Gabriel told her about not reacting.

"Niamh, I am so sorry. I should have told you or Liam. I was wrong. This is my fault," she cried.

"His drinking is not your fault. His gambling is not your fault, only not telling us was your fault, and I forgive you," Niamh said sweetly.

"Can you fix him?" asked Deliah hopefully.

"I'll fix him, but I've never dealt with anyone with an alcohol problem. I'll have to go through my mother's books and see if she ever dealt with anyone in this condition. I'll ask the doctor if he knows of anyone who Mother might have worked with who had this situation, and maybe he will remember such a time so that I might find it more quickly. Mother dated her journal entries. I'm sure that if anyone knew a cure, it would be her."

Suddenly remembering that Deliah was pregnant, she asked, "How are you feeling? Are you ill? You are so thin, Deliah. I wouldn't have guessed you are pregnant."

"I've been dizzy and throwing up in the mornings. Morning sickness. Other than that, I'm doing fine, just worried and nervous about Donal."

"Did you tell your parents yet?" Niamh asked worriedly.

"God, no. They will not only kill Donal, but me as well."

"How about your brother?"

"He knows but told me not to tell our parents. He won't tell anyone. You know how protective he is."

"I'm going to wash Donal up unless you want to. We need to freshen up that room."

At that offer, Deliah smiled and took the water to Donal's room, along with a washcloth and a towel.

The doctor had been standing outside, talking to Liam, but knowing that Liam would come into the kitchen soon, Niamh made some hot tea and heated up some soup for him. She cut off some bread that she had made the night before and spread some of their farm-churned butter on it, to go with his soup.

When Liam came in, he looked old. Beaten down by the horrible news of his son's illness and Deliah's pregnancy, he looked like he had aged ten years in a day. He sat in his usual seat at the head of the table, drinking his tea, while Niamh served his soup and bread.

"Don't be upset with yourself, Father. You didn't know. None of this is your fault," Niamh said lovingly.

Liam looked up at her with tears in his eyes. It always amazed him that she seemed to know what he was thinking. He had blamed himself, without justification. He felt that somehow this was his fault, and he was suffering deeply in his soul.

"Take some soup, Father. It will restore you. I'm sorry I was gone so long. Fintan and I were out exploring the day."

"I'm not upset that you were out with Fintan. It's your birthday, Daughter, and I wanted you to have fun. I think we should talk about Deliah. I don't think it is going to be safe for her to stay at home with her parents, being like they are. What would you think if we asked her to stay here? She could help you out and help with Donal. I was going to hire her brother to work in Donal's place. I guess we could even make him a place over the shed."

"Father, whatever you choose will be fine with me. I agree that Deliah won't be safe at home, and as long as her brother isn't working right now and is available, he is welcome here," she said lovingly.

"Can you fix Donal's organs?" he asked.

"I will, although, truthfully at this moment, I'm not sure how. I will find a way, I promise. I was wondering if you ever knew of Mother taking care of anyone with this condition. Perhaps she has some mention of it in her journals."

"I'll have to think about that. Your mother was usually pretty private when it came to people's business. The only way I would know anything about her work would be from the neighbors. She would talk about happy things, like the birth of a baby or someone getting well, but as for personal issues, she always kept those to herself. She was very respectful of others, always."

"The doctor said to keep giving him water every hour. I'll start with that, and in the meantime, I'm going to go through Mother's journals and see if I can find something that will help. Back to Deliah and Roger, I think it would be fine if they live here, but the only thing is...her parents will be furious, and we will have to deal with their rage. I guess it would be better to deal with it here, rather than having her over there," Niamh said pensively.

"Well, I'll talk to Deliah and Roger and see how they feel about it. How do you like Fintan Wild Fire?"

"He's incredible. I love him. He is smart too. He seems to know what I'm thinking before I know what I'm thinking," Niamh replied, smiling.

"I found out from Deliah today that Donal won that horse gambling in town," Liam told her sadly.

"Donal, gambling?" she said in shock.

"Deliah told me that he's been in town drinking and gambling at night ever since we lost Brigid," he replied questioningly.

"And sleeping with my best friend?" she said sarcastically.

"Yes, apparently so. They are probably going to need to get married now, since there's a little one on the way."

"Yes, they had better do that. I'll talk with Deliah and see if I can find out what her plans for marriage are and help her out in any way I can," she promised her father.

In the midst of Donal's sudden illness, finding out that Fintan was won in a gambling debt, Deliah's pregnancy, and having the responsibilities of the homestead, Niamh barely had time to remember the experiences of the day, but one thing stood out the most to her and that was her dream of Old Sheniah. Old Sheniah was a healer like her mother, and also strangely resembled her. As Niamh and her father sat at the old wooden table discussing this new twist to their lives, they both were thinking the same thing. If Brigid were here, she would have known what to do to make things right again. She would have instantly known how to heal Donal, what to do about letting Deliah and Roger move in, and how to deal with the up and coming anger that was sure to take place when Deliah's parents found out about the pregnancy.

Deliah's parents have never been easy to deal with. The easiest way to deal with them is to stay away from them, but that hasn't always been possible since the girls were best friends and their community wasn't that large. Some people always seem to want to get into other people's affairs, but Deliah's parents were a mystery to everyone. They were rarely seen in town and most considered them to be very angry and dark folk. They were people who held deep secrets and were not to be trusted.

Now that Deliah was pregnant and unwed, her life might be at risk of incurring their fiery temperaments. Liam was right: it would be much safer for Roger and Deliah to stay at Liam's homestead. Liam wouldn't be able to manage the entire responsibility of the farm chores on his own, and Roger's help would be invaluable. After thinking it over a bit, he decided to ride into town to talk with the parents first, before mentioning anything to Deliah and Roger.

"I'm going to ride into town to talk with their parents," he told Niamh.

"Let me go with you," she asked.

"No, until we find out more about Donal's condition, I want you to be here with him, and I'm not sure about you taking Fintan into town right now...not until we make sure this 'deal' about the gambling debt is free and clear. I'm going to leave Roger here, and I've found some chores for him to do. If anything comes up in the meantime, send him in to get me. Keep Fintan in the barn for now," he told her worriedly.

"Alright, Father, while Deliah is here looking after Donal, I suppose I will clean up in here and then go through Mother's journals to see if I can find anything about curing him," she replied. "Father, you aren't planning on telling Deliah's parents about the pregnancy, are you?"

"Not yet. Deliah doesn't want anyone else to know, for now, other than our family. We need to respect her wishes, but I don't like keeping things from people. Considering who her parents are, though, it is better to keep this quiet for now."

"Is there any chance that I might lose Fintan?"

"There's always a chance, Honey. I'm going to make sure things are settled up, though, and hope and pray all of this won't cause any more hardship."

After Liam left for town, Niamh hurriedly set out some soup for Deliah and Roger, then she went to Donal's doorway and tapped gently.

"Deliah, I left some soup and bread out for you and Roger. I'm going to go through some of my mother's journals to see if I might find a cure for Donal. How is he doing?"

"He's quiet and sleeping for now. I've cleaned him and given him water," Deliah told Niamh, before bursting out into tears again. "I don't know what

I'm going to do, Niamh. I've brought all this shame on myself and my family, on Donal and your family. I wish I could turn back time. Donal means the world to me, and we talked about getting married someday. I'm sorry for not telling you all this before. Now, with Donal being so sick and a baby on the way...and my parents..." she said between sobs.

"You know things always have a way of working out. They always do," she reassured her. "Right now, you are with child and need to take care of yourself and your baby. Why don't you get your brother and both of you have some food and tea? You trust Roger with the news about the baby?"

"Yes, I had to tell him. I needed his help to get Donal here, and I was crying so hard I couldn't think straight. Should I tell Liam to come in and eat also?"

"No, he ate. He had to go into town for something. Deliah, on second thought, you stay and I'll get Roger. I have to do something outside anyway," she told her as she remembered that Fintan needed to be in the barn. She first found Roger, who was walking toward the house.

"How's Donal?" he asked.

"He is sleeping right now. Deliah is in the house with him. I'm going to put Fintan in the barn, so go ahead in and eat with Deliah. She's crying and upset and I need to do a few things."

"Niamh, did she tell you?" he asked embarrassedly.

"She did, Roger."

"Our parents are going to kill her for this, you know. It's a shame this had to happen right now since she and Mother have been getting along so well for the past few months and working so closely together."

"Oh, they're finally getting along? I'm glad to hear it. What are they 'working' together on? Do you mean in the gardens?"

"Yes, in the gardens and the kitchen. Mother has been teaching her about herbs and things."

"I haven't had much time to spend with Deliah since Mother left, and I hadn't realized she and your mother had gotten closer."

"Oh, they stay up late talking and spending time together. Pretty strange after all these years, isn't it? Now, Mother will probably kill her."

"No one will be killed, Roger. Things have a way of working out. Do you know who Donal got Fintan from, by any chance? I know he supposedly won him in a gambling debt, but I've never seen this horse around here. Whose horse was it?" she asked.

"I only know they were from Limerick. Two old men who were at the pub were playing cards with Donal. Those men stopped me in town and asked where they could get a good drink and I told them at O'Shaunessey's pub. I gave them directions. That's when I first saw Fintan. One of those men was pulling him on a lead. I asked where they were from and they told me Limerick, then they said they had certain 'business' to tend to and would be heading back to Limerick in the morning. Then, two days ago, I found out that Donal won your horse in a card game and was keeping him at Freddy O'Reilley's farm until your birthday, today. Not a very happy birthday, is it?"

"Roger, some parts of it have been happy for me. Getting Fintan was incredible, and hearing that I will be an aunt was happy news. Yes, there are rough times included in this day, but things will work out. They always do, one way or another." She smiled, trying to cheer Roger up, as she headed toward Fintan.

"Fintan, what a day!" she said as she approached him. "Come on. We need to go to the barn. Papa wants you to stay in here for a while until we find out some details..." She didn't finish her sentence because she noticed movement in the trees to the right of the field.

"It's alright, Niamh. It's me, Gabriel."

"Gabriel. What are you doing here? How did you know where I live?" she asked, startled by his sudden appearance.

"I was leaving and suddenly thought that I should take Fintan back to the mountain with me. He'll be safe there, Niamh. I'll watch over him," he told her.

"Safe from what?"

"From forces who want to hurt your family. That's all I can tell you for now. Will you trust me?"

"What will I tell Papa?"

"Tell him that you hid Fintan away and he is safe. I'll keep him with me and take care of him, Niamh, until things are clear."

"Fintan, what do you think of this plan?"

Fintan walked toward Gabriel and nuzzled him.

"Well, take him then. When will I see you and Fintan again?" she asked, tears in her eyes.

"You'll know when the time is right. We will meet you at the shore, right where we landed earlier today," he told her while reaching into his pocket. "Here, make this into a tea and give the tea to your brother tonight and again in the morning," he said while handing her a bundle wrapped in a leaf. "It won't completely cure him, but it will help to get the poisons out of his system."

"You mean the alcohol?" she asked.

"No, I mean the powder that he is being poisoned with. Deliah's mother has been putting it in his tea, to cause him to be too tired to come home. She wanted Donal to have a baby with Deliah."

"How can this be real? How could anyone drug my brother, and why did she want them to have a baby?"

"I need to leave and get Fintan out of here quickly," he told her as he began walking away. "As long as you trust me, things will work out fine, Niamh. I will guard over Fintan with my life, I promise you."

Niamh stood very still, watching Fintan and Gabriel as they walked into the woods until they were out of sight, then she went to the barn door, latching it carefully before going back into the house. She had a circus of thoughts doing curious aerobics in her mind. From the time she woke up and looked out her bedroom window, the day had left her mind reeling. From the early morning arrival of Fintan to crossing the Owenglin to Solomon's Tower, meeting Gabriel, seeing the monstrous dragons, having the strange dream on the mountain, to coming home and finding Donal deathly ill and Deliah pregnant. And now, to find out that Deliah's mother was poisoning Donal, and the very idea that Fintan might be taken from her was more than her innocent mind could handle. At this time, all that would have made anyone collapse, but Niamh showed what she was made of and was determined to stay strong, just as she had when her mother had disappeared.

Niamh somehow trusted Gabriel, who she didn't know, and knew he would watch over Fintan. Knowing this gave her some peace, as Fintan had already taken over the most significant part of her heart. In only one day, the laws of her life changed, and she remembered what Gabriel told her about her birthday while standing in Solomon's Tower. *'Your birthday is the ending of one year of your life and the beginning of a new year of your life. I feel that whatever we are about to see will be a precursor to lead you to the experiences of the next year of your life.'*

She knew the meaning of the winds before leaving with Fintan and how the arrival of such winds could bring intensity and destruction along. She remembered what Gabriel told her about how the dragons were controlled by someone who had darkness in their spirits and adding it all up, she knew that her simple life had quickly become very complicated. It would no longer be just her, her brother, and her father. If things went according to Liam's plan, Deliah and Roger would be with them, and at some point, a new baby. She wanted to handle things in a way that would make her mother proud of her and hoped that she would possess at least half the skills her mother had. Donal needed to be healed, quickly.

Chapter Eight
The Elders of Iona

Gabriel and Fintan, after crossing the Owenglin's currents, quickly headed up the mountain path to the cave. Nightfall would soon be upon them, and Irish nights in the fall can be unusually cold, especially near the ocean. Gabriel quickly built a campfire near the mouth of the cave and then went inside to get some food for Fintan, the food he had stored for him days before.

Fintan was remarkably calm, considering that he was whisked away from Niamh, but he instinctively knew that by going away with Gabriel, there would be fewer problems for Niamh and her family. He knew Gabriel for many years and cared deeply for him, having confidence that Gabriel would do whatever it took to help Niamh and her family.

"Fintan, we have company tonight, my friend. The Gypsies are coming here for a special meeting with the Elders of Iona. They should be here soon, and I'm looking forward to talking with them."

Gabriel spent a lot of time with the Gypsies, especially his dear friends Analine Cleary and his wife, Isabelle. They were Tinkers and traveled throughout Ireland making and fixing all types of metal pots and pans, along with trading horses.

Gabriel smiled when he remembered the first time he met them, over fourteen years ago. The Clearys' daughter, Ocean Marie, had been about five years old and had wandered away from their camp, following a trail through the brush and then falling down a slippery hillside to the ocean's edge. While at the beach, Gabriel watched her while she was so thoroughly absorbed in communicating with a baby seal pup that she didn't seem to realize that the tide was coming in. It would have stranded her, had Gabriel not rescued her and brought her back to her camp. Upon arriving back at the camp, Ocean's parents were ecstatic. They had just returned to the campsite after looking for her for several hours. Feeling disheartened that their efforts were in vain, they were organizing a search with some of the other Gypsies who had just returned from work.

"I found her on the beach," Gabriel said to her parents. "The tide was about to come in and she was talking with a young seal pup, hardly aware of the impending rising water. Judging from the marks on the hillside, it appears that she fell and slid all the way to the beach," he told them.

After finding out that Ocean Marie was uninjured, they invited Gabriel to dinner. Gabriel found their company to be quite exciting and found them to be very spiritual and generous. They had been friends ever since. Tonight, after meeting up, they would be escorting the Elders of Iona to Solomon's Tower.

Fintan and Gabriel had met with the Elders of Iona on several occasions, and both had the most profound respect and admiration for their wisdom. There was never a challenge that the Elders were not able to see a clear path through, and Gabriel hoped to discuss the arrival of the dragons with them and what could be done to prevent the impending destruction, particularly on the O'Brien homestead. He knew that the storm that was about to hit Connemara was going to be no light matter. Hell was getting ready to enlarge itself, and the focus of hell's intent was the O'Brien family.

Once the Gypsies arrived with the Elders of Iona, Gabriel offered them seats by the fire, along with warm drinks and food. Although Gabriel saw the Gypsies reasonably often, he was surprised by how quickly Ocean Marie had grown up, now a young woman, and known for her wisdom. Analine and Isabelle did an excellent job raising her.

They all greeted one another and sat by the campfire exchanging short stories about their journey and discussing the situation at Niamh's homestead. Upon hearing about Donal's condition, Ocean Marie closed her eyes. She needed to focus her attention inward on what she was thinking and feeling.

"Donal will not be healed until he sheds himself of the unknown guilt," Ocean said respectfully.

"How do you know this?" asked her father.

"If he hadn't felt guilty about something, he wouldn't have been drinking and gambling," she replied. "His jaundiced condition is the symptom of the thought; therefore, the thought of guilt is the originator of the illness. The guilt must be taken away, dragged out at the roots, and he must forgive himself for the thing that he originally felt guilty about in order to begin the healing process. No herbs will cure this. The herbs will help some, but as long as the original thought of guilt remains, the chance that he would go back to drinking and be unhappy would be great. This, along with an antidote that will work against the poison will be what is needed now."

Analine knew his daughter and recognized her wisdom yet worried that the Elders would counteract her attempt to bring healing to the situation. As enlightened and spiritually advanced as they were, they might not be ready to accept the fact that all illness begins with a thought. He studied their severe expressions in the glow of the campfire, hoping to find one whose appearance showed acceptance. Analine felt that it would take the Elders some time to accept what Ocean was presenting to them, yet she expected that someone would respond to her. It's a father's pride that caused his heart to yearn for her to be accepted as a Wise Woman.

"My daughter has a soft heart for all who are suffering; not only people, but animals as well," Analine finally spoke.

"You needn't convince me of this. It is very apparent," spoke Artair, the youngest of the Elders of Iona.

"Her wisdom appears to have exceeded our own," said Connall the Ancient. "Of course, it must begin with a thought. Brilliant! Thank you for sharing this wisdom with us, young lady. Now, tell me, if you will, what would your suggestion be about how to collect this thought from Donal?"

"I know if I could go there, I could meet with Deliah and Niamh and explain to them the importance of this work. Donal's healing will be through the spoken word. Someone needs to understand this," Ocean Marie offered.

"I am willing to take her there. Fintan and I could be there and back in no time," Gabriel offered.

"No," spoke Connall, "it is far too dangerous for Fintan to leave the island right now. You can take Ocean Marie by boat later after we hold council in the tower. There is more work to be done there, and we need to make decisions on how we will counter the attack shown by the dragons. If you would, please wait until we finish our discussions and make these decisions—that would be better. We may be sending Faolan, if he gets here in time, along with you. He had some business to attend to in Dublin and said he would be along sometime during the night."

"Yes, of course, I will wait," promised Gabriel.

"Thank you. I will wait as well," declared Ocean, eliciting a caring smile from her father. Although she was his youngest daughter, he trusted her and knew that she was protected from all evil. Analine knew this from the moment Gabriel brought her back from the beach that day when she was only five years old.

"What is the purpose of the Dark Ones focusing their energies on the O'Brien family?" asked Analine to the Elders of Iona.

"The O'Briens are from the sacred lineage of Brian Boruma. The Dark Ones know that they, the O'Briens, contain a seed of the ancient lineage from the Beautiful People, the Tuatha de Danann. The Tuatha have abilities that others don't possess, such as the ability to heal others. The Dark Ones believe that it is their mission to kill off all remaining traces of the Tuatha, which in turn, according to how they believe, will make *them* the most powerful beings on earth. As the Dark Ones focus their powers, they call forth the dragons, which bring the dark energy to, in this case, the O'Brien homestead. It was the

Dark Ones who orchestrated Deliah's fall from grace. Her pregnancy and the plan to trap Donal was all part of their master plan," explained Connall the Ancient.

"There has been a constant and ongoing war between the Tuatha and the Dark Ones. From the time the King of the Sea's daughter left the underwater world of her father and ran away to the Slieve Mish Mountains with Brian Boruma, the Dark Ones have taken the side of the King of the Sea. I might add that the King of the Sea had no intentions of working with the Dark Ones. They have taken it upon themselves to create havoc against the Tuatha and those that carry their seed. The Dark Ones can only maintain their level of power while in the air and have no powers within the sea. They believe that by waging war for the King of the Sea, he will grant them special privilege in or on the sea. These battles are in hopes of eventually gaining power over all the elements," added Artair.

"Deliah's mother is one of the Dark Ones. She is the reason that Donal is suffering now. Yes, he drank, but not enough to cause the damage that is wreaking havoc in his body now. She waited and observed for many years, hoping for her chance to drug him, which she did in small doses over the course of several weeks," Connall the Ancient explained carefully.

"What was in it for her?" asked Analine.

"Well," continued Artair, "she mostly did it for revenge against Brigid. She has been jealous of her since they were young and always wanted everything that Brigid had. Brigid was beautiful and carried the gift of healing; everyone loved her. She had the life that Moira thought should belong to her. Deliah also had Liam for a husband, someone that Moira had always wanted as her own. Moira wants power and will stop at nothing to get it. By orchestrating the union between Donal and Deliah, she knew that eventually there would be a grandchild who carried the gifts of the Magic Ones through her bloodline. She plans to take that child and manipulate its powers to rise against the O'Brien family, particularly to control Niamh and get her and Donal out of the way so she can finally marry Liam. Now that Brigid is out of her way and Donal is ill, with a baby on the way, if this story is true, I imagine that this woman feels pretty content with herself and her plan."

"Gabriel, when Faolan gets here, take him and Ocean Marie and leave them at Liam's. Then, I want you to head straight over to town and see if you can find out the names of the characters who had possession of Fintan before Donal got him and where they are now. I have a hunch that they are deeper in this plot than they are letting on. Ocean, take this medicine pouch and put it on Donal's neck. I put something in it to help counteract the potion that

Deliah's mother put in his drinks," said Artair as he handed Ocean a small pouch made of leather.

"Faolan, there you are! I trust you have handled the business in Dublin with success? Will you go with Gabriel and Ocean to the O'Brien homestead? I want you to stay with Ocean and don't let her out of your sight. Liam's son, Donal, has been poisoned and is in very dire condition. His daughter, Niamh, is there, along with a friend, Deliah. They are doing all they can to help Donal, but they need the medicine pouch and some herbs that I have given to Ocean," Artair explained.

"Of course I will go. When do we leave?" Faolan asked.

"You can leave right now. We were waiting for you to come back. We don't want the girls left alone there, and Gabriel is going on into town."

"I see that Fintan is here. I heard he was with the O'Briens."

"Gabriel will explain all this to you on the way. Waste no time!" said Connall the Ancient. Ocean, Gabriel, and Faolan bid their goodbyes as they quickly headed down the narrow dirt mountain trail to the water where their boat was tied to a rugged piece of wood on the rocky beach.

Chapter Nine
Message from the Sea King

The night of the meeting at Solomon's Tower, Ocean Marie's brother, Niko, was walking along the shore, when suddenly a beautiful mermaid appeared, swimming close to the beach. She smiled as she floated close to him, holding something in her hand, reaching out to him.

"The Sea King has sent me with a message for the head of the Elders of Iona. Will you please give this to him? He asks that he please read it and interpret it in the spirit in which it was intended," she said as Niko waded out into the water to accept the scroll that she was offering to him.

"I'm happy to deliver it to him."

"Will you deliver it on this night?"

"Yes, I will see him tonight and deliver it myself," he promised. "And will The Sea King require a response? Niko asked.

"He didn't say. I will come back tomorrow at dawn. If there is a message, I will deliver it to him."

Niko bid her farewell and put the scroll in his pack before ascending the long trail up the mountain to find Connall the Ancient and present it to him, as promised. As he approached the campfire, his mother, Isabelle, greeted him with a hug and offered him some food. Analine, her husband, motioned for his son to sit at the fire with the Elders.

Niko motioned for his father to come away from the fire so that he might speak to him privately before joining the rest of the group.

"Father, a mermaid gave me a scroll from the Sea King to give to Connall the Ancient. Shall I give it to him now or would you like to?"

"Son, please go ahead and give it to him. Thank you for showing me this respect."

Niko went to the fire and sat next to Connall the Ancient. After greeting him appropriately, he offered the scroll, along with the message that the mermaid gave him to convey. When Connall opened the scroll and realized how long it was, he decided that he needed first to read it alone, and excused himself. He knew the wisdom of the old Sea King and how he wouldn't write something that could be interpreted easily by anyone who might have foul intentions. He realized that he might need some privacy to figure out exactly what the Sea King wanted to convey to him.

After studying the following message for a while, Connall the Ancient came back to the fire and said, "I know where Niamh's mother is."

To Connall the Ancient,

I'm confident that you will understand and take the necessary actions.

Once upon a time, in a beautiful kingdom far, far away, there lived a very scholarly Prince. Out of all the princes in all the lands, this Prince was the kindest and most loving. He loved all the mountains and valleys, the sky and the ocean, the trees and the flowers, and all the animals and people in his whole kingdom. This scholarly Prince might have been pleased, but some of the people in his country had turned evil and went on wild rampages. This hurt him in his heart, and every day he felt sad and wished the people would stop fighting. He wanted them to stop fighting, but he didn't know how to make them stop, so he read many books to find the answer, but in all the books he read he didn't see the solution. One day, while out walking by the ocean, a beautiful Sea Turtle was swimming close to the shore and spoke to him;

"Hello, Scholarly Prince. Why do you smile but there is sorrow in your heart?"

"Hello, Sea Turtle. I am sad because I have read many books to find out how to get some of the people in my kingdom to stop fighting but I cannot find the answer."

"Oh, Prince, that is certainly a large dilemma. Perhaps I can offer some assistance," the Sea Turtle said caringly.

"I would welcome your assistance, as you are old and wise. Please tell me if you know the answer," the Prince said gently.

"I don't know the answer," said the Sea Turtle, "but I know of a Princess who lives in a kingdom far, far away and she might know the answer. She has read many books and has known many wise people. She is very nice and loving, like you, and I'm sure she would be pleased to help you."

"But how will I get my message to her, since she lives so far away in another kingdom?"

"I will deliver it to her myself. I am going on my yearly migration soon and will drop off your message to her and then wait there until she sends her reply, which I will bring back to you," offered the caring Sea Turtle.

"How can I thank you? You are an exceptional friend to me. You are always trusted and true."

The Prince had to figure out how to write a message without a pen, ink, or paper...or a way to keep his message dry while the Sea Turtle traveled with it. He looked all around and found a feather.

"Ah, this feather will work nicely for a pen."

He then looked harder and found an empty bottle on the shore. "Yes, this bottle will make a wonderful container to put my message in and will keep it dry while the Sea Turtle travels the wide ocean in her migration." He walked a little further down the beach and saw a piece of cork.

"I can take a rock and cut this cork to stop up the bottle after I put my message in."

"You are brilliant," spoke the Sea Turtle as he watched the Scholarly Prince in his search for supplies to write his message to the Princess in the faraway land.

Now, the Prince had a feather to use as a pen, a bottle to keep his message dry, a cork to close the top of the bottle so that no water would get in, but he was still missing two essential and necessary articles.

"I need paper and ink," he said to the Sea Turtle.

"I have an idea. I will be right back!" said the Sea Turtle as he dove into the water.

While he was gone, the Prince had an idea of his own. "I'll be right back," he yelled into the ocean, hoping the Sea Turtle would hear him and not think he had gone away. He then took off running as fast as he could to the forest near the ocean and didn't stop until he found a birch tree that was shedding some of its bark.

I can use this instead of paper, he thought as he rolled up a piece of birch bark quickly and ran back to the beach.

He was out of breath from running so fast, so he sat down on the beach to rest while he momentarily waited for the Sea Turtle to return. Suddenly, he remembered that there was one more thing he needed and didn't have any idea about what to use. *I have no ink*, he thought sadly. How would he ever be able to write his message without ink? He had plenty of ink at his castle, but it was far away and he wouldn't have time to run all the way there and get back in time before the Sea Turtle had to leave for migration. *I am beginning to think this is hopeless*, he thought, yet he knew deep inside that there was always hope in every situation.

Suddenly, he saw the Sea Turtle's head bobbing up and down in the water, coming closer. He was swimming more slowly than usual and appeared to have something that he was holding in his mouth. As he swam in closer, the Prince ran toward the water to meet him. The Sea Turtle swam up to the edge of the water, and with one quick wave of his head, the big thing that he was carrying flew up onto the shore and sat glistening in the morning sunlight. The Sea Turtle looked very proudly at the Prince and said, "This will help."

"Well, thank you for the shell, but what will it help with?" asked the Prince, still looking puzzled and wishing he had some ink.

"This is a Murex shell, and he has agreed to give us some ink," the Sea Turtle said confidently while the Murex stuck its head out of its shell.

"But won't the Murex have to die to give us the ink?"

"Well, usually the answer is yes, but this Murex is a scholar and very wise. He has figured out a way to collect ink from each of his friends and travels around with it in case anyone needs to write any messages," said the Sea Turtle proudly about his friend, the Murex, as he pulled a beautiful little bottle of ink out of his shell and handed it to the Scholarly Prince.

"I am so thankful to both of you. How will I ever repay you for all your kindness?"

"Oh, there is no need to repay us. We are delighted to be able to help you and your kingdom. You have always been so good to us, protecting us from fishing nets and trappers, and now it is our chance to repay you," said the Sea Turtle.

"Well, let's see. I have the feather and the Murex ink to write with, the bottle to keep the message dry, and the cork to keep my message from getting wet," said the Prince happily as he sat down by the water's edge, the Sea Turtle and the Murex by his side, to write his message to the Princess in the faraway kingdom.

Dear Princess of the Faraway Kingdom,

My dear friends are here, by my side, as I write this message to you. My friend, the Sea Turtle, offered to bring this letter to you, and my friend, the Murex, has shared ink for me to write. The birch tree gave her bark to write on, and the bird shed its feather for me to use for a pen. I am very thankful to all these friends for their help, but I need one more friend, which I hope you will become, to help me with my quest. My kingdom, which is far, far away from yours, needs to cultivate peace. Some of the inhabitants of my realm have been taken under an evil spell and are on a wild rampage, hurting others. I was told that you have read many books and know many wise people. I too have read many books and am a scholar, but I have unfortunately not come across the answer. Would you please share your wisdom and give me advice on how to take this evil off of my people so they might return to their peaceful ways, ensuring that my kingdom will be quiet once again? I will appreciate your kindness in this matter. I will eagerly await your response, which you may send back with my friend, the Sea Turtle.

With much gratitude,
The Scholarly Prince.

He finished writing his letter on the birch bark.

"Why does this ink look so pale and yellow? Is it because it is written on birch bark?" he asked the Sea Turtle and the Murex.

"Well, this ink is very, very special and very, very magical. It will turn other colors as it is exposed to the sunlight. When the Princess receives it, she will not be able to see it until it is taken out into the sunlight. Then, it will turn from yellow to green to blue, and finally to the most beautiful shade of royal purple. This is the magical nature of Murex ink," said the Murex proudly.

It was starting to get late, and the Prince hurriedly rolled the birch bark that his message to the Princess was written on and placed it carefully into the bottle. He then found a sharp rock and whittled down the cork until it was just the right size and put it in the top of the bottle, with only a small part of the cork sticking out of the top, so that the Princess from the faraway land could take the cork out quickly. When he had finished getting the bottle ready, he wiped it off carefully on his sleeve and handed it to the Sea Turtle.

"Here it is. Thank you for your help."

Everything was ready, but there still existed one small challenge. The Sea Turtle couldn't carry the bottle in his mouth because he wouldn't be able to eat. The Prince went running around all over the beach looking for a piece of rope, but there was none to be found. The Sea Turtle went to the bottom of the ocean looking for a rope, but there was none. The Murex dug deeply into the sand on the beach but found nothing. What would they do?

Well, there was one option that occurred to the Prince. The Prince took off his belt and used it to tie the bottle around the back of the Sea Turtle. The Murex, this time, rather than riding all that way back home in the mouth of the turtle, climbed on the Sea Turtle's back and used the belt to hang on.

"Go in peace, my dear friends. I will anxiously await your return," said the Prince as the Sea Turtle took off into the ocean with the Murex on its back, holding on to the belt, with the bottle containing the message securely fastened on the top.

Many days and nights passed after they left to bring the message to the Princess from far, far away. Every morning, the Prince would go out to the beach and gaze toward the horizon for any view of the Sea Turtle coming back with a message from the Princess, but each evening, he went back to his castle, disappointed that there was no news.

After dropping the Murex off, the Sea Turtle traveled day and night and night and day, thousands of ocean miles, through storms and rough seas, feeling as if he had to keep going quickly to bring the message to the Princess as soon as possible. In all his travels he had never experienced so many storms. One dark storm followed after another until the Sea Turtle began to wonder if all these storms were a bad omen. Finally, on the day that he reached the island where the Good Princess lived, he noticed a small ray of sunshine peeking through the dark clouds. As he approached the island, he saw a beautiful young woman sitting on a high rock, combing her wet hair in a little ray of sunlight. *This must surely be the Princess,* he thought to himself, after swimming up close and seeing how beautiful she was.

"Greetings, Princess," he called out to her as he swam up close to the shore where she was sitting on the rock.

"Greetings, Sea Turtle," she responded boldly.

"May we talk, please? I have come a long way to bring you a message from the Scholarly Prince in the faraway lands."

"Yes, of course, please come and tell me the message."

"Here, if you could untie this belt, inside the bottle on my back is the message," he told her.

"I think you should tell me the message, rather than waiting for me to read it. This way, we can save time if the Prince's message is as urgent as you say it is," she demanded as she roughly untied the belt from the turtle and held the bottle in her hand.

"If you say to tell you, then I will, as I know the Prince needs a solution quickly to his dilemma. His message is that he is asking the Good Princess, you, to help him get rid of the evil curse that is on some of the people in his kingdom." Suddenly, the Princess came upon an awful idea, for she was not the Good Princess, but her evil twin sister. She thought quickly and determined that she would continue to deceive the Sea Turtle into thinking she was the Good Princess, and she said that she needed to go to see the Prince in person to remove the curse. Her real motive was to go there and lure him into marrying her so that she could take control of his kingdom. She was a very greedy and evil Princess who thought only of herself.

She insisted on riding back to the Prince's kingdom on the Sea Turtle's back but first wanted to go to her castle and grab a few items to take with her. She ran off, carrying the unopened bottle in her hands, straight to her sister's room. There, she stole her sister's magic purse—filled it with her magic fairy dust that could always help in times of curse and trouble—and her green woolen magic cloak with the ermine trim that kept the wearer dry. The cloak had the Sea King's royal emblem embroidered on the front in rose-colored satin threads. Then, she ran back to the Sea Turtle and wrapped the Prince's belt around him and climbed on his back. "We had better go as fast as possible and not lose any time," she sneakily told him.

"There have been fierce storms all the way here. I hope we have better weather for traveling on the way back to the Prince's kingdom."

"So, tell me about this kingdom we are going to. Is the Prince very wealthy?" She loved riches more than anything.

"I imagine he is. His kingdom is more beautiful than many other kingdoms." The Sea Turtle was very wise, and although the Evil Princess didn't let on about her true identity, the Sea Turtle was beginning to feel that something just wasn't quite right about her. He stayed quiet, though, and waited to see if he could figure it out. The further they got in their travels, the rougher the seas became. Lightning and thunder began crackling all around them, and often the Sea Turtle would have to go underwater, which the Evil Princess hated, even though she stayed dry because she had stolen her sister's magical cloak. They traveled day and night to get to the Prince's kingdom, and finally, on a Thursday morning, just as the sun was rising, they got to the shore where the Prince had just arrived. The Evil Princess took one look at the Prince and realized that luring him into marrying her would be more fun than she had thought because he was so handsome.

"Here," he said as he offered her his hand to get off the back of the Sea Turtle. "I didn't expect you to make such a long voyage for my sake, Princess. I will be forever in your debt for such a great act."

"It is my pleasure," she smiled. She knew the Scholarly Prince would marry her, now that he had said that he was in her debt.

"Please, come to my castle and get warm and have some food."

The prince thanked the Sea Turtle and walked to the castle, leaving him by himself. She was happy to have some time to rest after traveling so many miles.

When she got to his castle, he called for his sister to come and help the Princess change into something warm and for his mother to bring them some food. Both his sister and mother were amiable and hospitable to their guest and had no suspicion of her evil intentions. The Prince's sister handed her one of her beautiful green satin dresses and some soft green slippers to wear, and she put the Princess's cloak and bag in a spare room for her while she was changing. When the Evil Princess was finally ready, she walked out into the hallway where she met the Prince's sister, and together they went to have breakfast. The mother came out of the kitchen carrying beautiful fruit, bread, and jam, along with yogurt and eggs, and placed them carefully on the table in front of the two girls before sitting down with them.

"Thank you for coming to help my son with the bad situation in our kingdom," the mother told her softly.

"I'm happy to help," she lied.

"May I ask what your plan is?" the Prince's sister asked.

"I have a plan, a good plan at that, but I cannot speak of it yet, if you don't mind. I can tell you this much. Whatever I say must be done very quickly; otherwise, your whole kingdom can become infected with this evil."

Both the mother and sister gasped and looked at each other with their eyebrows furrowed.

"Part of my plan is to marry the Prince, and by doing so, he will have my power as well, giving us enough power to defeat the evil."

"Does my son know of this plan yet?"

"Oh, he will know soon enough because the wedding has to take place immediately." She didn't want to waste any time getting this kingdom into her own hands, and as soon as she could achieve this, she would get rid of the mother, the sister, and maybe even the Prince.

"How soon does the wedding need to happen?" asked the sister.

"No later than 7 o'clock tonight!"

"Tonight? I don't know how we can plan a whole wedding by tonight. We would have to prepare food, invite the guests, and make the flower arrangements, along with having the wedding clothing made," said the mother in a hurry.

"Do you want your kingdom to be saved or not?" asked the evil twin sarcastically.

"Well, yes, of course, I do. We will have to make this work," the Prince's mother submitted.

In the meantime, the kind and sweet Princess had come back to her castle in her kingdom and found the bottle that the evil twin had dropped on her floor. She opened it and pulled the birch bark out but didn't see anything, so she put it in her pocket. It was raining outside, and the Good Princess went to get her magical cloak out of the closet, so that she could go back outside without getting wet, but found that it was missing. Then, she went to get her bag with the magical fairy dust, which she needed to help heal a sick frog that she had been visiting earlier in the day and found that to be missing as well. She thought to herself for a minute and then decided that she would have to go anyway, even without her cloak or bag, and see what she could do to help the frog.

Suddenly, when she went outside, the sun broke through the clouds and she hurriedly ran to see the frog, who had realized it was sunny and gone outside to feel the heat. As the Good Princess approached him, she apologized for not having her magical fairy dust with her. He assured her that he was feeling much better now since the sun came out. She was happy to hear this and decided to go for a walk in the sun.

She quickly realized that the birch bark was in her pocket and decided to see if she could read it in the sunlight. When she pulled it out of her pocket, she saw the words beginning to form, first yellow, then green, then blue, and finally royal purple. Now able to make out the words, she read the letter. Her hands began to shake, and she ran all the way to the beach to see if the turtle was still waiting for her response. As she approached the beach, she couldn't see him anywhere, so she climbed up on a high rock to see if he was swimming out further in the sea. Suddenly, a white beluga whale appeared and greeted her.

"Have you seen the Sea Turtle today?"

"Yes, I saw him a few hours ago with your evil sister riding on his back, going through the storm," he told her. Quickly, all the pieces fit together in her mind. Now she understood why the cloak and purse were missing.

"Was she wearing an iridescent green woolen cloak with an ermine trim and hood?"

"Yes, she was wearing a beautiful cloak like the one I've seen you wear in the past."

"I have to follow her and get to her before she destroys a whole kingdom. Do you know the way to the Prince's kingdom?"

"Yes, I do, and I would be happy to take you there. I know a shortcut, but first let me call some of my friends to go with us," he said as he let out a loud call.

Within no more than a minute, several other white beluga whales appeared and agreed to go along. About halfway through the trip, they ran into the Sea Turtle's cousin swimming toward them.

"Have you seen your cousin, the Sea Turtle, with my evil sister?" the Good Princess asked.

"Yes, she is at the Prince's castle getting ready to marry him. The wedding will be held at 7 o'clock today."

"Don't worry," said the white beluga whale that she was riding. "We can get there in plenty of time." He swam faster than ever before to get the Good Princess there on time so that she could stop the wedding. In the meantime, the Good Princess knew that she had to devise a plan so that her sister wouldn't recognize her and decided that she would have to disguise herself. The Sea Turtle's cousin was swimming as fast as he could to keep up, and she yelled down to him from her high seat on the whale.

"Can you find me any clothing in the ocean, perhaps in an old trunk or in a shipwreck?"

"I'll try," he promised as he dove quickly under the water.

She then spoke to one of the whales, "Can you get a message to the Prince's kingdom, directed at all of those under an evil curse? Tell them that I am inviting them to my island today and that there will be plenty of riches for them when they land, but they have to leave the kingdom of the Prince before 7 o'clock tonight."

"Yes, I will do that right now," he promised.

"We will meet you on the shore of the Prince's kingdom as soon as I get into my disguise. We don't have much time to stop this wedding!"

In the meantime, everyone at the Prince's castle was busy preparing food, making flower arrangements, and sewing wedding outfits. They were almost finished when they heard the doorbell ring.

"May I please speak to the mother of the house? I am here for the wedding and the bride is a friend of mine from long ago," croaked an old, bent-down woman with a cane.

"Yes, of course. Please, do come in," said one of the servants.

As soon as the mother heard that she had a visitor from long ago, she tidied her hair and apron and hurried to the doorway.

"Well, hello. Please, do come in. Do I know you?"

"Please, may I have a private word with you and your daughter?" she croaked.

"But of course," the mother said while leading her to a private room.

As soon as they entered the private room, the Good Princess took off her disguise, showing that she was the Good Princess from far distant lands.

"My evil twin sister got the note your son sent to me. She will destroy everything unless we stop her from marrying your son. Please help me to stop this wedding," she pleaded.

The mother and sister of the Prince knew that the Good Princess was telling the truth because they were wise and had begun to have a bad feeling about the evil twin sister but were afraid to say anything, just in case she was telling the truth.

"Here is my plan. I have to stay hidden so that my evil sister won't see me here, but one of you can give her a message. Tell her that three ships will be leaving here at 7 o'clock to take the evil ones out of your kingdom and they have trunks filled with gold and silver on them. She will hear this and leave your son before she has a chance to marry him. I know my sister well, and she will go get the gold and try to come back with a good excuse to marry him."

While all the ones who had an evil curse, which had caused problems in the Prince's kingdom, were boarding boats to go to the Good Princess's kingdom, music had already begun to play to announce the bride's entrance into the church to be married. The Prince was already waiting for her at the altar, willing to marry her to save his kingdom. Suddenly, a messenger came to the bride-to-be with a note that read, '*There are trunks filled with gold on the boats in the harbor, but you must hurry to catch the boats before they leave at 7 o'clock.*'

The bride thought to herself, *I can run to the boats, take the gold, and be back an hour late for my wedding. The Prince will have to wait for me!*

At that thought, she took off running in her wedding dress all the way to the boats and boarded the first one she saw. She was the last of the evil ones to get on the ship, and as soon as she boarded, the plank was removed and the ships took off. She didn't even notice that the boats were moving because all that was on her mind was finding the trunks filled with gold and jewelry. All three ships were well out into the deep water when suddenly the group of white beluga whales got underneath and shoved them in another direction. No matter how hard the captains tried to steer their ships, they could only go in the opposite direction from where they wanted to go. No one on board knew that the white belugas were underneath.

For many days and nights, the whales guided the ships farther and farther away, until they found the most remote island, which had no inhabitants, and stopped. By now, everyone onboard thought this must be the kingdom of the Good Princess, so they all got off the ships. Even the evil twin sister got off the ship and went to the dry land of the island. As soon as the whales saw that everyone was safely out of the ships, they began shoving the boats far, far away from shore. They kept pushing the empty boats for several days so that there would be no chance for the evil ones, including the evil twin Princess, to get back to the kingdom of the Prince.

When the white belugas returned to the Prince and assured him that all evil was gone from his kingdom, the whole kingdom cheered and celebrated. The Prince was so grateful to the Good Princess that he invited her to stay and live in his kingdom. She thought that the kingdom was so beautiful and everyone was so kind that she decided to stay. When the Prince's sister heard that the Good Princess's magic cloak and a bag containing the good magic fairy dust had been stolen, she knew exactly where to find them and brought them to the Good Princess.

"Please, keep these for yourself. You see, I don't need them any longer. I was able to help without using either my magic cloak or my good fairy dust. We were able to get rid of all the evil in your kingdom by working together," the Good Princess told the Prince's sister.

Because the Good Princess decided to stay in the Prince's kingdom, he became the happiest Prince who ever lived because he loved her so much for saving his kingdom and preventing him from marrying her evil twin sister.

From then on, there was no evil in his country; only joy, love, and laughter, and they all lived happily ever after.

With the Highest Regards,

The Sea King.

This is the story the Sea King sent to the Elders of Iona on the night of their meeting on Slieve Mish Mountain, at Solomon's Tower. The Sea King obviously wanted to let them know something by writing it in the form of a fairy tale, but what could it mean? The old Sea King was known to be a sagacious man, although he did have an awful temper at times. His hurt over losing his daughter to Brian Boruma was very tragic for him. Had he ever forgotten it? Was he over it?

Chapter Ten
Donal

Gabriel, Faolan, and Ocean Marie climbed out of the small boat, and while Faolan tied the boat to a nearby piece of driftwood, Gabriel checked to make sure they had gotten everything they needed to take to the O'Brien homestead. They all walked up the trail through the birch trees and headed toward the house. The first person they saw when they reached the property was Niamh, who was outside feeding the chickens. Gabriel cleared his throat carefully, hoping to get her attention so that she wouldn't be startled upon their arrival.

"Gabriel!"

"Niamh, these are my friends, Ocean Marie Cleary and Faolan. They are here to help you with Donal. How is he doing?"

Niamh smiled and greeted each of them, and then explained Donal's condition.

"He's had a rough night. He was shaking and trembling, coughing and having nightmares. I've been giving him water every hour, and I've given him the tea that you gave me. I went through Mother's journals and couldn't find any notes about possible remedies for him."

"How is Fintan?" Niamh asked.

"He's missing you. I can tell."

"Well, I'm missing him more. I wish this mess would get straightened out so that Fintan could come home. How I wish he could be here with me now."

"Ocean's brother, Niko, is looking after Fintan while I'm here. He has been around horses his whole life, and Fintan likes him a lot. Fintan is in good hands, so please don't worry. Niko'll take excellent care of him until I get back," Gabriel assured her.

"Please thank Niko for me. I'm glad to know that Fintan is in good care. I can hardly wait to see him again."

"Do you mind if we go inside? Ocean Marie has something for Donal, a medicine pouch that the Elders have made for him," asked Gabriel.

"Where are my manners? Of course, we can go in. Can I offer you some food and drink?"

"Thank you. Perhaps we will have something after we meet with Donal. Is your father home?"

"Yes, he's here. He went to Deliah's parents' house yesterday to see if they would allow Deliah and her brother Roger to stay here with us, at least while Donal is ill. He's been going through Mother's journals since he came back. He hasn't spoken much but said he would talk to me later today."

"Did he get their permission, do you know?" asked Ocean Marie.

"Yes, I believe so. He seemed very perplexed when he came home and said that Deliah's mother, Moira, was more than willing to have them stay here. He also said that Moira had sealed her destiny with her evil deeds."

Upon hearing this, Ocean had one of her 'feelings.' She tried not to frown, and smiled instead, saving this information for later, after she assessed the entire situation.

Deliah had been watching the three of them from the kitchen window, while doing the morning dishes, and wondered who they were and what they were doing here. She didn't have a good feeling about them being here and secretly wanted them to leave, but when they entered the house with Niamh, she smiled sweetly and greeted them.

"Deliah, these are my friends, Gabriel, Faolan, and Ocean Cleary. They came to see Donal," Niamh explained.

"Very pleased to meet all of you. How do you know my Donal?" she asked, primarily interested in Ocean Marie's reply.

Gabriel and Ocean Marie both noticed the way Deliah said 'My Donal' and how she looked at Ocean Marie when asking how they knew him. They recognized those hints of jealousy instantly, while Faolan and Niamh paid them no mind.

"He's in this room," Niamh said as she gently tapped on the bedroom door where Donal was staying.

"Donal, these are my friends, Gabriel, Faolan, and Ocean Marie Cleary. They wanted to visit you and offer their help," Niamh explained to her brother.

"I'm not at my best right now, but it's very nice to meet all of you," Donal said quietly as he reached out his hand to each of them.

"How are you feeling?" Ocean asked.

"I've seen better days, that's for sure," he smiled.

As they all talked, Gabriel noticed that Deliah, who remained quietly in the doorway, was becoming more irritated as the minutes went by. He decided to distract her so that Ocean Marie could give Donal the medicine pouch and speak with him privately.

"Niamh, Ocean Marie needs to speak with your brother privately. Can you somehow get everyone to leave the room?" Gabriel whispered so that no one else could hear. She gave a small nod and thought for a moment.

"Deliah, would you mind going outside to find Roger and see if he would like to join us for some tea?"

"No. Roger is probably rushed right now. I'll give him tea when he comes in."

"That's fine, then. Will you please help me get some tea and food ready for our guests?"

"They said they didn't want anything, didn't they?" she said, standing her ground. She didn't want Ocean Marie around Donal. She was too pretty, with her dark, curly, long hair and pale-green eyes.

"Oh, I would love some tea and a little something to eat," said Gabriel.

"Well, come on in the kitchen, then, and Deliah and I will make something for you," she said while holding Deliah's arm, leading her toward the kitchen. Before reaching the kitchen, Deliah headed toward the back of the house, saying that she needed to fetch another chair. Faolan and Gabriel followed Niamh into the kitchen, while Ocean Marie stayed behind with Donal.

"I might not have much time in here with you, but I want to give you this medicine pouch. Do you mind if I put it on you? It has herbs in it that will help you to heal." Without waiting for a response from Donal, she leaned over and held his head up from the pillow gently and tied the medicine pouch around his neck.

"Thank you," he smiled while feeling the pouch. "Haven't we met?" he asked.

"Yes, we have met, once, a long time ago. I'm surprised you remembered. Listen, Donal, I know that you are probably feeling exhausted and confused after all you've been through, and I don't want to tax your energy, but I need for you to talk to me and tell me something. Are you blaming yourself for your mother's disappearance?"

Donal's eyes teared up, and he turned his head away from her. His mind felt like it was about to unravel and he began coughing from holding in his tears.

"I know this is hard for you but I need for you to tell me. Why are you blaming yourself? What happened, Donal? You can trust me. I won't tell anyone, and I can help you heal."

Through teary eyes, Donal stared into Ocean's eyes and suddenly realized that she did want to help and could be trusted. He felt the words of all his pain for the last two years rising to his throat. As hard as he tried to hold them in, he couldn't. Salt tears became a silent stream, finding their way to Ocean.

"She wanted me to go with her," he said between sighs. "She asked me to go, and I wouldn't go with her. I didn't want to go to Deliah's house and deal with her parents. I just wanted to stay here and play my guitar. I stayed here and worked on the song I was writing and she left by herself. I never saw her again."

"Why was she going there?" Ocean asked, puzzled. "Did anyone else know where she was going?"

"No one knew but me. Mother didn't want my father to know because he was so tired from working all day and she knew he would insist on going with her. She didn't want Niamh to know either, for the same reasons. I'm the only one who knew, and I never told anyone. When she was believed to be missing, I went there many times, trying to get answers and find my mother, but they kept telling me that she never made it there. She was planning on going there first and to the doctor to help with one of his patients afterward. She only told my father that the doctor wanted her to help with one of his patients."

"Why didn't you tell this to anyone in these two years that she's been missing?" Ocean asked carefully.

"First off, I promised my mother that I wouldn't tell when she asked me to go with her. Second, I knew she wouldn't have wanted my father to know that she didn't tell him the whole truth. My mother would do anything for anyone, especially if they were sick. There is nothing I can do about it now. She is dead, and I'll never see her again. I've been a mess since that night, and I can't even think straight. I've been drinking too much, and I feel like I can't even focus anymore. I have to get my life back on track, now that a baby is on its way."

"Donal, how much have you been drinking?"

"Not enough to make me feel this sick. I rarely had more than two drinks a night, if that. Alcohol takes a quick effect on me, I suppose."

"I know that your mother loved you, Donal. She would want you to forgive yourself for that. You know she would forgive you for not going, don't you?"

"Yes, of course. Mother was the most forgiving person I've ever known."

"And do you think that she would want you to be this unhappy?"

"Of course not."

"You need to forgive yourself. You made a mistake. It isn't your fault your mother isn't here. Things happen exactly the way they are supposed to. Your mother would have wanted you to be happy and realize that people make mistakes. The most important thing you can do right now is to forgive yourself. That is what she would have wanted. Don't you agree?"

"I do agree... But...how? How will I forgive myself for being so selfish that I wouldn't go with her?"

"Try looking at it from another angle, Donal. Try looking at it the way your mother would have looked at it. She loved you, right? She knew how important your music was to you and she would have wanted you to complete your song and share it. She knew that you loved her, and I'm sure she understood why you wouldn't have wanted to go to that house."

"True...she said she understood. She wasn't upset with me at all when she left."

"Donal, listen to me. You need to be the man your mother would have wanted you to be. You made a mistake...we *all* make mistakes. It's what we do after we realize that we made a mistake that counts. What will you do now? What do you want?"

"I want to get well and do the right thing. That's what she would want from me."

"Then do that. Give up on all this guilt, forgive yourself, and move on. You should be feeling better soon, and when you do, play your guitar and write your music."

"I threw my guitar into the ocean."

"Understandable, but that wasn't the only guitar in the world, right?" she asked. "What did you say about a baby on its way?" She suddenly remembered what he had told her.

"Deliah is pregnant with my child."

"Really?"

"Yes, she told me a few weeks ago, and I didn't handle that very well either. I was cutting down on drinking and trying to help out here at the homestead. I was beginning to see some light at the end of this darkness, and she came and found me. Honestly, I don't even remember being with her. I remember falling asleep on her mother's couch after talking with her for a few hours, but she said we were together that night, a couple of months ago."

"I see."

"So, do you now understand how I'm such a mess?"

"Yes, I do see it, but I doubt that this entire burden you are carrying is real."

"What do you mean?"

"Donal, the times that you saw Deliah, where were you, at her house?"

"Yes, all the times I saw her were when I went there to talk with her parents about my mother's disappearance."

"And how did Deliah's parents treat you when you went there?"

"They were nice to me. Deliah's mother always insisted on making me drink tea and eat...almost every time I was there. Her father wasn't around much. He kept to himself most of the time."

"And had they ever been nice to you before your mother was missing?"

"Never. Deliah's parents must have felt sorry for me about losing my mother."

"Donal, I have a feeling that you are going to be feeling better soon. It's a strong feeling. I'll be back to check on you, and I want you to do something for me, please?"

"Yes, of course," he promised.

"Promise me that you will only drink water...no tea, until I come back, even if Niamh gives it to you. I will explain all this to you later, but promise that you will only drink water."

"I promise."

"Don't take that medicine pouch off, and don't let anyone take it off you. Not even when you are washing up."

"Do you think my mind will ever be clear again?" he asked, hopefully.

"Yes, I do."

Ocean Marie grabbed his hand as she bent over and gave him a soft kiss on his forehead. His fever was already subsiding, and his eyes were beginning to look much brighter than when she first came into his room.

"I'm going to go out and join the others now. I'll be back soon. Remember, no tea, and keep the medicine pouch on."

"Thank you. I just remembered where we met. I was playing my guitar and singing by the ocean."

"Yes, I remember. You will be playing and singing again soon."

"I believe you."

"Yes, I know you believe me," she smiled as she walked out of his room.

Ocean Marie walked into the kitchen where Gabriel, Faolan, and Niamh were sitting at the table talking and having tea and soup, with bread and butter.

"Please, sit and have something," offered Niamh.

"I will, thank you, but first I need a word with Gabriel, privately. Would you please come outside with me for a minute?" she asked.

"When are you leaving?" she asked when they got beyond earshot, outside. "Let's walk toward the barn. I want to make sure that I am far enough away that no one can hear me, as this is of a very private nature."

"I was planning on leaving very shortly, why?"

"I'll tell you when we get close to the barn."

They walked a few minutes, and when they got to the barn, Ocean Marie told him what she found out, as promised.

"Donal's life is in extreme danger here, and we don't have much time. Deliah is making up this pregnancy and is still poisoning him with her teas. She's working with her mother, Moira, unfortunately. Donal will be fine, but we have to get him out of here. Can you think of some way that we can get him away from here and to a safe place without upsetting Niamh?"

"Yes, I'll think of something. I'm not sure what it is right at the moment, but I'll come up with a plan."

"As I said, we don't have much time. I told Donal not to drink any teas, only water, and to not take the medicine pouch off, no matter what. I'm not sure Deliah won't slip something into the water, though, so we need to remove him from here, or else remove her. Gabriel, let's focus now. There must be a solution. Where is Liam?"

"Niamh said that he's been reading, so I assume he is in the study or wherever Brigid's books are kept, why?" asked Gabriel.

"I think we will need his help for this."

Suddenly, Niamh came running toward them. "Gabriel, help. Some men have taken Deliah. Come quickly."

"Which men took her and how?" he asked while running with Niamh and Ocean toward the house.

"There were two men. They said that Deliah's mother, Moira, owed them. They were looking for Fintan, and seeing that he wasn't here, they took Deliah instead. Faolan has gone after them. They came through the back of the property and must have been waiting there without our knowing."

"Niamh, does Liam know about this? Did Donal hear them taking her?" Ocean asked.

"Donal didn't hear. I checked on him as I was running to get you. Deliah made some tea for him. He drank it, and now he's fast asleep. I'm not sure where my father is. They had guns and threatened us to be quiet. One of them hit Faolan in the head with his gun, and he was knocked unconscious, but he came-to very quickly. They are on horseback and Faolan is on foot. I pointed out a shortcut over the ridge where he might be able to get to them."

"Where is Roger?" Gabriel asked.

"Father sent him back, earlier, to his house to collect things for himself and Deliah, things they will need to live with us."

"Do you have other horses?" he asked.

"There are two that we use for plowing, but there are no saddles for them," she quickly responded.

"In the barn?"

"No, they are in the field. Father hasn't brought them in yet. Do you want me to get them?"

"I think you and Ocean should stay here with Donal. I'll get the horses and try to catch up with Faolan. Can you show me the direction that you pointed out to him?"

"Yes, there is a trail between those birches. I sent Faolan through there. It leads across the ridge, and the road is below it. You can take the horses through there, and it is much quicker than the road."

"Niamh, can you find your father and tell him what has occurred? Ocean, would you stay with Donal and try to keep him from finding out about this?"

Niamh went to the house but couldn't find Liam anywhere. "Father, where are you? Are you here?" she whispered loudly but didn't get a response. *Where could he have gone?* she wondered after looking carefully in each room and around the outside of the house. She saw Gabriel riding one of the old mares and leading the other one into the birch tree opening leading to the trail. She was relieved that he had found it. Niamh was surprised that those horses could sprint, considering their ages.

After checking on Donal and securing his windows, so that they wouldn't open from the outside, Ocean went into the kitchen and sat at the table.

"Do you have any guns here?" she asked Niamh.

"Yes, my father keeps two rifles in his room."

"Would you please go get them and some shells, just in case we end up needing to chase anyone else out of here."

Liam made sure that everyone in his household knew how to shoot the rifles, not that he thought anyone would ever need to use them, but he wanted to make sure they knew how to, just in case. Niamh ran to her father's room and looked under the bed, where he had always kept the guns, but they were gone. She looked all over the place, in case he put them somewhere else, but they were nowhere to be found. She came back downstairs to the kitchen where Ocean was waiting.

"My father is not here, and I cannot find his guns."

"Does he normally leave with the guns?" Ocean asked.

"Never. Those guns were there only two days ago. When I was cleaning, I saw them."

"Where do you think he is? Did he tell you he was going somewhere?"

Chapter Eleven
Niko

While the Elders of Iona were at the top of Solomon's Tower, Niko and the Gypsies set up their camps along the edge of the tree line. Niko helped his parents and brought them some fresh water from a stream he found on the other side of the mountain. After making sure his parents and family were all set, he decided to take Fintan to the stream for a drink of fresh water.

"Come on, Boy. Let's go get some fresh water for you," Niko said while climbing on Fintan's back. Fintan already knew the way to the stream and seemed anxious to get there. Niko loved horses, and especially Fintan. He remembered looking after Fintan in the past, when he was Gabriel's horse and had ridden him many times. He knew that no one ever had to lead Fintan...you just had to think of where you wanted to go and Fintan led the way. At least, that was the way he used to respond, but today Fintan seemed to have a mind of his own. When he got close to the stream, he took several long drinks of the cold, refreshing water while Niko was still on his back, and then like a lightning bolt, he took off at a fast run straight toward the Owenglin River. All Niko could do was hang on as Fintan ran directly to where Gabriel kept his small boat tied, but it was gone. When they got to the water, Fintan jumped right in and swam hard, with Niko holding tightly to his mane. Niko held the reins back tightly, to no avail.

"Fintan, what are you doing, you crazy thing? You've got a mind of your own. Where are you taking us?" he yelled while trying to hold on.

Fintan swam hard across the currents and then straight to where Gabriel's boat was docked. After smelling the ground, Fintan took off again, running like the wind on the trail that led to the O'Brien homestead. Ocean was the first to hear the sounds of hoof beats and ran to the window.

"Oh, Niamh. Come quickly. My brother is here with Fintan," Ocean said while running to the door to meet her brother.

"Niko, what happened? Why are you here?"

"I'm not exactly sure. Whose home is this?" he asked.

"This is the O'Brien place. This is Niamh. It is her brother, Donal, whom I came to help. How did you find me?"

"I didn't even know you were here. Fintan was out of control. When I took him to the stream on the mountain for a drink of fresh water, he took off running down the trail and finally to the river. He swam across the river with me on his back and wouldn't stop until we arrived here. I have no idea what he is thinking and I must say, he sure doesn't listen like he used to."

"Brother, this is Niamh. Niamh, my brother, Niko."

"Pleased to meet you, Niko. Can I offer you something to eat or drink?"

"Thank you for your kindness. I will wait, though."

"Niko, I'm glad you are here with Fintan. We've just had a situation here. A young lady was taken from here by two armed men. Gabriel and Faolan have gone after them. Niamh's father, along with his two rifles, is missing."

"Do you think the men stole the rifles?"

"I hadn't thought of that," Niamh admitted.

"Have you checked all the property for your father, Niamh?" Niko asked.

"No, actually, we have only checked the house."

"With your permission, I'll go around and check the rest of the property. It might be that those men stole the rifles and put your father somewhere on the property to keep him out of the way."

"Yes, of course. Do you want me to go with you?" Niamh asked.

"No. It would be better if you stay with Ocean and Donal. I'll be right back. I'm going to take Fintan. I can get around a lot faster with him, rather than walking."

Niko mounted Fintan and headed off in the direction of the barn while Ocean and Niamh watched from the porch. They saw Niko ride up to the barn and leave Fintan outside. He opened the barn door and hurriedly ran inside. After checking out the barn thoroughly, he ran around to the other outbuildings, now out of the view of the young women. They could still see Fintan standing near the barn door, looking restless. Suddenly, they heard a whistle and Fintan went running to the back of the shed.

Ocean became concerned and went running to where she last saw Fintan, calling for Niko as she got closer.

"Niko, where are you?"

When Fintan heard Ocean's voice, he raced around the building to show her where they were.

"Niko, is everything alright?" Ocean asked.

"I've found Liam O'Brien," he yelled. "Bring Fintan and help me here, quickly."

As Ocean ran after Fintan, around the building, she noticed small patches of bloodstained grass and feared the worst. She found Niko dragging the body of a man out of the shed.

"Oh my God, is he dead?" she asked.

"No, he's lost some blood, but he is still alive. Help me get him up onto Fintan, and we'll get him to the house."

As Ocean was helping her brother lift the man onto the horse, she realized this couldn't possibly be Niamh's father. This was a young man, although it was hard to tell because of the dried blood and dirt.

"Who is this, Niko?"

"I have no idea. He seems to be in his early twenties. Not Niamh's father."

They got him up on the back of Fintan and quickly but carefully led him up the pathway to the house. Ocean ran inside to tell Niamh and get some hot water ready to clean the man's abrasions. She quietly opened the door to Donal's room and motioned for Niamh to come talk to her, giving her a signal that she couldn't speak in front of Donal.

"Niamh, Niko found an injured man in the shed in back of the barn. He's bringing him in now. Will you come and help?"

"Oh no! It must be my father."

"No, I'm sure it isn't your father. This man is very young."

Niamh hurriedly poured some water in a large cast-iron pot and started the fire under it, while Ocean and her brother brought the young man into the house, laying him down carefully on a blanket on the floor. When Niamh looked at the young man lying there on her kitchen floor, covered in dried blood and dirt, she gasped.

"Do you know him?" asked Niko.

"It's Deliah's brother, Roger. Is he breathing?"

"Yes, he's breathing but he took a hard hit to the head, as you can see. It looks like he was hit with something pretty heavy," Niko said.

Ocean gathered up some cloth and began ripping it up, making bandages, while Niamh started gently washing his face, hands, and head.

"Roger, it's me, Niamh. Can you hear me? Roger, talk to me," she said as she gently patted his face with the wet cloth and cleaned the dirt off his eyes. "Roger, who did this to you and why?" she asked.

"He's not answering me," she said to Ocean.

Niamh was beginning to become very flustered thinking about all that had happened while trying to get Roger to regain consciousness. Suddenly, an image from her dream flashed quickly into her mind, and she remembered being Trini and sitting in the garden with John, Fintan, Basil, and Dillis, talking about the importance of staying calm and not blaming anyone. It was a sudden image that left her mind almost as quickly as it came, but it was enough to cause her to take a deep breath and stay focused. Even though her brother was in the next room, Ocean was there in the kitchen with her, and Roger was there lying on her floor trying to regain consciousness, she felt very alone until she remembered that dream. Then, she remembered that Fintan was here on the property and felt comforted.

"Roger, smell this," she said as she waved a small bundle of mint leaves in front of his nose.

"Niamh, he's coming around," whispered Ocean.

"Roger, can you hear me? It's me, Niamh."

Roger opened his eyes very slowly and tried to sit up, startled to find himself lying on the kitchen floor with Niamh and Ocean kneeling next to him, supporting his head. He recognized Niamh but felt confused when he saw Ocean, as he was expecting to see his sister.

"Where is Deliah?" he asked groggily.

Ocean and Niamh gave each other a quick, knowing glance, one that communicated to each other that the best plan was to not tell Roger what happened, yet.

"Here, have some water, Roger. Can you sit up a little and drink this?" Ocean said as she helped him.

Roger sat up and looked around the kitchen, remembering.

"Your father is in town," he said, as he remembered seeing Liam right before he was hit.

"Roger, what else can you remember? Where did you see him?" Niamh asked.

"I saw those men that Donal won Fintan from coming out of my parent's house right as I was going up the walk. When I was leaving, your father was just arriving. I held the gate for him, but he didn't say anything. It's not like him to not speak to me."

"Those men must have waited until Roger left and followed him here," Ocean said to Niamh.

"Can you remember anything else?" Ocean asked.

"Yes, I remember my sister coming after me with the shovel and striking me."

"You must be confused by the head injury, Roger. One of those men hit you, right?" Niamh asked.

"No, Deliah hit me, with the shovel."

"This isn't possible, Roger. Your sister wouldn't hurt you," Niamh said.

When Ocean heard this, she quietly went outside and told Niko to go back to the shed and see if there was a shovel nearby, perhaps one with blood on it. She knew that Roger was coherent and knew what he was saying. Niamh, however, didn't know who the real Deliah had become.

So many questions ran through Niamh's mind. *What was Father doing back at Deliah's mother's house? Why does Roger think it was Deliah who hit him?* And at the same time as the questions went flying through her thoughts, she was grateful for the feeling that her father might still be alive and that Fintan was here.

"Ocean, will you stay with Roger while I check on Donal?" Niamh asked as Ocean came back.

"Of course I will. Would you like for me to check on him?" she asked.

"Yes, that would be nice of you. Thank you."

Just as Ocean was about to walk into the room where Donal was, she heard Niko on the porch. "I'll be just a minute, Niamh," she said as she stepped around Roger and went to the porch, closing the door behind her.

"What did you find?" she asked Niko.

"Here is the shovel, and it has blood on it. It looks like there was a fight inside that shed, but there is also blood on the grass outside the shed. If Roger was the only one hurt, and he was hit inside the shed, why would there be blood leading up to the door?"

"Yes, I noticed that blood when I was running down there. Roger is saying that his sister is the one who hit him, not the men. He is coherent and knows what he's saying, but I see that Niamh doesn't believe him. I need to go back in and check on Donal."

"I'm going to stay out here and keep Fintan company. He's sensing something. Now and then he lifts his head up, smelling the air. I don't want him taking off on his own."

Inside the kitchen, Roger was feeling well enough to sit at the table and have a cup of tea. He told Niamh that he had something important to say to her.

"Niamh, I don't know how to tell you this, but my sister, prompted by my mother, lied to your family. She's not pregnant. I found out this morning when I went to my house to get the clothes. When I came back, my sister came out to the shed to get her clothes, and that is when I confronted her with the truth. She told me that if I told anyone, she would kill me. I told her that she was wrong for whatever she was up to and that I was going to tell Liam when he got back, and that is when she grabbed the shovel and came after me."

"Why would she lie about it? What plan might she have to do such a thing?"

"I overheard my father arguing with my mother when I arrived there this morning. It appears that he was angry with her and Deliah for devising a plan for her to marry your brother. They didn't know I was there. My father was furious and said that he'd had enough of this folly and it had been going on far too long. He was threatening to leave if my mother didn't set things right. I stood outside listening for quite a while before going in. Father was also upset about my mother giving Donal some 'remedy' and how it could have killed him."

"Did he say what it was?"

"I know there was belladonna in it, but I don't know what else."

"Father said that he had put up with her witchcraft long enough and was upset that she'd gotten my sister involved in it as well. Apparently, she had been teaching my sister for a couple of years now. Niamh, I am so sorry. I can't stand the thought of this being my family and I am going to move as far away as I can, as soon as I can."

Niamh assured Roger that she didn't hold any of this against him and she told him that the men had taken his sister when they couldn't find Fintan.

"We have to find them. My sister has lost her mind and is dangerous. Not only that, but I don't want those men to hurt her. Something else that I found out, Niamh, your mother is still alive." Before having a chance to respond to Roger, Niko came running into the kitchen.

"Niamh, we need to get your brother out to the boat, and we all need to leave here. We need to get back to the Elders. I'll help you get Donal ready, and he can ride Fintan to the boat. Roger, you can ride with Donal; the rest of us can walk. Niamh, leave a note for the others."

Chapter Twelve
The Seal Cave

Ocean Marie, Niko, and Niamh hurried along the trail leading to the shore, while Donal rode Fintan with Roger sitting behind him. They all boarded the boat and headed into the Owenglin River with Fintan taking the lead. Just as they entered the water, the skies turned dark gray and the winds picked up, causing the small boat to rock violently when they got to the currents. Fintan swam close to the boat and helped to keep it from tipping over. When they finally reached the shore, they saw Analine waiting for them. Donal and Roger got back on Fintan, and they all headed up the trail, fighting the winds and rain, which were picking up considerably.

Rather than heading to Solomon's Tower, they went around a large wet rock to the cave Fintan had retrieved Niamh's cloak from, just a few days before. Fintan led the way as he walked in, respectfully carrying Donal and Roger, while Niamh and Ocean Marie followed them, finally followed by Niko and Analine. Sitting inside by the fire was Isabelle, Analine's wife. When she realized how drenched they all were, she ran to a small room in the side of the cave and came back carrying blankets and cloaks, while Analine dried Fintan and placed a warm blanket over his back. When everyone had changed and were seated by the fire, she passed out pewter plates of food for each of them and cups of hot linden tea.

This was not a cave of impenetrable darkness filled with moisture and hog-faced bats, nor was it a dank, dark home of mountain beasts, like bears or mountain lions or shiny, slithering snakes, but more like a room in an ancient Irish castle. The walls, though made of thick gray-brown stone, were clean and smooth, radiating soft buttery light and warmth from the crackling fire, which was placed strategically in the middle of the main chamber. There were furnishings: a large wooden trunk with metal strappings and iron hinges with locks; a large wooden couch; and thirteen chairs, hand-carved with images from the sea; and a broad chest of drawers, each locked. On top of the chest were pans and utensils, pewter plates and cups, along with vessels of pottery. The cave didn't smell like a cave, but rather like the inside of an Orthodox church. It had the distinct smells of angelica, frankincense, and sage, along with the scent of wax from the few large, white candles burning in ornately carved bronze holders.

Holding the images of all their unanswered questions within a particularly quiet place in their minds, they sat in silence, taking a moment to warm up and renew their energies. Most were still too tired to talk and sat quietly by the fire, slowly and carefully eating and drinking, except for Niamh, who was walking around the cave with Fintan, looking at the carved symbols on the cave walls. When Niko placed more wood on the fire, it became bright enough that she suddenly noticed a large stone disk in the far back of the room and headed toward it with Fintan.

The disk, which appeared to hover upright in midair, measured approximately five feet in diameter and was about two feet thick, made out of bluestone. It had a spiral beginning in the center, with symbols carved into it all along the spiral. Niamh went to touch one of the symbols, which she recognized from her mother's journal and was suddenly taken aback by the presence of a being dressed in long white robes with a hood, coming from a doorway behind the disk. It stood around six feet tall. She was startled yet remained composed, hoping for a chance to see its face. Knowing that Fintan was right next to her gave her courage. If this were something to be feared, Fintan would have moved in front of Niamh or reared up, as horses do when threatened or protective, yet Fintan didn't move. As the being moved closer, a flicker of golden light from the fire illuminated the face under the hood, and Niamh became weak from what she saw. It was the face of a seal, and out of its whiskered mouth, it spoke to her.

"Niamh, do you remember the symbols?"

"I do remember some of these, and the spiral is very familiar, but I don't know where I remember them from," she responded.

"Come; let us sit by the fire. I have something to share with everyone," the Seal said while motioning for Niamh to follow along with Fintan. He appeared to glide above the ground as he went toward the fire where the others were sitting. When Analine saw him coming toward the light, he got up and carried one of the elaborately carved chairs for him to sit on. As he settled in the chair, he took his hood off. Underneath, rather than the head of a seal, was the kind and gentle face of the King of the Sea. The only ones who were not shocked by this transformation were the Gypsies, Analine's family, who knew the King well. Silence permeated the entire cave, so much so that even the crackling of the fire was hushed. He sat quietly for a moment, looking at the faces of those who were before him and staring into each of their eyes while he read their hearts.

"Niamh, I would like to address you first. How are you, my dear?"

"I'm fine, sir...Your Honor."

"You and your family have been through quite an ordeal, and I feel somewhat indirectly responsible. I'm here in hopes of helping the situation. Would you be willing to allow me to help you, Niamh?"

"Yes, of course, but I'm curious, how can you help?"

The King glanced lovingly at her and smiled. Niamh looked at her brother, who was still ill, at Roger, whose head was bandaged, and then at the rest, who were looking very hopeful. Then, she looked at Isabelle, who smiled softly and nodded gently. Without having her mother to guide her in making important decisions, and with her father missing, she appreciated Isabelle for her support; even if it was only a smile and a nod.

"Yes, sir...Your Honor. I would be more than happy to have your help, and I appreciate your concern."

"And how about the rest of you? Would you care to come to my kingdom?"

Niamh suddenly remembered stories that her mother told her about the Sea King and how he was always mighty on land, but even mightier in his kingdom. *This must be why he wants us to go there with him, so that he will have his full powers*, she thought.

Analine looked to his wife for her approval on the King's plan, and after he saw her nod, he agreed. Niko was always up for an adventure, and Ocean would love nothing more in life than to fulfill her greatest desire, which was to go to the kingdom of the Sea King. The King saw Donal and Roger showing signs of hesitancy and reassured them that they would feel much better there and that he would ensure their safety and health in those travels.

"When will we leave?" asked Analine.

"Early tomorrow morning. We should all be ready to travel by the time the sun rises. We must first speak with the Elders of Iona, who are still meeting in the tower, and see if they are willing to stay here until we get back. Then, we can all leave as soon as the sun comes up. If they find it necessary to return to Iona quickly, then they will need escorts."

"But what about Gabriel, Faolan, and my sister?" asked Roger.

"I'm quite sure we will hear from Gabriel shortly," the King assured him. "Niko, will you go to the shore now, where you will find a mermaid waiting? Please, tell her that we will leave in the morning, to send the escorts, and to open the portal shortly after daybreak. Ask her to have the kingdom prepared for exceptional guests. Fintan will be joining us, so have them make the necessary arrangements for his stay as well." Niko left immediately into the dark, rainy night, through the forest path and down to the ocean.

After the King finished speaking, Isabelle ushered the girls through a dimly lit hallway leading to a room where there were beds and a fire to keep them warm, while the King, Analine, and Donal curled up next to the fire. Fintan stayed with the men, much to Niamh's dismay. The girls fell asleep instantly, except for Isabelle, who like many a good mother would do, waited to hear that her son, Niko, had arrived back safely. As soon as she heard him come in, she floated off to dreamland.

Chapter Thirteen
The Scuabtuinne

Niamh thought she was the first to wake up, perhaps awakened by the excitement of going to the Sea King's underwater kingdom, and the idea of the possible help she might get from going there. She tiptoed through the room, past Isabelle and Ocean Marie, and out into the main room in the cave, expecting to see all the men awake, only to find them still sleeping. Noticing that Fintan was not there, she quietly made her way past the sleeping men and outside into the early morning light. The sun was just barely peeking its way into view, causing small nearby birds to begin their greetings to each other and the new day. She looked around, taking in all the pre-dawn beauty; the mist on the grasses, the dew on the leaves, the way the patterns in the tree bark began to pick up light and change form. Taking a deep breath, she smiled softly, thankful for the King's presence and his offer to help her family.

She quickly realized that the campfire was still going from last night, but that there were fresh logs on it. *Someone must have gotten up and restarted the fire then gone back to sleep,* she thought, still wondering where Fintan might have wandered off to. Hearing a quiet rustling of leaves, she looked up, and there was Gabriel, riding Fintan, coming down the trail from the direction of the tower. When Fintan saw Niamh, he quickened his pace to get to her a little faster.

"Fintan, where have you been? Good morning, Gabriel. Have you only just arrived? Is Faolan with you?"

"Good morning, Niamh. I arrived during the night, with Faolan. We brought Deliah back with us and left her with the Elders at the camp by the tower. Faolan is still up there, at the camp, but will be joining us shortly. We found out that Deliah stole two of your father's rifles and was giving them to the two men who were coming after Fintan. She had no idea that they would take her. When they found out Fintan wasn't there, they took Deliah as ransom until the mother could pay off the large debt she owes them."

"And what about the men who took her?" Niamh asked, hoping they weren't here also.

"We left those men with the sheriff in town. The sheriff also has Deliah's mother."

"Any word about my father?"

"Yes, he was tied up and held at gunpoint at Moira's house. The sheriff found him when he went to arrest her. He's fine. We escorted him back to the homestead, and he knows that you and Donal are safe."

Gabriel explained as much as he could while dismounting Fintan. Niamh had her arms around Fintan's neck, hugging and giving him soft kisses, while Gabriel threw a few more branches into the fire.

"Gabriel, the most remarkable thing happened yesterday. The Sea King is here. He has offered to help with my family's situation and has invited us to his kingdom," she told him excitedly.

Gabriel feigned innocence in order not to diminish Niamh's excitement while telling him her news, but he already knew about the King. When the King had heard of the arrival of Gabriel, Faolan, and Deliah in the middle of the night, he'd come out of the cave. It was the King who decided to leave Deliah with the Elders, rather than allowing her to accompany the rest of the group to his kingdom. He thought Deliah would be too disruptive to bring into such a peaceful nation and more than likely would end up causing a lot of trouble.

"I'm so thankful that my father is fine and at the homestead, and I'm very grateful to you for all your help. Deliah's brother, Roger, is with us. He had a nasty head injury and claimed that Deliah hit him with a shovel right before she was kidnapped. Ocean and I bandaged him up, and her brother, Niko, arrived at the homestead with Fintan. He is the one who found Roger and brought us here. I was even told that my mother is still alive!"

"Not to change the subject, Niamh, but Faolan and I would love to go with you to the kingdom. Do you think you could arrange for this to happen?" he asked, but he knew that he had already been invited. It was his way of testing her, trying to see if she enjoyed his company or not.

"I will ask the King," she quickly replied.

Gabriel smiled, getting his answer in her eagerness, and realized that she was, indeed, interested in having him around. Their conversation was interrupted by the other guests who began walking out of the cave, one by one. Isabelle came out with her husband, Analine, carrying some food, followed by Ocean, who was holding two large pitchers filled with fresh birch bark tea. Roger was next, with a clean bandage on his head, and finally the Sea King, carrying a large scroll.

Niamh greeted everyone, but it was the King she walked over to and asked if she might have a word with him. She tried to remain calm and hoped she was not overstepping any bounds as she told him that Gabriel and Faolan were here and how helpful they had been to her, and she then asked if they might be welcome to join the rest of them on their trip to the Sea King's kingdom.

"My dear, if you would like for them to join us, then so be it," he said, holding her shoulders, while she sighed in relief.

"Thank you, sir...Your Honor."

When the Sea King and Niamh finished their short talk, they sat at the campfire, joining the others, along with Faolan, who had just arrived. After eating their breakfast, everyone packed up their things and started on their way toward the portal that led to the kingdom of the Sea King.

The way to the portal can't be explained. Neither can the directions, or the scenery. I can't even give you clues because it is a huge secret. Even clues are forbidden; if people knew how to get there, they would never leave the King and his kingdom alone. He would be bothered day and night, never getting any peace. Once outsiders saw how beautiful and opulent the kingdom was, they would never want to leave; their families would be missing them and searching forever, unable to find them. It is hard enough on the Sea King to see the oceans being overfished, suffering from oil drilling and oil spills, and whales being slaughtered, and that is only at the top of the kingdom. One can imagine the destruction and pollution that would occur if the way to the kingdom were revealed and got into the hands of those who are greedy. The only ones who know where the portal is, other than the King and those whom he invites, are the ravens and crows, and they have too much respect for life to ever divulge the secret whereabouts. What can be shared is that, while walking, the Sea King led the way, his guests following behind, and somewhere on the beach a bright aqua and golden-colored light appeared, in the shape of a triangle. The closer the group came to the pyramid of light, the brighter it shined and came closer to the beach where they were.

The Sea King smiled softly at Niamh as he reached for her hand to guide her forward, and the others followed behind until all were secure within the light. As they entered the shimmering light, Niamh noticed that it was a chariot with an iridescent, golden floor translucent enough to see the ocean beneath. Fintan headed to the front of the chariot, and the Sea King threw three golden braided cords into the air that gently flew over Fintan's neck, while the ends attached to the chariot.

"Bring us home, *Enbarr*," said the Sea King to Fintan as the chariot led by Fintan traveled calmly across the waves.

"Gabriel, why has the Sea King called Fintan *Enbarr*?" Niamh asked.

"*Enbarr* is his spiritual name, Niamh. In full, his name is *Enbarr of the Flowing Mane*. The Sea King has a name too; it is *Mannan Maclear*. This chariot is named *Scuabtuinne – Wave Sweeper*. Fintan is the Sea King's horse. He can transcend between the kingdom of the sea and the earth. He takes on his magical nature to be able to lead the *Scuabtuinne* when called by his spiritual name."

Niamh's eyes began to tear up as she became very still, thinking, "*Fintan isn't mine. He will be taken from me, and I might never see him again.*"

"Niamh, stay hopeful. Keep your thoughts in the moment you are in. Try not to look backward or forward," Gabriel said lovingly as he put a comforting arm around her shoulders. Niamh looked up into his eyes and saw peace and confidence, which assured her that all was well. Then, looking out to the sea, she realized that her challenges were only temporary.

The sea became a glistening image of golden diamonds as the sun gently made its ascent higher into the sky. Gentle breezes swept by the passengers of the *Scuabtuinne,* refreshing their souls and taking every worry from their minds. The sea, the magical, majestic sea, became a comfort for Niamh.

After traveling for some enchanting time on top of the sea, the chariot, still being led by Fintan, slowly submerged, heading down into an area that looked like an underwater forest. Although they were traveling underwater, they were able to breathe and did not get wet.

As the *Scuabtuinne* lowered to the ocean floor, Niamh noticed that they were traveling along a well-worn pathway through an ancient underwater forest, yet it seemed as if they were now on dry land, with air and the appearance of a soft pale-blue sky overhead. There were openings in the forest where she could see clearings that contained fields of flowers and beautiful aqua lakes shimmering from an underwater sun. She also noticed birds and animals of every kind and description. At one point, she saw a family of white deer who quickly looked up in perfect stillness as the vessel passed.

Finally, the Sea King's magnificent castle was in clear view and the *Scuabtuinne* lowered to the ground, landing on a radiant crystalline platform next to the King's moat. As the *Scuabtuinne* opened its plank doorway, simultaneously the large double doors of the castle opened and the residents of his city began crossing the moat in eager anticipation of the new guests' arrival. The Sea King was the first to disembark from the craft, and as he did, a loud cheer emanated from the crowd. As he walked into the group, he was greeted with hugs, flower garlands, and kind welcomes.

The passengers of the *Scuabtuinne* began their ascent into the crowd and were greeted in the same manner as the King. Standing in the doorway of the vessel was Niamh, sitting atop Fintan, with Gabriel standing with his hand on Fintan's neck. Suddenly, the crowd became quiet in respect of this site and a little dark-skinned girl with aqua eyes and a golden ring on one of her little toes ran through the crowd. As she approached the Sea King, he picked her up and held her in a warm hug. Niamh saw the little girl whisper something in the Sea

King's ear, and after he nodded, he gently placed her back on her feet on the ground. She ran as fast as she could to the entrance of the vessel and Gabriel helped her up on top of Fintan, placing her carefully in front of Niamh, then he gently walked the trio down the ramp and into the crowd.

The residents of the Sea King's great village hurriedly crossed the moat's bridge and entered the city, while The Sea King walked with his visitors, smiling and talking as they entered the kingdom. Niamh, still sitting with the little dark-haired girl on top of Fintan and being led by Gabriel, remained perfectly quiet, but each of them had lingering questions in their mind that would be addressed later. Niamh recognized the little girl but couldn't remember where she knew her from; Gabriel wondered if Niamh would get her full memory of who she was back on this trip, and Dillis wondered how long Niamh would stay in the kingdom.

Chapter Fourteen
Donal's Healing

Only having arrived at the castle the day before, Brigid waited anxiously in a quiet sitting room within the Sea King's palace, knowing that soon she would see her children for the first time in two years. Her heart was overflowing with joy, yet at the same time, she was nervous, as she knew that she had to tell them a story that they wouldn't be pleased to hear. She hoped that when she explained where she had been, her children would not allow hatred to enter their hearts toward her abductors.

She thought of various options she might employ to assuage their anxiety upon hearing her story but decided that being direct and truthful was the best course of action. She knew her children and counted on their inner character of being loving and forgiving to get them through the pain of her story. Brigid had lost weight since she last saw her children, and her countenance was pale and colorless from being locked indoors for the past two years. Her hair was dull and lacked the beautiful shine that it used to have and her skin had wrinkled from remaining dehydrated, as she was only given small amounts of water each day. Although her abductors did feed her, it wasn't the type of food that she was accustomed to and it lacked taste and nutritional value. She was kept indoors in a very dark room and only saw the people who her abductors brought in to be healed, usually criminals with stab wounds or injuries from falling off their horses while being chased.

Brigid had no idea of her son Donal's condition, although she did know of Moira's plot to entrap him with the pregnancy story. The last time she saw Donal, he was in his bedroom working on a song when she came in and asked if he would go with her to Moira's house. Brigid, for the past two years, felt very thankful that Donal had refused to go because he might have been seriously hurt or even murdered. He surely would have tried to fight against the abductors, and they were too embroiled in their evil plot to allow anything or anyone to interfere with it. She knew that Donal must have felt guilty when she didn't turn up, and she prayed hard he would know that she would never hold it against him for not going with her.

She would never forget the look on Moira's face; a look of contempt, yet pleasure at Brigid's downfall. She seemed to take great delight that her plan was working and believed that, with Brigid out of the way, Liam would be free to marry her. Brigid knew that Liam would never marry again and, unless some power of darkness drugged him and coerced him into it, he would never go along with any of Moira's plans. He, being the kind-hearted and loving man that he was, was wholly dedicated to his wife and children. He would do nothing to jeopardize not only his family but his standing within the village.

Moira, on the other hand, had a dark and jealous heart, one that longed for all that wasn't hers. She could easily give up her husband for another, and she could just as quickly use her children as a means to her corrupt plan's end. She had always been jealous of Brigid and thought that Brigid needed to be out of the picture, but that was only part of her plan. She used her daughter as a pawn in her game, hoping that Deliah would carry Donal's child, and give her even more reason to be close to Liam. Knowing that Liam's family carried the pure light lineage of the Tuatha de Danann, a child of the family would inherently carry certain magical powers, which she planned to use to her advantage. Deliah's mother thought it was advantageous that neither Niamh nor Donal knew that they had any power, as it would make it easier to manipulate them. She inwardly laughed at their innocence and how naïve they were, thinking them dull in intellect.

The two men who eventually kidnapped Deliah were the same ones who had abducted Brigid and had stolen Fintan, before losing him to Donal while gambling. Those two men were as corrupt as Moira and were distantly related to her.

When Donal was led down the corridor by one of the Sea King's attendants, he didn't know that he was going to meet his mother and thought he was being led to a room to freshen up before their meal. Being deep in thought, Brigid barely heard Donal's footsteps as he approached the room she occupied until he was right at the door. The very second she became aware of his presence, she ran to the door and held him tightly.

"Mother," he said tearfully, startled and unsure if he was dreaming. "Can it be you? Are you real? How can you be here?"

"Donal! My dear son!" she sobbed. As she held him, she instinctively knew that he was ill and held his shoulders to take a closer look into his eyes. Being a healer, and of the lineage of the Tuatha de Danann, she was well attuned to people's energies. Being Donal's mother, she was attuned to his energy even more and instantly felt healing energy transmitting from her body to his. This was one aspect of the Tuatha de Danann's magical powers: when one was exercised in their magic, they did not have to think things through or ponder how to heal someone. Brigid had been a healer her whole life, and although her children carried the healing gift within them, they had not yet become practiced in it. Once being exercised in it, they would be very attuned to other people's energies, and if there were a need for healing, the energy would intuitively travel from them to one who needed healing.

The two, mother and son, stood facing each other, looking past their rough conditions and more into their wounded spirits while something very magical began occurring. They both started to be healed. Each cared more for the other than they did for themselves and each knew that, within one another's presence, all would be well.

"Donal, forgive me for being away," she finally said, softly.

"I'm thankful to have you back in my life. We thought you were dead," he replied. "I know all of this is my fault, for not going with you, and I'm the one who needs to apologize. I haven't been able to live with myself since that night. I don't know how you will ever forgive me for this, but I swear I will make it up to you."

"Donal, there is nothing to forgive. If you had gone with me, they would have killed you, and that would have been far more painful for me than anything either of us has endured. I have never held that against you. It's good that you didn't go. Can you imagine the pain that your father and sister would have gone through if both of us were gone for two years?"

"Mother, Niamh is with me. She's here. Should we go and find her?" he asked.

"Yes, I am aware that she is here, but I asked to see you first and spend a little time with you alone. I could feel how you have suffered and the guilt you must have felt, and I also knew that you would want to see me alone at first. Let's sit for a bit and talk, and then we will go together to see your sister. The Sea King wanted to surprise you and your sister, but I asked specifically if I might see you alone first and was granted his blessing to do so."

As the underwater sun's rays flowed in through the castle windows, it illuminated their thoughts, allowing them to have clarity and share their plights. As they shared, Brigid instinctively knew that her son was being healed, not only in his body but in his conscience as well. Knowing that he was being healed allowed her to release her pain, and her youthful appearance began to return to her. She explained to him how Deliah's mother had devised the plan to have a grandchild, and then she told him about his heritage and their magical abilities. Donal accepted all that she told him, without question. He told his mother about his drinking and gambling, how he won Fintan at O'Shaunessey's pub and gave him to Niamh for her birthday. Brigid listened intently, until Donal mentioned Deliah's pregnancy, and then interrupted him.

"She is not with child, Son. It was a plot derived from her mother. Together, they have been drugging you, and this is how you got the damage to your liver. Between the tea that Ocean Marie gave you, along with the

131

medicine pouch you are wearing, and being here hearing the truth, you are being healed. You must let go of all the guilt you have about not going with me on that night. Guilt creates pain and illness. This is not your fault. When you let go of the last remnant of guilt, your organs will be completely healed."

"Ocean told me the same thing, Mother. She told me that I had to get rid of all my guilt."

"I hope to meet Ocean someday, Son. She sounds like a sage young woman."

"You will meet her today, Mother. The Sea King brought her here with us," he smiled. "I told her that I threw my guitar in the ocean because I was so frustrated with myself for not going with you. She was very understanding and told me that there are other guitars in this world and that I would have another one someday."

"I'm sure you will, Donal. It would be a shame for you not to play your music again. I've waited two years to hear the song you were working on when I left. I trust you have finished it?" she asked.

"I can finish it now. As soon as I get another guitar, I will sing and play it for you. Mother, Niamh somehow knew in her heart that you were alive. She never gave up believing that, you know. She did everything the right way. She took care of Dad and me, cooking and cleaning and all the chores. You would be so proud of her."

"I'm proud of both you and your sister. You feel as if you have done something that is 'less than' your sister, but you haven't, Donal. Each person deals with the pain of loss in their own way. You were deceived. This was not your fault. I cannot say it enough, Donal. If you want to help me now, you must believe that this is NOT your fault!"

"I knew that you would forgive me, Mother. I never doubted that. Now, I have to learn to forgive myself and those who took you away."

"What good will it do to hold onto that feeling, Donal? You can't help yourself, or me, by holding on to that hurt. It will profit nothing to keep that feeling against others. We are fortunate to have our family safe, and soon we will all be together again. For this, we should be nothing but thankful. With the dark forces aiming their energies directly at our family, we need to do all we can to keep our minds and thoughts clear of hatred, revenge, and guilt. We will need to unite to prevent incidents like these from happening again. We will need to know who we are and the gifts we have been given."

"And this is why I love you, Mother."

At this, Brigid smiled and gave her son a warm hug. "Let's go and join the others now. I'm anxious to see Niamh. I've heard that she has grown into a lovely and sweet young lady while I've been away."

"She rides like the wind, Mother. You should have seen her riding Fintan across the ridge, without a saddle. The saddle was out being repaired when I gave her Fintan, on her birthday. She just hopped up and took right off, like she'd been riding all her life."

"I'm curious, Donal, why did you want to give her a horse for her birthday?"

"It wasn't that I wanted to give her a horse, but I wanted her to have that horse in particular. When I saw Fintan and looked in his eyes, he reminded me of her. There is something about him that is the same as Niamh. I can't explain it, but I knew that I had to find a way to get that horse, in particular, to her. She told Dad that Fintan seems to know what she thinks before she even knows it. I also had a feeling that the two men who had Fintan would hurt him. They didn't seem like very good people, so in a way, I thought I could kill two birds with one stone. I knew that Niamh would keep him safe and that he would keep her safe."

"Donal, those two men were the same ones who abducted me. They are related to Deliah's mother, and she hired them to help her orchestrate the demise of our family because she wanted me out of the way, thinking that she might marry your father if I was gone. Those two men had stolen Fintan from Gabriel before bringing him to our village."

"Oh no! Does this mean that Niamh won't be able to keep Fintan?"

"I'm not sure yet. We will have to see what Gabriel wants to do," she told him. "The horse is rightfully his, so it will be up to him to determine Fintan's destiny. I've never spoken with Gabriel, but I have heard about what a good person he is from the Sea King. I am anxious to meet him, and Ocean, along with her family."

"Roger is with us. He is pretty banged up. He has a head injury," Donal told his mother.

"Let's go now and join the others. It sounds like I have some healing work to take care of."

Just as she said this, one of the Sea King's attendants knocked at the door and Brigid welcomed her inside. "The Sea King has organized a feast and is hoping you and your son will be attending. It will be in the grand dining room hall. Shall I escort you? He sent this note to you, Ma'am," she said as she held out a beautiful abalone shell containing the envelope that the Sea King sent to her.

Brigid kindly took the envelope from the shell, opened it, and read it aloud to Donal.

My Dearest Brigid,

I haven't told Niamh that you are here yet. In light of our recent victory in overcoming the forces of darkness, I have organized a special surprise for her and would be honored if you would attend our feast and share in the joy of this magical occasion. Please bring Donal with you.

Forever,

The Sea King

After reading, Brigid was handed a piece of paper and an envelope to reply to the Sea King. She wrote:

My Dearest Sea King,

My son Donal and I would be honored to attend your feast, and we both thank you for all your unending love and support of our family.

Forever,

Brigid

Brigid carefully folded the note, inserted it into the envelope, and laid it gently in the beautiful shell being held by the Sea King's attendant.

"I will deliver this to the Sea King and come back to escort you to the feast," she said, smiling.

"Donal, what do you think the surprise is for Niamh?" she asked her son.

"I'm not sure, but whatever it is, she deserves it. She has been the most amazing sister that anyone could ever hope for. There isn't a surprise that could be too great for her. I only wish I had half of her courage. When I was weak and fell apart after you left, she stayed strong for all of us."

"I can't wait to see her," Brigid smiled as she thought of her daughter and how she longed to see her again.

Just as she thought this, the attendant came back to lead them to the banquet hall. They passed through a beautiful corridor whose walls were glass and looked out into the ocean. Donal loved fish and sea life, and he knew the names of all the coral and fish, pointing each out to Brigid as they passed. Beautiful fish swam among the coral reefs, formed by two coral species, *Lophelia pertusa* and *Madrepora oculata*, which interconnect with tubes of the worm *Eunice norvegicus*. Amongst the coral branches, they saw, redfish, saithe, cod, ling, tusk, squat lobsters and other crustaceans, mollusks, starfish, brittle stars, sea pens, and sea urchins. A wide variety of animals were growing plant-like beings attached to the reef, including sponges, bryozoans, hydroids, and other coral species. Brigid and Donal were intrigued by all they saw but continued forth with the attendant, anxious to see Niamh.

"Donal, it amazes me how you know the names of all these beautiful plants and fish. I'm very impressed," said the attendant.

"Oh, I have loved sea life since the day I was born. I am always drawn to the sea," he told her.

Brigid smiled as she thought about their lineage and their relation to the Sea King. *Of course, my children would love the sea and all that the sea holds. It is their heritage,* she thought.

"Donal, what is that large fish called, over there, it looks like a plate with the large spikes on it?" Brigid asked.

"Let me see...oh, that one is called *John Dory,* and they usually like to hide and lie in wait, hoping for smaller bait fish to swim by so they can have their supper," he told her.

"Your son knows a lot about the sea. I have lived here my entire life and didn't know the name of that fish," the attendant said to Brigid, who smiled with pride.

"Ah, here we are, through this door to the banquet hall," the attendant said as she opened the elaborately carved wooden door.

Brigid grabbed Donal's hand as they were ushered into the elaborately ornate banquet hall. As soon as Donal was seated, the attendant guided Brigid up the stairs and to the left of the stage, where behind a curtain was a comfortable chair waiting for her, along with a meal. She wouldn't be eating with the others since she was going to be part of the surprise the Sea King had arranged for Niamh.

Chapter Fifteen
Initiation

Niamh sat quietly in her room, thinking about all that had transpired since acquiring Fintan on her birthday while waiting for an attendant to bring her into the banquet hall. Many questions entered her thoughts, yet she was peaceful. *I recognize that symbol that keeps popping up everywhere, but where do I remember it from and what does it symbolize? Will Fintan and I be reunited when we leave here? Where is my mother? Is she well? Will I see her again?* Finding out that her mother was still alive was the most significant blessing she could imagine, but she didn't know her mother was here, in the same castle, or that she would be seeing her soon.

She looked around the room and saw all the beautiful, elaborately carved furniture and bookcases. While looking at the carving on one of the cabinets, something glimmered, but when she looked up to see what it was, there were only more books. She continued to look around, and again, something gleamed in the same area as before, so she got up from her seat and walked over to the shelf where she noticed the glimmering coming from. In a higher shelf than she could reach, even while stretching and standing on her tiptoes, was a book she recognized from her dream. The book took on a golden glow and began glowing brighter and brighter. Niamh stretched harder and reached higher, but no matter what she did, she couldn't reach the glowing book. Her mind became flooded with memories of her dream of Trini O'Brien, trying to reach the book in the library in Dublin. *This feels all too familiar. What is this book, and could it be the same book that was in the dream, the Golden Glows?*

"Is everything well with you, Miss?" the attendant asked after seeing Niamh's flushed cheeks from jumping up and down to retrieve the book.

"Oh, yes, of course," she responded, embarrassedly, while she smoothed her dress and hair. *I hope no one heard me jumping around in here.*

"The Sea King sent this to you," the attendant stated while holding out a sizeable radiant abalone shell that contained an envelope addressed to Miss Niamh O'Brien. Niamh noticed that there was also a significant package that the attendant sat down on the floor next to her when she opened the door.

Niamh gracefully took the envelope from the shell and opened it. It read:

My Dearest Niamh,

It is my most sincere wish that you will accept the gift that the attendant brought along, and honor me by wearing it while attending my banquet, which will be held in the banquet hall very shortly.

Sincerely,

The Sea King

Niamh smiled while she carefully placed the note on the dresser in the room, feeling very proud that the Sea King sent her a personal invitation, along with a gift. When the attendant saw her smile, she reached down and grabbed the package and handed it to Niamh, then she stood quietly while waiting for her to open it.

Niamh carried her package to the couch and offered the attendant a place to sit with her as she began carefully opening her present. *My heart feels as if it could beat right out of my chest,* she thought while opening it. *If only my mother could see me now, in this fantastic underwater castle, opening a gift from the Sea King.*

Niamh carefully took the present that the Sea King sent and held it to her chest. It was the green cape bordered in ermine skins, embroidered with the sacred symbol in rose-colored thread, the one Fintan gave her to wear on the mountain. As she tried on the cape, once again, her eyes misted with tears. *This wrap felt familiar to me when I wore it on the mountain, and now again it is familiar. I recognize this symbol, yet I still don't know what it means or why it is so familiar to me. When I wore it on the mountain, on my birthday, it felt as if I had worn it many times before, and now again, this same feeling overtakes me.*

"You are very beautiful in your cape, Miss O'Brien," the attendant said while admiring how beautifully the cape fit her.

"Thank you. I will take good care of it to return it to the Sea King in good shape," she replied.

"Oh no. This cape is for you. The Sea King wishes you to keep it. It is yours," she replied as she ushered Niamh to a gilded, full-length oval mirror.

When Niamh looked in the mirror, not only did she see herself, but she also saw the reflection of the window on the opposite side of the room where the outside world was teaming with schools of brightly colored fish, making it seem as if she were completely underwater. This was not an entirely realistic or accurate portrayal because, in the reflection, Niamh was holding a long, richly engraved, ornamented golden scepter. As she stared at the reflection in the mirror, she saw herself for who she was, the heir to the Sea King. Her eyes, now filled with the clear, quiet mist of hope and remembrance, stared longingly into the mirror, remembering long-lost times, ancient wisdom, and ocean magic, long-hidden dreams of the Tuatha de Danann. She was so absorbed in the process of regaining her memories that she didn't notice when Gabriel came into the room or when the attendant quietly walked out.

Gabriel stared with pride as he realized that the reflection in the mirror of Niamh contained the royal scepter, her scepter that signified that the times of remembrance were upon her and that the power of the magic of the ocean, her inheritance, was now able to be used. Gabriel saw that she was lost in the reflection, and he stood quietly while sacred energies flowed from the representation in the mirror into Niamh. As this transformation took place, a soft, golden light enveloped Niamh, surrounding her with a golden glow.

"Gabriel! I didn't see you standing there. Where is the attendant?" she asked suddenly.

"The Sea King needed her. I will accompany you to the banquet. Shall we go now?" he asked, knowing that she was now ready for her future; a future that was held in place by a long lineage from the ancient past.

"Yes, of course. I am ready," Niamh said confidently, still enraptured by the experience reflected in the gilded mirror and not yet realizing the magnitude of her situation.

As they began to leave the room, Niamh turned one last time to look in the direction of the mirror, making sure that it was real and securing all that occurred into her memory.

"One second, Niamh. I have to retrieve something for you," Gabriel said as he quickly walked to the bookshelf, pulled the still-glowing book from one of the top shelves, and handed it to her. Niamh took the book from him and realized that it was the very book she had been jumping up to reach—the one that reminded her of her dream when Trini and John were in the library in Dublin—the book that contained the mystery of the Golden Glows.

How did he know that I wanted to see this book? Just as she thought this, she realized a strange similarity between Gabriel and John from her dream. She suddenly realized that Fintan was also in her dream. Holding the book close to her heart as they walked, she remembered the dream and the beautiful little dark-skinned girl with the light eyes, Dillis, and her interpretation of the Medicine Wheel; "*Everyone's life is a circle, and we all go round and round it. These stones are directions, and the stick that I threw in the center is to show which direction you are in now. Each direction has a meaning. When you have a lesson to learn, the lesson is born in the top of the circle; the top is like your mind or heart, where ideas come from in the North. Then, you go around the wheel to the right, where your ideas become inspired by creativity in the East. After your ideas collect the energy of creativity, they travel to the bottom, to the*

139

South, where your innocence and your purity gather up your ideas to carry them up to the top to be born. When you are negative, or if there is negativity around you, the South loses its strength and cannot carry your idea back up to the top to be born. After the creative thought takes on its highest form of purity, it travels further along the wheel to the west, to the place of introspection, where you meditate on it, allowing it to rest in your mind before it completes its journey. It is important to stay calm and peaceful so that your ideas can be light enough to get carried to the top to be born," she told the group seriously.

"Is this what the glowing book is about?" asked John.

"It does contain this, but this is not all it is about. There is a lot more, but you won't ever understand the book until you understand the Sacred Circle and how to stay peaceful," Dillis said as she stared into each of the group's eyes, one at a time. "Lesson Number One in the glowing magic book begins with this. When any lesson or time comes up in your life, whether it is a hard lesson or a natural one, staying peaceful is the most important thing you can ever do..."

As she walked, remembering every detail of her dream, word for word, her memories began to fix firmly within her mind. The Medicine Wheel, the Sacred Circle, staying peaceful no matter what, and Lesson Two, blame no one. As she thought about Lesson Two, she remembered what Basil, the talking cat from her dream, said to the group, *'As long as there is someone to blame, you never get to really grow up. It is a childish thing to blame your parents, your teachers, your siblings, or worse yet, blame life. Once you make up your whole mind that your life is yours and you are going to be happy and good, no matter what, and decide that you will never blame anyone, including yourself, you have Lesson Number Two.'* She also remembered that all animals could talk, but only a few people could understand them.

Chapter Sixteen
Starfish Quartet

Niamh, escorted by Gabriel, entered the banquet hall through a back entrance. Many of the other guests entered by crossing a footbridge that passed over a crystalline stream where there were cascades of water falling over dark rocks on either side. These were bordered by lush lime and olive green ferns and beautiful tropical flowering plants, which looked as if they grew right out of the rocks. Once inside, they were ushered to a table in the front of the enormous hall where most of the group that traveled with her to the kingdom were seated next to what appeared to be a stage; and in the far-left corner sat the musicians, a starfish quartet. These were huge starfish, the size of humans, and dressed in excellent long-tailed black linen tuxedos and top hats. Two starfish played violins and sang soprano and alto; one starfish played the viola and sang tenor, and the fourth starfish played the cello and sang bass. When the Sea King entered the stage, they stopped singing and performed Mozart's string quartet in D major, the Sea King's favorite.

Although Niamh had no idea of her relation to the Sea King, when the other guests saw her wearing the green royal cloak, trimmed in ermine skins with the rose-colored symbol embroidered on it, they realized who she was and stopped their conversations and stared humbly. No one approached her or spoke to her, they only sat quietly and respectfully until she was seated.

Eight large wooden octagon tables were decorated beautifully for the banquet, each having a silk tablecloth in shades of teal, aqua, indigo, and pale sky blue, forming a mesmerizing composition of iridescent patterns, and embroidered with various colored silken threads in designs unique to the underwater kingdom. Upon each of the large octagon tables sat clear crystal seahorse candelabras containing crystal globes that held pure white candles, which gave the whole room a warm and inviting ambiance. Small starfish and shells were placed around the candelabras, some leaning against them.

Roses of all sizes, shapes, and colors were everywhere, with sprigs of baby's breath sprouting from each arrangement; they were on the tables, in large urns throughout the room, placed in arrangements strategically on the stage, and hanging from the ceiling on evergreen garlands wrapped in small white lights. The entire hall contained the now-familiar combined scents of roses, angelica, and frankincense mixed with the sweet scent of the sea. *This smells like the Tower of Solomon,* Niamh thought.

Crystalline waterfalls cascaded peacefully across shiny dark-lava rocks spouting from the wall, into small fishponds beneath, which also contained clusters of floating roses. The soft ivory-colored sand on the bottom of the fishponds held clusters of family crystals and small clams and oysters. Seahorses, starfish, and schools of little turquoise, orange, and violet-colored fish swam peacefully through the brilliantly shimmering water.

Surrounding the room were large, potted white birch trees, covered in tiny white lights that had white peacocks with long, flowing tails sitting on their branches. The white lights from the trees reflected not only on the waterfalls and shimmering fishponds but also on the brilliant gold leaf picture frames on the walls, which contained the portraits of various family members from the Sea King's lineage. As Niamh tried to take in all the enchanting sights of the exquisitely adorned banquet hall, she noticed that two of the large golden frames were entirely covered by royal-purple velvet cloth so that the portraits underneath could not be seen without removing the fabrics, and she wondered what was underneath.

The royal wait staff consisted of eight giant Pacific octopuses, one assigned to each table. The hundreds of suction cups on their eight sinuous tentacles made it quite easy for them to hold large platters, therefore be able to serve at least six guests at one time, while standing on two of their long tentacles. They had beautiful dark eyes, similar to labradorite gemstones, with colors ranging from gray-green, dark gray, black, or grayish-white, and had streaks of royal and cobalt-blue iridescent bands throughout them. Their skin changed color to match their environment, taking on a warm golden glow from the candles and white lights. They were dressed in gold and silver brocaded, long-tailed jackets, white ruffled shirts, and each wore a midnight blue tie, tied loosely at their neck. Rather than noses, they had long, sharp, dark-orange bird-like beaks. They were very polite and friendly, and you could tell that they were knowledgeable and loved the work they were doing.

The mermaids all sat together at the same table, and each was unique in appearance. Niamh hadn't noticed they were mermaids, as they were all wearing shawls, until she saw one of their long, shiny emerald-green flippers peeking out from under the embroidered tablecloth. They were very dainty in appearance and had beautiful eyes and lips. One mermaid Niamh was particularly drawn to was sitting facing her and had the most luxurious lavender-frosted, orchid-colored hair, long and hanging loose around her shoulders, with several aqua braids wrapped carefully around the sides of her head, tied in the back. She had ashen skin and deep cerulean-blue eyes, outlined in black. Her shawl was shades of aqua, saturated with deep blues and greens in an endless pattern. When she saw Niamh looking at her, she smiled sweetly before continuing her conversation with one of the smaller mermaids who was sitting close by.

Suddenly, one of the tiny starfish that sat on Niamh's table stood up and walked over to her. Pointing to the beautiful mermaid who smiled at Niamh, it said, "Her name is Adia, and I'm sure you will find her to be a valued friend," and then, after shaking Niamh's hand, it walked slowly back to where it had been sitting with the other starfish and seashells and settled in quietly.

Niamh had never experienced such a magical world; filled with talking animals, mermaids, castles, and the grandeur of the Sea King's kingdom. She was overwhelmed and awestruck by not only the surroundings but the incredible personalities of all the people and creatures she encountered. So many thoughts rushed through her mind that she could barely grab hold of even one of them, as everything was happening so quickly. She was glad that Gabriel was by her side, as his presence brought comfort to her, and seeing the Sea King, who was also a great comfort to her, caused her to feel that even more experiences were about to unfold. She slowly looked around the room while the quartet finished playing Mozart's string quartet in D major in the background of her thoughts.

When the Sea King's favorite song finally ended, he made his way down the steps and sat down at the guest table, next to Niamh. While lighthearted music continued, each of the guests dined on their exquisite delicacies, sipped their delicious drinks, and the Sea King carried on a jovial conversation with the guests at his table. When their meals were finished, and the wait staff cleared their plates, the Sea King graciously excused himself and headed toward the back of the stage, slipping behind an ivory brocade curtain.

"Gabriel, have you visited here often?" Analine asked.

"Yes, as a matter of fact, I've been here on several occasions. The Sea King has been very generous in his invitations and company," he told him modestly.

"I'm surprised you could find it in you to leave at all," Ocean Marie said, wide-eyed with wonder. "I love it here and find that it is far more beautiful than my mind ever imagined."

"Yes, I'll admit it is challenging to leave this beautiful kingdom but necessary at times," he said thoughtfully.

"The Sea King is most gracious," said Isabelle, and everyone agreed.

"Niamh, you've barely said a word. Are you enjoying yourself?" asked her brother.

"Oh, yes, it is exquisite. If I am quiet, please forgive me, everyone. I only wish my mother were here to see this. She often spoke of her desire to see this kingdom," she smiled sadly. "And there is a lot to see and experience here. I could never have imagined how beautiful it is."

The music became softer as the Sea King came out from behind the brocade curtain and stood center stage until the audience was hushed, and then he spoke:

"I would like to thank all of you for being present at my banquet this evening, and I would like to introduce my guests." As he called out each of the names sitting at Niamh's table, they each stood up, in turn, and gave a slight smile, nod, or wave. He didn't introduce Gabriel since they all knew him well, nor did he call Niamh. After each guest's name was called, there was applause and greetings. "Finally, I would like to introduce you to my great-granddaughter, Niamh O'Brien," he said while smiling directly at Niamh.

"Gabriel, please lead my great-granddaughter to the stage, as I have a few surprises for her," he said mischievously.

Gabriel took Niamh's soft hand in his own as she lifted herself from her seat and walked toward the stage. She had no idea why the Sea King called her his great-granddaughter unless it was a form of endearment, used in this kingdom toward young women. She allowed Gabriel to walk her up the stairs to the stage, where the King hugged her warmly.

"Niamh, it is my greatest pleasure that you have arrived here and honored me with your presence. I would like to return your kindness by presenting you with this gift, from Gabriel and myself," he said while motioning toward the right of the stage. There, being led by Dillis, the beautiful little girl from her dream, was Fintan Wild Fire. When Niamh saw Fintan, her worries melted away and her eyes teared up. She hugged the Sea King and Gabriel, thanking them from the bottom of her heart, and then little Dillis, and finally Fintan, who was adorned beautifully for the occasion. She stood next to Fintan with salt tears pouring down her cheeks, feeling more gratitude than could be imagined, while the audience clapped and cheered.

The Sea King finally motioned for stillness when he noticed a look of confusion cross Niamh's face as she wondered what she should do now. *Should she lead Fintan off the stage or would Dillis take Fintan somewhere until after the banquet?*

"My dear, I have saved the best gift for last," he said as he motioned to the left side of the stage, where stood Niamh's mother, dressed beautifully in a royal-blue dress with emerald-green designs.

Dillis knew that Niamh was about to faint from shock, so she took a firm grip on Niamh's hand and led her to her mother.

"Ladies and gentlemen, my granddaughter, Brigid O'Brien, mother of Niamh. They have been separated by strange circumstances for over two years,

144

and this is their blessed reunion. My granddaughter, Brigid, is a healer, like her mother before her, my beloved daughter. Brigid had been captured and held hostage for two years and forced to care for those with criminal intentions. Gabriel searched high and low for these two years, and he finally found her and brought her to me, for which I am forever grateful to you, Gabriel."

Niamh looked down at the table, to her brother Donal, and motioned for him to come up to the stage while holding her mother tightly and pouring kisses and affection on her.

"I've met with Donal already, love. We talked for a while before the banquet. The Sea King wanted to surprise you, so I told Donal not to mention a word at the table," Brigid told her.

"So you know about his health?" Niamh asked. "I wanted to heal him but didn't know what to do," she told her worriedly.

"Yes, he is healing. Please, don't worry. I've started the healing process for him," she explained quickly.

The Sea King stood proudly watching as Niamh experienced the happiest day of her life. Knowing that Gabriel gave Fintan to her, and now seeing her mother, made her heart so full that she could barely contain her joy.

"And now, last but not least, I have a surprise for you, Brigid, and for your children," he said while motioning in the direction of the back of the stage. The cream-colored brocade curtains with the golden silk tassels opened, and there stood Liam, Brigid's husband and Donal and Niamh's father.

What a glorious day it was for the O'Brien family, being reunited, all thanks to the Sea King's kindness and Gabriel's quick thinking. Gabriel came up with the idea after finding out that Liam was in danger from the dragons, and he went in the *Scuabtuinne* to pick Liam up before the banquet. Applause roared throughout the exquisitely decorated banquet hall, and each of the O'Brien family, in turn, embraced Gabriel and the Sea King, thanking them again for all their devotion and care.

"Now, if you will please place your attention on the right side of the room... Attendants, it is time," the Sea King said as he nodded to two of his attendants. The attendants carefully removed the royal-purple velvet cloth from one of the golden picture frames, and underneath was an oil painting of Brigid and Liam. As the audience gazed admiringly at the portrait, Niamh finally began to realize who her mother was and her relation to the Sea King.

"Now, finally, Attendants..." he said as he motioned for them to unveil the next painting. As he nodded, the attendants carefully pulled the velvet cloth from the final covered frame, and Niamh couldn't believe what her eyes revealed to her. It was an oil portrait of Niamh sitting atop Fintan, who was standing next to her brother, Donal. She wore her royal-green cloak and held the royal golden scepter she had seen in the mirror within her right hand.

"Now, after all this excitement, shall we all go to our tables and partake of the luscious desserts that our chef has been so kind to make for us?" the Sea King asked while motioning toward the serving table being wheeled through the hall toward the first table, where he and his guests sat.

As they ate their beautiful delicate pastries and flavored cream desserts, one of the Sea King's attendants came and asked him if he could please have a word.

"Excuse me, please. I will return shortly," the Sea King told his guests. He knew that the attendant would only interrupt their celebration if it was of the utmost importance, and he knew that if it were anything trivial, the attendant would have waited until the banquet feast had ended. He braced himself as he walked out of the hall and into the corridor with his attendant.

"I'm very sorry to bother you, your Honor, but this is very important."

"Yes, I assumed so. Please, what is it?" the Sea King asked kindly.

"Moira made a potion that caused her prison guards to follow her orders, and they turned over the guns and let her out of jail. She then went back to her house and tried to kill her husband, and called on her dragons. The dragons came and brought her to the O'Brien homestead. Gabriel took Liam out in the nick of time because they arrived shortly after Gabriel and Liam left. Moira was so angry that Liam wasn't there that she had the dragons burn down the entire property—house, barns, and sheds. She and the dragons are headed across the Owenglin River now, toward the Tower of Solomon. She intends to free her daughter so that both can work together to become more powerful. They hope to find the O'Briens and continue with their original plan of killing all but Liam. Moira still plans to marry him."

"Thank you for the message. Please, send for Gabriel right away. We will have to prepare to move the guests to Paroisse Saint-Pierre, on Cape Breton Island, where Moira and her dragons won't have any power. Please, have the *Scuabtuinne* prepared, and Fintan as well."

After giving his instructions, the Sea King went to his private library and sat at his desk, waiting for Gabriel. *How will I tell Liam and his family that they have lost everything their family has worked for? I must keep the family safe, at all costs.*

"Gabriel, thank you for coming. I'm so sorry to disturb your meal, but I have just been informed of something that requires our undivided focus and attention," the Sea King told him, along with the details that the attendant had told him. "After all that Liam's family has been through, I truly hate to disappoint them again, but we must get them out of here and to safety. I've called for the *Scuabtuinne* and for Fintan to be readied to take them to Paroisse Saint-Pierre. Will you accompany them?"

"Yes, of course, I will. Will you be staying here?" Gabriel asked.

"Yes, for now, I must stay. The Elders of Iona will be attacked soon, and I must be ready to do whatever is necessary for them. Moira has summoned the dragons and burned down Liam's entire homestead. She is on her way with the dragons to rescue her daughter and then will be on her way here. Leave quickly with the guests and bring them into the church through the underground passageway, ensuring that they won't be noticed by anyone. I will go out to the banquet hall with you and explain it to our guests, but they must leave as quickly as possible. Please, take this golden scepter that was my daughter's and give it to Niamh. She will know how to use it when the time comes."

Gabriel carefully took the scepter and walked quickly with the Sea King back to the banquet hall, where they found their guests talking happily and enjoying the rest of their desserts.

"I'm sorry to impose this horrendous task upon all of you, but I must speak frankly and honestly," the Sea King told them as he recounted the story of Moira and her destruction upon their property, along with telling them her plans. He then explained how they must leave with Gabriel as quickly as possible. He told them that they would be taking a route that would require opening a portal, and as soon as the *Scuabtuinne* passed through the portal, it would be closed until the matter was resolved. He ended with, "This makes me feel terrible, after seeing you all together, reunited after so long a time. Be safe and stay together. Gabriel will be with you." He hugged each of them quickly, and when he came to Roger, he told him that he was very sorry to give him this news about his family, then he quickly left the hall.

Isabelle Cleary, being the compassionate woman that she was, went to Roger and told him that everything was going to work out and not to worry. She held his hand and said, "Stay strong."

The Sea King returned to his study and sat quietly at his desk, staring out the window, thinking, when he heard a little tapping at his door. He motioned for his attendant to tend to the door.

Dillis walked in, followed by Basil, the talking cat from Niamh's dream who lived at Old Sheniah's.

"Dillis, Basil, is everything well with you?" he asked.

"We want to go to Paroisse Saint-Pierre with the others," she said firmly.

"Yes, we feel a *need* to go with Niamh and the others," said Basil, who had gone behind the desk to be closer to the Sea King.

"You feel a *need?*" he asked both of them.

"Yes, we feel a *need*," they replied in unison.

"Then I suppose you must go with them," the Sea King replied earnestly.

The Sea King knew that there was little time before the *Scuabtuinne* left, so he hurriedly motioned for his attendant, and all four of them, the Sea King, his attendant, Dillis, and Basil, walked quickly to the ship. After Basil and Dillis boarded, they headed directly to Niamh and her mother.

"Gabriel, I see that you have gathered my guests together and boarded the *Scuabtuinne* for your travels. I have given my permission for Dillis and Basil to accompany you. They sensed a *need* to go to Paroisse Saint-Pierre."

"Yes, of course," Gabriel replied while helping Dillis and Basil aboard, while the Sea King's attendant placed the royal bells on Fintan, causing him to become *Enbarr of the Flowing Mane.*

"You must leave now, as the portal must be closed quickly behind you and we haven't much time," the Sea King told Gabriel as he waved to Niamh and her mother. "Stay safe, my loved ones."

Chapter Seventeen
The Dragons and Solomon's Tower

After destroying the O'Brien homestead, Moira and the three dragons under her command flew across the Owenglin River and straight to the sandy beach at the foot of the mountain where the Tower of Solomon stood. While giving the dragons a command to wait for her, Moira quickly donned the disguise of an old beggar man and grabbed a nearby walking stick and headed toward the tower to infiltrate the camp of the Elders of Iona in hopes of retrieving her daughter. She knew the Elders of Iona could not refuse to feed a beggar, and she truly believed herself to be more deceptive than they were wise.

As Moira made her descent, what she hadn't counted on was Faolan's watchful eye. He had been standing guard over the trail with a clear view of the beach since the early morning. His gut instinct told him that there was a threat, and without consulting with the Elders, whom he knew would have told him to relax and have faith, he set out on his own to ensure the safety of the Elders and Deliah. As he observed the beach, he saw Moira command the dragons and take on a disguise and watched as the dragons listened to her harsh commands.

Quickly, he ran to warn the Elders and escorted everyone into the cave, securing Deliah in one of the soundproof back rooms that had an ancient and secure metal lock on the door. Artair quickly grabbed some plants on his way into the cave, and crushing them with a stone, carefully placed them in a pouch along with a clear liquid from a vial he had in his possession.

"Faolan, we must cause these dragons to sleep while we deal with Moira. Can you make it back to the beach and pour this concoction into the pool they are drinking from without being seen?" Artair asked quickly. "Let's just hope they haven't taken their fill of water and are still thirsty."

Faolan took the pouch from Artair and hurriedly tied it to his belt and headed down another trail toward the beach. He hoped to figure out a way to distract the dragons, so they wouldn't see him and he could pour the liquid into the pool before they spotted or smelled his presence.

After racing quickly for a minute, he saw a clearing down to the ocean where one of the royal mermaids, Eva, was swimming with three dolphins. It would take a little extra time to get to that side of the rock cliff where they were swimming, but he decided to go anyway, as he would need their help to distract the dragons. Suddenly, a white raven appeared flying over the trail and Faolan wasted no time calling for it to come to him. He quickly let the white raven know that he needed to get Eva and dolphins to cause a distraction to draw the dragons' attention. The raven flew swiftly to where they swam and delivered the message. Faolan saw Eva look in his direction and motion that she was heading to the other side of the rocks and would try to distract the dragons. He let her know through sign language that she was to wait until he signaled her from the next clearing before she was to distract them. He saw her and the three dolphins quickly head toward the rock, knowing they would hide behind it until he signaled.

The three dragons, the same three that Niamh and Gabriel had watched from the Tower of Solomon on her birthday, sat sunning themselves on the eastern shore, occasionally walking to a clear crystalline pool to drink. Gabriel ran at lightning speed, as quietly as he could, down the steep trail until he got to the clearing where Eva could see him but the dragons could not. He had to move very quickly before the dragons got a whiff of his scent.

Just as Eva came out from the rock to distract the dragons with her beauty, a loud, dark, and eerie shriek came from somewhere higher on the trail. It was Moira, calling the dragons to her assistance. All three dragons quickly sprang into action and headed straight into the sky, flying to the top of the mountain where Solomon's Tower was. Faolan watched as they circled in the air above the tower, and saw the green dragon slowly fly downward to where Moira gave him instructions. Faolan couldn't hear what she was saying, so he raced up the hillside and moved in quietly behind the tower to listen to her more easily.

He watched as the green dragon lowered his head and Moira's voice became almost a whisper. Faolan was gazing so intently on Moira and the green dragon, trying to hear what she was whispering, that he wasn't aware of what was right behind him. Before he had time to realize his precarious circumstances, the black dragon with eyes like a cesspool grabbed him with his wickedly long talons and quickly flew into the sky. Moira immediately took on the appearance of Faolan and fled toward the cave, pretending to be him.

Disguised as Faolan, she ran to the cave and told the Elders of Iona to release Deliah so they could all move to another location. Artair quickly unlocked the door and told Deliah to come out fast as they had to leave. As the Elders were gathering up their things to go, Moira, in her Faolan disguise, grabbed Deliah and ran toward the tower, where the green dragon was waiting to lift them off into the sky to find the O'Briens. The Elders quickly realized her trickery and ran after them, but it was too late.

In the meantime, Eva, whose plan was to distract the dragons, saw the whole scenario unfold and swam with the dolphins as quickly as she could to the Sea King's kingdom to tell him of Moira's evil actions. One of the Sea King's attendants met her just as she was swimming into the underwater moat next to the castle's entrance. "I must speak to the Sea King. It is an urgent matter," she told the attendant.

"Yes, come through, and I will get him for you," the attendant told her.

The Sea King came running alongside the attendant to the underwater doorway leading from the moat into his kingdom. He had sensed in his heart that something had gone awry at the Tower.

"Please, Eva, what has happened?" the Sea King asked the mermaid.

"Your Honor, Faolan wanted me to distract the dragons, but before I could, the black dragon with the cesspool eyes carried Faolan away. I know not where. Moira has captured Deliah and is flying on the green dragon toward our kingdom," she told him quickly.

"Come through now, and we will close the portal," the Sea King told her. It was unfortunate that they had to close the portal since no messages could go in or out of the kingdom while the portal was closed. Not knowing the fate of Faolan was bothering the Sea King very much, yet he had to do all he could to protect his kingdom.

"Please, Your Honor, may I stay outside of the Kingdom and see if I can find Faolan?" she asked.

"It is far too dangerous for you, Eva," he told her sincerely.

"It is a risk I am willing to take, for Faolan," she replied. "I will have the whales, selkies, and other creatures of the sea to help me, if necessary. Please, allow me to stay on the outside and be of service," she pleaded.

The Sea King's heart went out to her, and knowing that she was from the royal lineage of mermaids, considered that she had special powers beyond the power of many who were not of her sacred lineage.

"Yes, but first you must know something. I've sent Gabriel and Fintan to Paroisse Saint-Pierre, along with my guests. Dillis and Basil felt a *need* to accompany them, and I have given my permission. They should arrive shortly. I've closed the portal behind them. When you find Faolan, please try to bring him there, to be safe with the others. You know where the secret passageway is. Go through the passage to get through to the back of the church without being seen."

"I WILL find him, Your Honor, and I WILL bring him there."

The Sea King hugged her warmly and sent her on her way with his blessings. Eva immediately went through the gateway, out through the moat, and headed straight toward the coral reef where she knew several of her closest friends would be.

Chapter Eighteen
Paroisse Saint-Pierre

The *Scuabtuinne*, led by *Enbarr of the Flowing Mane*, traveled quickly through the underwater passageways, leading from the Sea King's kingdom to Cheticamp, on the western shore of Cape Breton Island, home of Paroisse Saint-Pierre. Father Pierre Fiset, a parish priest in Cheticamp since 1875, had raised the money to have the beautiful stone church built, overlooking the Cheticamp Harbor so that he could serve the community of French Acadian Catholics on the island. The first Acadians settled in the sheltered valley at the foot of the coastal highlands; however, after the northern end of Cheticamp Harbor was opened up, in 1874, the potential for developing the fishery there became apparent and community activities slowly relocated closer to the harbor.

The people were reluctant to abandon their substantial stone church at Le Buttereau, constructed in 1868, and remained in the valley until the energetic efforts of Father Fiset persuaded them to build a new church along the harbor. He established an annual levy to raise money for the church, but even after the levy ended, parishioners still contributed wood, mortar, labor, and even their fishing catches. Sandstone building materials were ferried across the ice from the northern end of the island to the building site. The older stone church in Le Buttereau was demolished, and its stone transferred to the new site, along with the rose window, the stone medallion engraved with St. Peter's keys, some of the stone steps, the altar (now located in the sacristy), and the bell from the old outside belfry, named 'Marie,' were also used in the new church

The rose window on the front of the church contained a potent symbol of protection similar to the image used by the Sea King's family. The church provided underground passageways leading out to the harbor, from which the *Scuabtuinne* would be able to make its entrance into the caverns beneath the church.

As the *Scuabtuinne* carefully approached the entrance, Gabriel recited magical words in Gaelic that halted the water in the harbor from entering the caverns but allowed *Enbarr,* leading the *Scuabtuinne,* to enter. Once inside, the ship was harbored carefully, close to an indoor dock, and Gabriel helped each of the passengers off safely. After each of the guests disembarked onto the wooden pier, Gabriel lit a torch and led them through a stone tunnel to a wooden stairway leading to a comfortably furnished room directly under the parish. Inside the room, Gabriel excused himself and went quietly to find the priest, careful not to let anyone else see him.

Gabriel found Father Fiset sitting quietly in a small stone room, used as a library, in the back of the church, reading. Father Fiset was an Acadian man of great faith, with a willing heart to help all in need. He believed in God, and at the same time he did not find it hard to believe in the Sea King, mermaids, flying horses, or talking cats. He looked up from his book and found himself to be very pleasantly surprised to see Gabriel in his doorway, yet he inherently knew that Gabriel was there on essential matters.

Gabriel explained the situation to Father Fiset as quickly as possible, letting him know how important it was to keep the guests safe and protected. Father Fiset felt exceedingly honored that the Sea King had entrusted the lives of his guests to him and vowed in his heart, and to Gabriel, to protect them at all costs.

"Now, shall I come with you and be introduced to them?" he asked Gabriel while placing his book carefully back on the shelf. "Let's get some food and drinks for them before we head down to meet them."

After gathering up some food and drinks from the church kitchen, Gabriel and Father Fiset left the kitchen through a side door which led down a steep stairway and into a stone passageway that led to the room where the guests waited. They carefully set the food on a table upon entering the room, and then Gabriel introduced them to the priest, who welcomed them all warmly and offered his hospitality. Each, in turn, showed their gratitude for the priest's generosity, thankful that they would remain safe until the recent matters were sorted out. When Father Fiset realized that Analine's family was of Gypsy heritage, he took great interest in conversing with them. He knew the Gypsies to be helpful, kind, and generous to a fault and had heard many stories of their unfailing devotion to those who had helped them in the past.

While they all enjoyed the fascinating tales, the conversation took a necessary turn to the matters at hand and the possibilities of an impending dragon attack. Although everyone was safe within the church, the villagers would undoubtedly be upset and endangered by the arrival of the dragons.

It was a long and tedious day, and everyone was beginning to tire from their travels, so each, in turn, started to retire to cots that had been placed against the walls bordering the large room where they stayed. Only one significant curtained window gave them a view to the harbor, but Gabriel, along with Father Fiset stressed the importance of keeping the curtain drawn until nightfall and then open them only if all lights were extinguished, as they couldn't take the risk of anyone knowing they were there.

Finally, sometime after midnight, each of the guests was sleeping comfortably; all but Gabriel, who walked carefully, silently to the window and gently pulled one corner of the curtain, free to glance out at the lights on the harbor. As he peered out into the beautiful, star-enchanted night, his thoughts quickly turned to Niamh, how beautiful she was, and how his feelings for her were developing rapidly. *Will she ever love me, again? Does she remember?* he wondered. Her regaining some memories intensified his questions.

Lost deep in thought, he was startled when he suddenly realized the presence of thick, low-hanging fog quickly rolling in over the harbor. Mentally drawing himself away from his thoughts and into the present, Gabriel looked carefully into the mist, squinting his eyes and focusing his perception, and then scanning the immediate view for any signs of activity. A still, quiet hush encompassed the room. He could no longer hear the soft sleeping sighs of his friends or the foghorn that had been regularly keeping time since they arrived. He could only distinguish the absence of sound, which caused him to become more aware. It felt like he was in the center, the eye, of a hurricane.

Being a seasoned warrior, Gabriel knew and understood that total silence was a presage to intense energy shifts, changes of a substantial nature. He was trained to be aware at all times, not only of his surroundings but his heartbeat, which is a sign in itself. He knew the call of every bird and how the tone of their calls would lower when danger was present. He knew to listen for the rustling of leaves, the change in the sounds of wave patterns, and the change in air pressure. He knew that total silence usually preceded sudden changes, and he purposefully heightened his awareness to detect its message. His teachers had trained him to know that when outward calm occurred, to use it as a sign, and silence himself inwardly for his senses to click into a heightened awareness without his heartbeat becoming elevated. He knew that there were different levels of consciousness and how to change his levels according to 'signs.' His most important lesson: stilling his body/mind/spirit and staying focused. There were other times available for daydreaming. His hopes and dreams that Niamh would regain her full memory would have to wait for another time. The silence warned him that his entire being should be at one with the stillness and be ready for action at any point.

In her sleep, Ocean also noticed a change in air pressure and quietly woke up out of her dream. She had been dreaming of the Sea King; he was giving her a warning, telling her to consider the 'signs' and 'pay close attention.' In her dream, the Sea King looked troubled as he spoke and kept looking out the window of his library. In her dream, she asked him why he was so worried and he replied, "We need to find Faolan, quickly. His life is in danger!" Ocean wanted to run from her bed and tell Gabriel of her dream but knew this was not the right time. Instead, she quietly left the room and went to look for the priest. Gabriel saw her move out of the corner of his eye and wondered why she would leave the place they were all supposed to stay in. His eyes scanned the cots where his friends were sleeping and checked to make sure that they were all comfortable. He took the blanket from his bed, carefully laid it across Niamh, and went back to his watch at the window.

As Ocean approached Father Fiset's door, she hesitated, as she heard a scratching sound on an outside door and the small cries of a kitten outside. *Oh, poor little thing. It must be Father Fiset's kitten, trying to get inside.* Ocean hesitated for a moment, trying to decide whether to open the door to the outside, as all the guests had been told to stay in the room and not venture outside. In that moment of hesitation, she chose not to heed the warning and thought it wise to let the kitten inside quickly before disturbing Father Fiset with her dream. She believed that the priest would be happy that she found his kitten and let it in, rather than leaving it outside in the night with the dense gray fog rolling in.

Analine awoke, startled from a dream, and hurriedly sprang out of bed. *Ocean. Ocean Marie!* he shouted in his mind as he ran toward the door, with Gabriel, Donal, and Roger not far behind, each running through the hall and up the stairs to Father Fiset's quarters, arriving just in time to see Ocean Marie being pulled out of the door and into the thick fog.

"OCEAN!" cried Donal as he ran out the door and into the night fog, blindly following his instinct.

"NO! DONAL! COME BACK!" yelled Gabriel just when Father Fiset came out of his room, awakened by the loud cries.

"Father, Ocean was tricked into going out into the night, Donal followed her and both are out there now!" explained Analine worriedly.

"I'm going after them, Analine, stay with the others. I'll find them. Father Fiset, lock everything tightly after I go out and don't open to anyone until I get back. I'm sure this is more of Moira's dark magic, and they may try to get in, disguised as one of us. Do you have a key to this door?" Gabriel asked the priest.

"Yes, I'll go and get it for you," he said while running through the open door to his quarters. "Here," he said as he handed Gabriel the key, which was attached to a golden coin. When Gabriel touched the key and the coin, attached by a small chain, he felt a quick surge of energy go through his entire body. He disregarded this to get to the task at hand: finding Ocean and Donal.

"Lock up, quickly, now," Gabriel said as he closed the wooden plank door behind him and ventured out into the fog. Although the matter at hand was pressing, he stood quietly for a moment, gathering up his energy and using all of his training and senses to 'feel' the energies around him. Gabriel couldn't 'feel' where Ocean was yet, but he had sharp images of Donal on a dock. He knew the dock was not far from the church and headed off quickly in that direction.

Donal had made his way to the dock by heading toward the faint amber glow of the harbor light that was at the end of the pier, thinking that Ocean's love of the sea would create a connection between them if he were by the sea. He made his way to the wooden dock, past several openings where ships were moored until daybreak, when the fishermen would head out to the rolling sea to collect their catch for the day. On his way to the end of the dock, he stumbled over something and almost fell into the water. After gathering himself up, he realized it was a man, quite inebriated, sitting with his back propped up against one of the tall wooden poles used for securing the boats' ropes, an empty bottle of Scottish whiskey lying next to him.

Donal knelt down and asked the man if he was alright and if he had been hurt from Donal stumbling on him, and almost gagged from the rancid smell of alcohol and tobacco emanating from the man. *What a fine sight! I probably used to look and smell like this when I was drinking. Never again! I hope I remember this sight if I'm ever tempted to live that lifestyle again. This smell would deter the devil himself!* Donal noticed that the man was beggarly, dressed in ragged clothing—the fingers were worn off his gloves. But in the fog, Donal couldn't see his fingertips and wondered if he had lost his fingers in some drunken accident.

Groggily, the man looked up straight into Donal's eyes, and staring at him earnestly, said, "I'm what you would have become."

"What? I need to find someone. Have you seen a young woman with long, dark hair, wearing a blue shawl?"

"She's with the old lady and the dragons," the old man muttered, barely audible.

"Where did they go?" Donal asked while moving in closer to hear him. He listened to the old man whispering but couldn't make out what he was saying. Just as Donal moved as close as he could stand without gagging again from the smell, talons issued forth from his half-gloves. Gray, gnarly, scaled finger-like talons with sharp, yellow-stained claws, reaching right for Donal's throat and eyes. Right as the talons were about to reach Donal's throat, something fish-like bolted out of the water and knocked Donal down into the depths of the sea. Donal quickly held his breath while the fish-like being held him tightly, swimming rapidly underwater toward an underwater tunnel. Just when Donal felt that he could no longer hold his breath or his lungs would explode, they reached the shaft and Donal felt himself being lifted up toward the air in the tunnel. He took in a gasping breath while the mermaid prompted him forward.

"You are from the Sea King's banquet," he said, recognizing her from the mermaid's table.

"Yes, I am Eva. I live in the Sea King's kingdom and he allowed me to leave the nation for a time, as it is crucial that I find Faolan quickly. I think that Faolan and Ocean are being held at Bald Mountain, by Lake Ainslie. There is a dragon's lair on the backside of the mountain. If we continue through this tunnel, we will end up at the east end of the lake. After that, you will have to go on your own. There is an overgrown pathway leading to the property at the old Campbell farm. You will follow that path to the road. Directly across the street is Bald Mountain. The dragon's lair is on the backside of the mountain, but it is heavily guarded by werewolves. Are you familiar with them? These are not the friendly sort, and it is best to avoid them at all costs, but if you do encounter them, you will have to outsmart them somehow. They gain their strength from barite, a mineral found in the mountain. If you can lure them away from the mineral deposits, you stand a chance of rescuing Faolan and Ocean Marie from the dragons."

"I understand. I will be fine. Where will you be when we come out?" he asked.

"I will go and get some help for bringing them back and will return by the time you retrieve them. I'll wait for you at the edge of the trail that I will show you," Eva told him.

Chapter Nineteen
Lake Ainslie

The underwater passageway began at Cheticamp and continued westerly under the island, into Lake Ainslie. Once Donal came out of the underwater passageway, he swam for a short distance with Eva until they reached the old Campbell farm. Donal bid her adieu and promised he would bring Faolan and Ocean Marie back. He had never encountered werewolves, was not familiar with the properties of barite, had never visited this island, and knew nothing of how to rescue people from dragons, but he did know that he could not fail at this mission. He had to bring all the courage he could muster to this task, along with any strength and endurance he held within himself. He had one gift that he was recently made aware of: he was of his mother's lineage and held her powers deep within his soul.

Donal, now soaking wet, quickly climbed onto the shore and found the path that led through the old Campbell farm. He ran as quickly as he could, moving overgrown plants and vines out of his way. He soon reached the road and saw the mountain straight in front of him. A child riding a blue bicycle pulled up next to him when he got across the road and asked why he was wet.

"I was fishing and fell out of my boat," Donal lied, knowing that the child would be safer in the long run if he didn't know about the tunnel. *Children are curious, and it wouldn't be good for this child to be out in the water searching for a tunnel. Besides, the tunnel should probably be kept secret.*

The child just shook his head and rode on, while Donal quickly continued toward the back of Bald Mountain. Finding an old mining path, he proceeded cautiously, while keeping his senses alert to the presence of werewolves, dragons, and danger. He traveled up the mountain for about fifty feet until he came to a small clearing which overlooked fields and woods. Stopping to get his breath, he saw a significant murder of crows circling silently, directly over him. *Hopefully, the smell of the lake will mask my scent from the werewolves,* he thought to himself, then suddenly he remembered the first conversation he'd had with Ocean Marie when she came to his house to bring him the medicine pouch when he was ill:

'Donal, listen to me. You need to be the man your mother would have wanted you to be. You made a mistake... We all make mistakes. It's what we

do after we realize that we made a mistake that counts. What will you do now?
What do you want?'

'*I just want to get well and do the right thing. That's what Mother would*
want from me.'

Donal reflected on this memory, and Ocean's amazingly loving and comforting words, and it gave him new energy to hurriedly find her and bring her to back to the church, safe and unharmed, where she could be with her family. *She came to me when I needed a friend and encouraged me at a time when I had no courage. She helped me to heal, and now I must find her and return the kindness she has shown me. Who knows where I would be today if not for her compassion and care?*

He took a deep breath and continued up the pathway, still viewing the circling crows at each clearing, wondering why they were so quiet. Crows typically caw and make noise, especially if there are a lot of them, yet these were completely silent, so much so, that he wouldn't have known they were there unless he saw them. The path became steeper and rockier the closer he got to the cave, and he was beginning to smell an unusual scent, musky and acrid. He stopped quickly and turned his focus and attention to the location of the smell. It was coming from the direction of a stand of elm trees, but he couldn't see clearly through them to see what was causing the smell. Suddenly, it dawned on him that the acrid stench was coming from at least one werewolf.

Now that Donal knew the location of at least one werewolf, he decided to stay very still, in hopes that the smells from the lake would mask his scent. He crouched down next to a tall sycamore tree and slowed his heart rate as he focused on sharpening his awareness. *I wish they would move out of here and go to the other side of the mountain. I need to get to that dragons' cave, quickly, and find Ocean and Faolan.* As soon as he thought this, they began making noises, short grunts, which gave the impression that they were communicating with one another. He realized there was more than one and quietly slipped behind a large fir tree, careful not to make a sound, just in the nick of time, as they began moving toward his location. He was right: there were three large adults. As they stumbled past his position, they paused for a moment, sniffing the air before going on.

Donal watched silently from behind the tree, noticing how dirty and matted their dark fur was, how long, sharp, and yellow their teeth were, and how recklessly they lumbered along, not mindful at all of stomping on flowers or plants. They were not at all like wolves, except in name. They had somewhat human-like hands at the end of their overly long, shaggy arms, which ended in lengthy knobby fingers with grayish-yellow, razor-sharp fingernails. They snorted, grunted, and gruffed to each other as they stomped through, unmindful of Donal's discreet presence. After they were out of view, Donal breathed a massive sigh of relief, thankful that he didn't have to deal with them, at least for now.

As soon as they passed by, he walked a little further along the steep trail, being careful to avoid the sharp outcrops of dark gray stones, until he reached the next clearing, which gave him access to a view of the path beneath him. Suddenly, something below him caught his eye. He had to climb up onto one of the jagged rocks to get a better view but still be careful not to reveal his location, in case he was being watched. It was a petite woman, perhaps in her early twenties, sitting on a rock by the trail he had just climbed from. She appeared to be in some pain, as she was looking around carefully, rubbing her arm, apparently trying to look for help. Donal couldn't call out to her, nor could he make his presence known, since the werewolves were not far away. He would have to go quietly back down the trail to get to her and hope that something else didn't get to her before he did. His mind felt torn between rescuing this woman and carrying on quickly to retrieve Faolan and Ocean Marie.

Within a split second, he had made his decision. He would quickly go down through the woods and come out on the trail, close to where the young woman sat. It wouldn't be right to leave her by herself, knowing that the werewolves were so closely lurking. The plan he devised in his mind was to go and check on her, direct her back down the path, and then go as quickly as possible back to help the other two. However, that isn't how things worked out.

As soon as he approached her and motioned for her to be very quiet, he heard a loud shriek coming from a place which was lower on the trail. It was a god-awful sound that shook the very core of his being; a sound he never could imagine hearing. It was another werewolf, following them up the trail. He had gotten a whiff of the woman's scent and let out the shriek to let the other werewolves know that he was on the hunt and had spotted his prey.

The blood-curdling shriek set every other creature and bird on Bald Mountain to attention. Donal surveyed the condition of the young woman's arm and quickly grabbed her by her other hand and started running as fast as humanly possible. The young woman, although injured, was able to keep up, and they ran as far as they could in the opposite direction from the sound until they reached a small cave nestled in the side of the mountain, facing Lake Ainslie. Donal hurriedly led the young woman into the cave, motioned again for her to be very quiet, and ran back outside to cover the cave entrance with pine boughs to mask their scents. As soon as he did this, he grabbed several of the most jagged rocks he could find and slipped back into the cave, carefully placing more pine boughs to enclose them in more securely.

It was pitch-black inside the cave and he whispered to her, "Are you alright, Miss?"

"I am. What was that noise?" she asked. Donal noticed that she had an American accent mixed with a little Irish.

"You may not believe this, but they are werewolves. I saw them up on the trail, right before I spotted you. What are you doing here, by the way, alone?" Donal questioned.

"I'm recently married. My husband, John, and I recently moved here from Ireland. I live right below here, in the old Campbell farmhouse. I've been hearing the loveliest sound of a nightingale in the evenings, coming from this area, and wanted to come up here and look at the mountain, but then I fell and hit my shoulder on one of the jagged rocks," she told him. "I'm Trini," she said, reaching her hand out to shake his in the blackness. "I think I should thank you for saving me from those creatures."

"I'm Donal O'Brien, from Ireland," he explained. "I think we should try to get a fire going in here and see how far this cave goes into the mountain. Do you have any matches with you?" he asked hopefully, realizing the matches he always carried in his pocket were soaking wet.

"Yes, I do," she told him while reaching into her pocket to retrieve them. "Here you go," she said as she handed him the matches. Donal quickly lit a fire and made a torch out of a stick and some twigs that he had gathered up before coming back into the cave. Then, he led Trini carefully deeper into the cave's recesses. The cave was dank with moisture and became chillier with each step. Donal watched over Trini carefully, grabbing her uninjured arm to help her stay balanced as she worked her way through the cave.

"This cave goes in quite a long way, doesn't it?" she asked.

"Yes, we have been walking for about ten minutes so far, and it still seems to me like we can go even further," he told her.

Shortly after their brief conversation, Trini noticed a tiny ray of light, coming from an area to the left of them, and pointed it out to Donal. They followed in the direction of the light for several more minutes, following along, but it never seemed to get any closer.

"Do you know if werewolves can see in the dark?" she asked.

"I'm sorry, Trini. I know little of werewolves. I know they smell horrible; have large, pointed ears that stick up; dirty, yellowish, fangs; long, dark, matted hair; and razor-sharp claws. I hid from three of the large ones before I spotted you. They went right past where I was hiding, and this was immediately before

I saw you," he said. "Whether or not they can see in the dark, well, I'd guess that they can."

"John should be coming home soon. I left him a note telling him that I was going to walk on the mountain. I hope he doesn't run into the werewolves when he comes to find me," Trini said worriedly. "By the way, what are you doing on this mountain, if you don't mind me asking?"

Donal struggled in his mind with this question, not knowing what, if anything, he should say to her. He realized that he had better just tell the whole truth since she was bound to find out soon enough anyway unless John found them first and brought her home. She didn't seem emotional about the werewolves and handled that very well, so perhaps her mind would accept the fact that one or more dragons were holding his friends hostage. Of course, he thought better than to reveal that he was formerly at the Sea King's underground castle and went through an underwater, underground tunnel from Cheticamp to Lake Ainslie, led by a mermaid named Eva. That might be left alone for now.

After explaining the part about his friends to her, he was amazed at her reaction;

"I knew it. I knew it. I knew it. I told John that I had three dreams about this very situation. Except in my dreams, it happened a long, long time ago, clearly back in the late 1800s," she said. "And there was a Sea King and a whole family of the lineage of the Tuatha de Danann who had magical powers, and..."

"Listen!" Donal told her very quietly. "I don't know what is going on here, but what year do you think we are in now? Because when I left home, it was 1889."

"It is 2019, of course!" she told him earnestly.

"But how can that be?" he asked worriedly.

"There has to be some explanation," she said gravely, unworriedly.

Before they could explore their quandary any further, the light they had been walking toward became bigger and a little brighter, so they started walking faster toward what might turn out to be another mouth to this cave. They began to see small glimpses of green, which told them they were close to the outside, but considering how far they had walked, it was hard to say which side of the mountain they would end up on.

As soon as they were at the cave's exit and Trini looked outside, she realized that her dreams had given her directions to finding Faolan and Ocean. After all of her spiritual training, she knew not to question and just 'feel' her way through any situation and all would be revealed. "I think I know how to find them," she said.

"You *do?*" Donal asked, amazed that she could have any part in this.

"Yes, just follow my lead," she told him as she began making soft whistling sounds, trying not to draw attention to herself as she walked carefully along the path that was outside the cave exit. Donal noticed that they were now on the back side of the mountain, as he could not see Lake Ainslie any longer.

"What are we doing?" he asked.

"I'm calling on Elk for protection and guidance. When I was in college and went on a long retreat, an elk followed me around the whole time I was staying in the woods. I never saw him, but he saw me. John pointed him out and called him 'your elk,' because he knew the elk was there watching over me. That happened before I ever realized that 'John' was the same 'John' I met in Ireland after my mom passed away. We were on the same flight and spent a few days touring Dublin and the surrounding areas before we each had to go our separate ways. Several years passed, and we hadn't stayed in touch, and then one day, when I was out spending time in the woods, I became ill and John came along and gave me tea which healed me. Of course, I didn't realize it was the same John that I met on the plane at first, because the John who gave me healing tea had on sunglasses—and because several years had passed in-between. We were both older and his appearance had changed quite a lot. Right after that, I went to one of his lectures, and all of a sudden, as soon as I looked into his eyes, I realized it was the same person I knew from all those years ago. To make a long story short, we dated until I finished college and then we got married. We both realized that we had to come to Cape Breton Island to live, so we came here and bought the old Campbell farm, just recently."

Donal listened intently as she told her story, and in the meantime, Trini's elk appeared from behind a stand of poplars. "He will show us what to do," she promised.

Chapter Twenty
Gabriel

Gabriel wandered silently near the dark water across the road from the church, in the thick gray fog, listening intently for any changes that might give him a clue as to where his friends were. He knew instinctively and believed wholeheartedly that all answers are found in the silence, through patience, and he reminded himself of these truths as he walked. Just as he was about to turn around and head back toward the church, he heard a splash in the water near the pier and headed in that direction, listening ever more attentively. He was right to follow his instincts because swimming up next to the pier was Eva. She explained how she saved Donal from the grasping claws of a demon, which was disguised as an old man on the dock, and then led him through the underwater passageway to Lake Ainslie.

"Do you know where Ocean Marie is?" Gabriel asked.

"She and Faolan are being held captive by Moira and her dragons in the dragons den on Bald Mountain. It is across the road from the old Campbell farm on the edge of Lake Ainslie. Werewolves guard it, and Donal is by himself," she hurriedly explained.

"Can you guide me there?" he asked.

"Yes, of course, but we must hurry and leave now," she told him.

Eva led Gabriel through the underwater tunnel and showed him the Campbell farm after they entered Lake Ainslie. Gabriel thanked her and told her that she should go back to the Sea King and report this news.

"I will go now. Be careful, Gabriel," she said sadly as she swam back into the underwater tunnel.

Gabriel climbed onto the beach, and spotting the mountain, began making his way through the trail in the back of the Campbell farm. He was almost to the road when he saw a young man coming out of the farmhouse, looking toward the mountain.

"Hello. I hope you don't mind if I cut through your property," Gabriel said quickly but politely.

"Where are you headed?" the young man asked.

"Just across the street, over to that mountain. Some of my friends might be lost up there and I need to get to them quickly," he offered.

"My wife, Trini, is over there also," he said while still holding the note she wrote earlier. "I'm just heading over there myself. Mind if I join you? I'm John," he said while reaching out his hand to greet Gabriel. John was outwardly composed, although inwardly he sensed that the situation was about to become intense.

"I think we had better hurry," Gabriel told him.

"Just give me one second," John told him as he rushed back into the entryway of the farmhouse and came out holding a dry shirt, which he offered to Gabriel.

John and Gabriel headed across the road, all the while listening and watching for any movement or change on the mountain. The fog was starting to roll in from the lake, and visibility was rapidly decreasing.

"John, we will have to be extremely cautious. There are werewolves guarding the den where I believe two of my friends, Ocean Marie and Faolan, are being held captive. Another friend, Donal, is up here somewhere looking for them. We now have four people, including your wife, Trini, to rescue," Gabriel explained.

"When I moved here, I found an old miner's map upstairs in my attic. I remember that there is a trail on the front side of this mountain that leads straight up to one of the entryways, into the back of one of the mining tunnels. I feel like we might save some time if we head straight toward that trail," he said, pointing to where he believed it to be.

The two men hurriedly hiked up the front face of the mountain, quietly and carefully pulling back overgrown weeds and stepping over anything that might alert the werewolves to their location. Both John and Gabriel were robust and healthy, so climbing the mountain quickly was not a problem for them, but climbing while keeping their senses alert for danger caused them to slow down periodically, to look around and listen.

"From what I remember on that map I found in the attic, that entryway should be right up ahead," John said, motioning a little to the right and higher than where they were.

Gabriel surveyed the area and noticed some freshly cut pine boughs leaning up against the mountainside, and realized that someone must have put them there recently, probably to mask their scent from the werewolves or dragons. He silently motioned for John to follow him as he went quickly to the area where the pine boughs were and started pulling them back from the cave entryway. John helped him, and they both went in, carefully replacing the branches behind them. After lighting a match, they ignited one of the boughs, and holding it up for light, saw the direction of the passageway. As they moved quickly through the dark, John knew that his wife had been through there recently and told Gabriel.

"She must have come in here to hide," Gabriel said. "Perhaps Donal found her, and he is with her."

Gabriel held their makeshift torch low to the ground to check for footprints. "Yes, they are together and went this way," he said while pointing to the right. "I see a faint light up ahead. They must have gone out through there. Let's go, quickly!"

Just as the two men arrived at the opening of the underground passageway and were getting ready to go out into the day, they smelled the stench of werewolves and heard their gruff sounds. They slowly went back inside and extinguished their makeshift torch. Gabriel, from where he stood, caught a quick glimpse of Donal and Trini, quietly sneaking to a large nearby rock to take cover. Gabriel, in an attempt to distract the werewolves, threw a rock in the opposite direction, which focused the werewolves' attention away from Donal and Trini, giving them the opportunity they needed to run again toward the cave where John and Gabriel waited. John quickly ran out of the cave and gathered more pine boughs, while Gabriel stood guard, helping the two back into the passageway.

"You are hurt," John said to Trini when he saw her.

"I'll be alright. I fell off a rock and hurt my shoulder, but it's nothing serious. We will be able to get out of here soon. I know where the dragon cave is, where Ocean and Faolan are being held. The elk showed me in a vision," she told her husband.

Quick introductions were made, and then they stood quietly, waiting for a sign from the elk that the werewolves were not nearby. While they waited, a heavy blanket of thick, grayish-blue fog traveled from the lake to their location and the elk appeared from behind large blue spruce, standing proud and regal, his now-solid bone antlers reaching high into the blue-green boughs of the tree.

Trini saw the elk and became very still while connecting with his spirit and building her inner strength to go where he would lead. She relayed the message she received to the others and motioned for them to quietly follow her as she headed in the direction of the elk, which stood quietly, only moving slightly to turn his ears to listen. He led them up a straight path to the mountain's summit where they would have a good vantage point and more visibility, then he stood entirely still again, listening. Trini watched him intently and saw that the elk wanted their party to split up before heading toward the dragon cave.

"The cave is directly under us now. We need to divide into two groups. Donal and Gabriel can go to the left, and John and I will go to the right. The

167

elk will stay here and stand guard to alert us to any changes. If the elk makes a low droning whistle, take cover immediately. He has let me know that your friends are in the cave, but the cave is guarded by one of the larger werewolves right now. The dragons, along with Moira, left several hours ago and headed east, toward the Atlantic Ocean. There is no telling when they will be back. John and I will distract the werewolf, hopefully, and draw him out toward us, while you and Donal go into the cave and rescue Ocean and Faolan," she instructed Gabriel. "After they are rescued, we will meet up at my house."

Gabriel and Donal knew that it was going to be hard for Trini to run very fast with her shoulder being injured, but she assured them that she and her husband would stay far enough away from the werewolf to ensure their safety. "I will be fine. I am protected. I know I will be fine because I have seen it!" she smiled assuredly.

Chapter Twenty-One
Eva the Mermaid

After Gabriel suggested that Eva go back to the Sea Kingdom and inform the Sea King of their whereabouts, she set off through the underwater tunnel, heading for the Cheticamp dock. When she came out of the underwater tunnel, she noticed that the fog had become darker and thicker and wondered how the others who were staying at the church were doing. She swam up close to the dock to see if anyone might be outside the church so that she could check on them before heading back to the Sea Kingdom. The drunken old man who had tried to attack Donal's throat with his long, disgusting talons was still sitting on the dock, surrounded by cigarette butts and empty Scotch whiskey bottles. Eva, being of a very fearless nature, approached the dock on the side where he was slumped over against the dock rail.

"Have you seen anyone here?" she asked him.

"Seen some people, but they ain't worth mentioning," he muttered. "Enjoy your last day," he said spitefully.

"Are you threatening me? Because if you are, I will have you know that I am not the least bit afraid of you!" she said sternly.

"Oh, it ain't me you have to be worried about. Enjoy your last day!" he said again.

"What are you talking about? You are obviously drunk and trying to scare me," she said.

"I ain't that drunk and I ain't trying to scare nobody. You are gonna die today, and I'm just telling you to enjoy your last day."

"And why are you telling me this? Do you think I would listen to the ravings of an old, drunken fool like yourself? Just tell me who you saw and where they went, and tell me right now!"

"I saw Moira and her dragons flying across the sky. They are going to kill you. You watch," he said mockingly.

"I'm tired of your ramblings. Did you see anyone else?"

"Doesn't matter now, does it? Cause you are gonna die."

At that, Eva had heard enough and dove down into the water to get away from him. She felt chilled from listening to his drunken warnings and needed to get away from him. *I wonder why he kept telling me to enjoy my last day, and that I was going to die? I need to get those words out of my head. I'm not going to die, and neither is anyone else. I just need to get back to the Sea Kingdom and tell the King what is going on with the others.*

As Eva swam out into the ocean, heading for the Sea King's kingdom, she let go of all the negative words the old drunken man had told her and decided to focus on the positive. Every once in a while, she would swim up close to the surface to check the weather, noticing that the clouds were beginning to darken and the waves were becoming stronger. A robust Gaelic wind from the northwest was starting to push the dark clouds quickly through the foggy sky.

Soon, Eva saw a small island that she was familiar with, where she had friends, and swam up to the shore to rest for a moment and collect her thoughts. She hadn't slept in a very long time, and with the recent tension of Moira and her dragons, she was beginning to be fatigued. Some seals were huddled together on the shore, trying to protect themselves from the winds, which were growing in strength. When the seals noticed her, they looked up to greet her and invite her to their circles to warm up and rest. Eva explained that she could only stay a few minutes and was on her way to the Sea King's castle to let him know where Gabriel and the others were.

One of the elder seals, Alby, named so because his coat remained white long after infancy noticed that Eva's brow was furrowed and knew there was something troubling her, beyond what she had told them. She explained to him that there was an evil drunken man on the dock in Cheticamp who was taunting her, telling her she would die today and that she didn't know where Moira and the dragons were. Alby listened with compassion and felt a knot in his stomach when she told him about the man's words. He suggested that she might stay with them until the winds passed, knowing that he and the seals could protect her, but she declined, saying that she wanted to return to her kingdom, to make sure the Sea King knew what was going on. She didn't want him to worry.

"Allow me to go with you then, Eva. I would feel more comfortable if someone was with you. I insist!"

"But with your light coat, you might be easily spotted from the air," she told him.

"It's OK, I'm a fast swimmer, and besides, we both know that it will be easier on a day like this to swim deeper. Going deeper will allow us to get there faster. We will be careful when we come up for air. With all this fog, it will be harder for them to see me anyway."

Alby went over to one of the seal circles and told them that he was going to accompany Eva to the Sea King's castle and not to expect him back tonight, as he would be spending the night there. They nodded their heads in approval and asked if Eva needed more than one seal to accompany her, but Alby declined, not wanting to put any of the others in any impending danger.

Alby and Eva dove into the cold water and started off on their journey. The journey from the island to the Sea King's castle was only a little more than an hour's swim, yet with strong winds disrupting the waters, they realized that it might take a little longer. They swam together, going deeper into the ocean where the swimming was easier, determined to get there as soon as possible because they both knew that the Sea King would be concerned about everyone and anxious to hear any news.

They swam for over half an hour, when suddenly, out of nowhere, a loud, blood-curdling shriek radiated through the sky. Eva's heart began racing, and against her better judgment, she came up quickly out of the water, followed by Alby, to see where the sound was coming from. At the very moment her head came up, she felt sharp, razor-like talons clasp her shoulders and pull her out of the water. As she strained to look up at whatever had grabbed her, she could see the pale-yellow underbelly of the black dragon, with Moira's feet dangling from the top of the dragon's back. The skin on her shoulders was pierced through by his talons, as he gripped deeper into her, and blood began pouring from the wounds. Each time she tried to struggle, his talons pierced her skin a little deeper until she couldn't bear it any longer and let herself be taken away. Alby looked up into the air, helplessly watching the horrible sight.

Eva could hear Moira's shrill voice giving commands to fly over the rocky cliff and felt the dragon speed up and turn toward an island with a very rough, jagged rock surface. *They can't possibly land on those sharp rocks. The dragon will pierce himself through if he falls there. Whatever could Moira be thinking to have her dragon land there? We will all die if he falls. I have to find a way to get him to drop me back into the water before they reach that island.* She tried to yell a coded message to Alby, who was watching helplessly from below, letting him know to take cover, in case they decided to snatch him out of the water as well. He was at risk because of his light coat, which stood out glaringly, even in the thick, dark fog.

Alby had a horrible, gut-wrenching feeling wash over him and knew that what the old drunk had told Eva was true. He knew it, yet he tried to deny it with all his might, hoping that the dragon would drop Eva into the water where he could rescue her. Alby's heart was breaking watching the scene above him, knowing that he couldn't help Eva. He went slightly under the waves to stay out of view but high enough that he could see what the dragon and Moira were doing with his beloved friend.

As hard as she tried, Eva couldn't think of a single thing to do to get the dragon to drop her into the ocean. Time was running out, as soon they would be over the island with the jagged rocks. She tried lifting her feet high into the air in an attempt to kick herself free. With every effort she made to break free, the dragon pierced her even more profoundly. She was beginning to feel very dizzy from losing so much blood and could barely stay conscious. The dragon sped up, then after hearing Moira's next command, shot straight up into the air another twenty feet and dropped Eva, head first, onto the jagged rocks. As soon as Eva fell, a lone seagull let out an eerie cry, then lowered himself to the stones where Eva lay in a pool of blood. He then flew out into the dark, foggy air to give the bad news to Alby.

Chapter Twenty-Two
Alby

Alby took the news very hard. He had known Eva ever since she was a little mermaid, just learning about life, and she always held a special place in his heart. She had a sincere concern for all living beings and still made the time to stop in and say hello whenever she was in the area. He often had lengthy conversations with her and knew her to have a heart of pure gold. Out of all the years he knew Eva, she never had a wrong word to say about anyone and showed genuine interest in all the seals and selkies they knew. His heart broke, and he cried great tears from his big black eyes as he asked the seagull to go to his island and have the selkies bring Eva's body to the closest cave and protect it until he could get instructions from the Sea King.

After giving the seagull instructions, he composed himself as best he could and swam as fast as possible to the Sea King's kingdom, dreading having to tell him about the accident, as he knew the Sea King loved Eva like his own family. When he arrived at his kingdom, he was recognized and allowed in immediately. He was careful not to tell anyone else of the news until he had talked to the King. He tried to think of the best way to convey the sad story and prepared himself to remain composed, but he was shaking and had a heavy heart.

Once he reached the castle, the Sea King's attendants led him into his study, where he was standing, looking out the window.

"Alby, come in, sit. Would you like something to drink?" the Sea King asked. The Sea King was very intuitive and knew, as soon as he looked in Alby's eyes, that something dreadful had happened.

"I have terrible news to tell you, and I am so sorry to be the bearer of this news. Eva is gone. She was abducted by Moira and one of her dragons. I am having some of the selkies bring her body to a cave for safekeeping, for now, until you give me instructions. I am so very sorry, as I know you two were close and she was dear to your heart."

The King sat quietly, unable to speak for several minutes. Alby understood the pain and knew that being quiet together was the only thing that could be done, for now. The Sea King was the first to speak, and said, "Why were you with her? Do you know anything more? Did she say anything to you?"

"Yes, she was on her way back from Cape Breton, Lake Ainslie, and told me that she had escorted Gabriel there to rescue Faolan and Ocean Marie. Ocean and Faolan are being held in a dragon cave there, which is guarded by werewolves. Donal went to rescue them. Afterward, Eva met up with Donal at the dock in Cheticamp and led him through the underwater passage to Lake Ainslie. When she came back, she found Gabriel and led him there in the same way. She told Gabriel she was going to come back here to give you the news, as she knew you would be anxious to hear. She also told me that there was a drunk man on the dock who was taunting her, telling her to enjoy her last day, and told her that she was going to die today."

"He must be one of the demons who work for Moira," said the Sea King sadly.

"Yes, I believe you are right," Ably agreed.

"Do you know where the Elders are staying, near Solomon's Tower? I think we need to get word to them. I will send someone out to give them a message and let them know all that has transpired. I think you should stay here with me, for the time being, and I'll also send word to the other seals and selkies that, once they bring Eva's body to the cave, they should stay close by it until further notice. I'm concerned that Moira will be devising more evil for anyone she comes into contact with."

"Can you tell me anything about the others, the ones I sent to stay with Father Fiset?" the Sea King asked. "Against my better judgment, I allowed Basil and Dillis to go in the *Scuabtuinne* and accompany the others. I'm very concerned about everyone, but particularly those two, as Dillis is merely a small child, although she has remarkable abilities and Basil is always more than interested in being involved in everything and may be getting himself into trouble."

"I am sorry, but I haven't heard anything about those at the church. As long as they remain in the church, they will be safe. I hope you aren't blaming yourself for allowing those two to go along. I'm sure you had every good intention of sending them there for their safety, and I know Father Fiset will do everything in his power to keep them safe and protected. They might be helpful to the rest of the group because of their intuitions and abilities."

"Yes, you are right. Basil said he had a 'feeling' that he needed to be there, and for as long as I've known him, I know his priority will be to protect Dillis, as well as the others. Those two are very near and dear to my heart, and I would love to know that they are safe. Now that Eva is gone, I'm leery to send anyone out there. We don't know what Moira will do to disrupt or even kill anyone else. My heart is feeling very broken over Eva right now," he stated while trying to hold back tears.

"I understand. I am very sad too. There must be something we can do. Is the *Scuabtuinne* back here now?" Alby asked.

"Yes, *Enbarr of the Flowing Mane* came back as soon as he dropped everyone off at Father Fiset's church," he replied.

"We would be safe in it, correct?" Alby asked.

"Yes, we would be safe. I was staying here, so that everyone would know where I am and be able to reach me," he told Alby.

"Do you think we should go to the church, pick up the others, and bring them back here? Should we go to the island and collect Eva's body?" Alby asked.

"Yes, I believe we should go. I am far too restless here, not knowing that everyone is safe. I will leave orders to my assistants to keep everyone inside the kingdom until we return."

Just then, the Sea King summoned one of his assistants and explained that they were to watch over the kingdom while he was away. He asked that they gather up everyone into the dining hall so that he could make an announcement before he left. After they were all gathered, he told them about Eva, how he was going to bring the guests back from the church in Cheticamp, and asked the mermaids if they would like for him to bring Eva's body back. They all agreed that her body should return to the Kingdom, but they worried about the safety of the Sea King and Alby's protection, as well. They told him to be careful and only bring the body back if he wouldn't be in any danger.

Alby and the Sea King then boarded the *Scuabtuinne* and headed out toward Cheticamp.

Chapter Twenty-Three
Basil and Dillis

Basil, after pacing back and forth between his cot and the window for most of the night, had been struggling with a feeling of anxiety. He was holding a secret deep within his heart, knowing that he needed to share it but struggling with trying to decide with whom to share it. He knew that Dillis also knew the secret and would never tell...and that she might be upset with him for sharing it. *Should I wake Dillis up and tell her that I am going to tell someone? Who should I tell? Who would be the most likely to help if I told them? The Sea King might never speak to me again for saying this. Gabriel knows, but he isn't here, and I have a horrible feeling that something terrible will happen if I don't tell someone soon.* Basil wrestled like this all night long until right before daybreak when he decided to wake Dillis up.

"Dillis, wake up!" he prompted while softly shaking her big toe.

"I've been awake all night, Basil. I know something is very wrong," she whispered, careful not to disturb any of the others.

She quietly got out of bed and walked with Basil to the door, gently opening it so that they could go into the hallway and talk privately. As soon as they were in the hall, Dillis motioned for Basil to follow her to the end of the hallway to make sure no one would hear them.

"What do you think we should do?" Basil asked. "We need to talk about this and see what our options are. I sure wish Old Sheniah were here. She would know what to do."

"We *know* what to do. We have to tell someone. We just have to determine who to tell," Dillis said, struggling with the idea of telling the secret.

"Out of the ones here, our options are Father Fiset, Niamh, or Brigid. Of course, the Gypsies are here, but they don't have the same direct power of the lineage, nor does Father Fiset," Basil reminded her.

"But Father Fiset *is* a priest, after all," Dillis told him.

"Yes, but he promised Gabriel he would stay here and watch over everyone. He won't break that promise. I think our choice has to be narrowed down to Niamh or Brigid. Brigid has already been through a horrible ordeal, but her powers are stronger than Niamh's. This is such a difficult choice to make," he told her.

"Niamh's powers are all there. She can use them if she needs to. I think she is our best choice because she won't talk us out of anything. Also, her powers are not 'less than' her mother's, it is just that she isn't used to using them," Dillis said.

"I agree. Niamh can use her powers. They are all there, inside her. She *is* of the royal lineage, and I know she will listen to us," Basil said confidently.

"Shhhh! I hear Father Fiset coming. I wonder why he is awake so early. Let's go back to our cots until he leaves; then, we can talk to Niamh," Dillis suggested.

The two quietly walked back down the hallway and were just about to open the door to the room where everyone was staying, when Father Fiset saw them and motioned for them to wait before going back in. He looked tired, as if he hadn't been asleep all night, and had a worried expression on his face.

"Dillis, would you please go in and wake up Niamh? Please bring her to my office, and Basil, come with me, please. I have something very important to share with the three of you."

Dillis quietly crept back into the room, gently shook Niamh's shoulder, and motioned for her to come out into the hallway, while Basil followed Father Fiset upstairs to his office.

"We must be very quiet and not wake the others. Father Fiset wants to see you and me. Basil is already with him, in his office. He said he wants to talk with us about something important," Dillis explained quickly.

Niamh took a quick glance around to check on everyone and then followed Dillis into the hallway. "Do you know what he wants to talk to us about?" she asked.

"I don't know, but when he finishes, Basil and I need to speak with you about something important too."

"Yes, of course. I hope everything is alright. It seems odd that Father Fiset would awaken us before dawn and only wish to speak with the three of us, rather than speaking to all of us. It is just the three of us, right?" she asked.

"I suppose so. Basil and I were in the hallway talking when Father Fiset came along and asked me to wake you and bring you to his office, and he told Basil to come with him."

They hurriedly made their way up the stairs and headed toward the priest's office, where they saw Basil standing outside the door. "Father Fiset said I could wait for you two, as he had to go to the library to get something first. He will be right back," Basil told them.

Father Fiset was back in no time, carrying a heavy leather book that appeared to be quite old. He let the three into his office and sat down behind his desk, thumbing through the ancient book while motioning for them to sit down.

"Ah, there it is," he said while coming upon the portrait of a man who looked similar to the Sea King but younger. He marked the page with a small piece of paper, then closed the book and looked directly into each of their eyes. His eyes were sad, tired, and concerned.

"Niamh, thank you for coming. Basil and Dillis, thank you as well. I know that you must be wondering why I would want to see only the three of you, and this early morning or late hour, however you choose to look at it. However, I have some critical things to discuss with the three of you. The Sea King has sent a message to me that he will be arriving here in a little while. He is on the *Scuabtuinne* and first has to stop off at an island. I will come right out and say it. Eva, the beautiful mermaid and friend of the Sea King, has been killed by Moira and her dragons. Her body has been moved to a cave where it is being guarded until the Sea King can retrieve it and take it back to his kingdom."

The three sitting across from Father Fiset could hardly believe what they were hearing and their eyes became wide with concern, while their hearts filled with sorrow.

"I'm so sorry to be the bearer of this news, and I know that each of you knows the pain the Sea King must be feeling right now. Alby, the white seal, is with the King and, of course, so is Fintan, *Enbarr of the Flowing Mane*. Now, I must go on and share the rest with you. Please be prepared to hear what I have to say, as it may shock you, but I must tell you because we will need to come together and make some important decisions. I will speak plainly. The Elders of Iona are in danger and need our help. Moira has taken Faolan to a cave where he is being held captive, along with Ocean Marie. The dragon's cave where they are being held is guarded by werewolves. Gabriel and Donal are there, trying to rescue them," he continued. "Eva helped Donal and Gabriel get to the cave through an underwater passageway, then left on her own to inform the Sea King. Before killing Eva, Moira sent one of her dragons to snatch Faolan away from his post and, disguised as Faolan, convinced the Elders to turn over her daughter, Deliah. It was after this that Moira and her dragons snatched Eva from the sea and dropped her onto sharp rocks where she died instantly."

"What can we do? Shall I tell my parents?" Niamh asked the priest.

"I have been praying about this, and I think it is better if we don't tell them yet. I know that your mother would want to leave the church and try to help. She has been through so much in the past two years, and it would be better for her to stay here with Liam and the Gypsies, where she can get rested. I think that the three of us can talk and come up with another plan to help. Also, your

179

father does not have the royal lineage. He would insist on going with her and wouldn't be able to operate with the same magical powers that she would. This might present a problem."

Basil and Dillis looked at each other, wondering if this was an appropriate time to share their secret, when Father Fiset noticed their expressions and asked them if something was going on. They both shook their heads a little and put their focus back on the priest. It is so hard to tell a secret, especially a secret that you have sworn NEVER to share, regardless of circumstances. Now here they were, struggling, knowing that by sharing the secret they might be able to save some lives.

"What is your suggestion, Father?" Niamh asked.

Father Fiset was wrestling with a secret of his own and apparently struggling, not knowing whether to share the secret and what the consequences would be if he didn't share it.

Basil, who had been sitting the whole time quietly, recognized the pained expression in Father Fiset's eyes and realized that they were all, other than Niamh, holding the same secret. *I can't stand seeing him suffer like this any longer. He knows! Dillis, tune into my thoughts! Father Fiset knows the secret! He will suffer within himself if he tells it. I am going to speak up!*

Dillis heard his thoughts and gave him a quiet nod but rather than having anyone else suffer, she decided to share it herself. "Father, before you say anything else, I have something that needs to be spoken. I have had a secret that I have been holding in for a long time and struggled with whether or not to speak it. By speaking it, I am breaking a sacred oath, yet by speaking it, we may be able to save some people."

"Dillis, before you continue, let me just tell you this; if your 'secret' is something that can save even one life, it is important that you share it. I cannot guarantee that the person who told you the secret would not be upset with you, but it is a risk you may have to take when lives are at stake," the priest told her sincerely.

"Then, can I please tell you privately?" Dillis asked.

"Yes, of course. Niamh, will you and Basil please wait out in the sitting room next to my office for a moment?"

Basil spoke up, "Dillis, I will tell him. You wait with Niamh." He didn't want Dillis to have it on her conscience and wanted to protect her.

"So, you know the same secret Dillis wants to share?" Father Fiset asked.

"Yes, it is one and the same," he told her.

Dillis kept shaking her head at Basil in an attempt to protect him from having it on his conscience. Telling someone's secret is no light matter.

Father Fiset made a quick decision and decided to send Dillis into the hallway with Niamh to listen to Basil, much against Dillis's protests.

"Alright, Basil, if you are ready to tell me the secret, then go ahead. I have been keeping a secret myself that I would like to talk to you about."

"But you can't tell a secret, you are a priest. I believe that we are keeping the same secret, and I will tell it. Once it is out in the open, perhaps no one else will have to decide to break a sacred oath. The 'secret' is that the Sea King has a son. He has been gone for a very long time. Not even Brigid or Niamh know about him. He is next in line to take over the Sea King's kingdom. The son left, thinking that the Sea King would stay alive forever because if there were no one to turn the Kingdom over to, he would have to stay to take care of it. He never let anyone know where he was, except for Old Sheniah. He told her that if she ever had a *feeling* or sensed that his son might be needed, he should be contacted. Only she knows how to do it and has his permission. Old Sheniah told me, just in case something ever happened to her, and Dillis psyched in the information because she was in the vicinity and picked up on it. The son has all of the powers of the Sea King, and it seems to me that he could help at this time. I feel that the Sea King and Alby, along with the Elders of Iona, are in danger. Moira isn't going to let the Sea King take Eva's body and will try to use it as a bargaining chip, perhaps to try to make an exchange for someone else, like Liam. The Sea King doesn't even know where his son is."

"Basil. Thank you for telling me. I did, in fact, know of the son. I had his photograph here in this book and struggled with the decision whether to tell anyone about him. I promised the Sea King I wouldn't ever tell anyone about him. He was very hurt that his son left and never knew the reason why. I was not aware that anyone else knew about him and was going to break confidence today and ask if you three would help me find him. I also *feel* things and believe that the Sea King and the Elders of Iona are in danger. Do you know how to get in touch with Old Sheniah?"

"Yes, Dillis and I know how to contact her together. I'm pretty sure she will help us find the Sea King's son. Dillis and I were discussing it this morning when you saw us in the hallway. We decided to talk to Niamh about it, since she is of the royal lineage and he would be related to her. We decided NOT to talk to Brigid because she has just been through such an ordeal and probably needs rest, although she is well aware of her powers, whereas Niamh is not used to hers yet. It is a hard call to make. We also thought that if we told Brigid, Liam would insist on helping, and since he is the object of Moira's desire, it would not be safe for him to leave the church," Basil told him.

"That is right, and that is the same process I have been going through, with the same reasoning. The message I received this morning, saying that the Sea King was going to pick up Eva's body and then come here, also said that he sent a messenger to the Elders to let them know what was going on. I feel that whatever messenger he sent will also be in grave danger. Let's call Niamh and Dillis to come back in and tell them what is going on; then, we need for you and Dillis to get in touch with Old Sheniah," the priest explained. "Please, let her know that it is important that we find the King's son immediately and request his help."

Niamh and Dillis came back in and sat down, waiting for Father Fiset to explain what was going on, while Basil told Dillis in his mind, '*I was right. He knows.*' They all sat quietly while the priest explained the situation to Niamh, who handled it very well. She was anxious to help in any way she could yet was not entirely sure about using her powers. After a short discussion, Basil and Dillis excused themselves to contact Old Sheniah, while Niamh and Father Fiset continued to work out the details of a plan. Father Fiset opened the ancient book that was sitting on his desk and showed Niamh a photo of the Sea King's son.

"This is Mannan Maclear, or commonly called Maclear, the Son of the Sea. He has been gone a very long time, to keep the Sea King alive. He is your relative, Niamh."

Old Sheniah agreed to contact the Sea King's son immediately and assured Basil and Dillis that Maclear would help. Old Sheniah offered her services, as well, and agreed to come to Paroisse Saint-Pierre, saying that she had sensed that was where she would be needed the most. Basil and Dillis were anxious to see her and hoped she would arrive soon. In the meantime, Father Fiset and Niamh continued to discuss a plan.

Chapter Twenty-Four
Son of the Sea

Maclear was outside in his garden when the white raven appeared; always a sign from Old Sheniah, letting him know that she would be visiting him. He wondered what was in store, as she didn't visit frequently, respecting his secrecy and privacy. He had known Sheniah his entire life and trusted her beyond measure. He had been living on one of the remote Scottish islands, Vatersay, in Bagh Bhatasaigh, to remain secluded. The only person who knew who he was, and his whereabouts, was Old Sheniah. The few islanders of Vatersay knew him to be a quiet, hard-working farmer who kept to himself but was always ready to help someone in need. Vatersay afforded him the opportunity to not only remain hidden from most of society but also to stay close to the sea, which he loved so dearly. Here, he could contemplate life and rest in the confidence of knowing that he had saved his father's life by leaving.

He missed his life in the Sea Kingdom but couldn't imagine what life would be like if his father passed away. By moving, he felt that he could forever prolong his death, yet moving came with a big price. He was lonely, longing not only for the Sea Kingdom but also his father and friends, and he could not marry unless he was back in the Sea Kingdom. In appearance, he was a young image of his father: muscular, with strong, chiseled features; long, thick, curly hair the color of autumn wheat; thick, dark eyebrows; and eyes the turquoise color of the Atlantic. His skin was naturally golden-brown, and his mustache and beard, other than in color, were a replica of his father's. Old Sheniah knew that all she had to do was ask Maclear and he would be willing to help, but at the same time, she worried that he would struggle inwardly since she knew the reasons why he left the Sea Kingdom in the first place. In character, he held the same traits his father held sacred, maintaining honesty, and intelligence. Spiritually, Maclear carried his lineage's gifts within himself yet used them sparingly. He was always happy to see Old Sheniah, as they had always been very close, and she was the only one who knew where he was and visited him.

She arrived carrying a bundle that contained food and herbs, brought from her home in Ireland, and following closely behind were none other than Basil and Dillis, who had spirit-traveled from the church to Old Sheniah's home to journey with her, each carrying a leather bundle. The white raven preceding their arrival stayed close by them in a nearby tree, observing, guarding over their every move and keeping an eye on the surroundings, knowing that Moira and her dragons could appear at any time. Old Sheniah knew that time was ticking, and they needed to act quickly, but she also realized that the subject had to be approached peacefully and carefully. *This might take an hour, an hour we may not have, but better to handle this request carefully now than carelessly and recklessly, where it might be denied,* she thought.

After they all greeted each other warmly, Maclear picked up Dillis and carried her, while leading them back to his humble home. After setting Dillis down, he offered them drinks as Basil and Dillis prepared the food they had brought from Ireland. Basil and Dillis loved visiting Maclear and enjoyed being in Vatersay, yet were serious, knowing the gravity of the situation that was about to be discussed. Old Sheniah walked slowly around the room, looking at the objects on the shelves and waiting for the right time to begin the serious discussion.

After the meal was laid out on the handmade wooden table, and they were all sitting down, Old Sheniah blessed the food and motioned for them all to begin eating. All the while, she prepared the words she would need to speak in order to convince Maclear to leave Vatersay and help not only his father, but also the Elders of Iona. She knew that she could convince him but didn't want to upset him in the process. She was on shaky ground when dealing with issues about the Sea Kingdom, as Maclear had some amount of guilt from leaving and tended to shut down emotionally when the subject was addressed. She did, however, know that he loved his father and would want to help him. Once the Sea King knew that his son was still alive, he would expect him to come home and want him never to leave the Sea Kingdom again, so that was yet another issue that would have to be handled carefully.

While Old Sheniah was quickly sorting through her thoughts about the various ways she might approach the subject, Basil, who had been restlessly sitting at the table and picking at his food, couldn't wait any longer and blurted out the facts quickly.

"Your father, the Sea King, is in danger, and so are the Elders of Iona, and Eva has been murdered, and everyone needs your help!"

Old Sheniah and Dillis passed a fleeting glance at one another with wide eyes and then turned their focus to Maclear, who was staring at Basil, looking rather sideswiped. He was speechless for a moment and dropped his fork onto the plate. For a quick moment of silence, he held his head in his hands and then quickly looked up at Basil, then Old Sheniah, who was casting a rebuking glance at Basil.

"Maclear, all that Basil says is true. You are needed, desperately needed. Your father is in the *Scuabtuinne* with Alby, the white seal, on his way to fetch Eva's body then pick up the Gypsies and the others, including Niamh and her parents, at the church in Cheticamp. Alby was with Eva when she was taken and made his way to the Sea Kingdom to give the sad news to your father. The Elders are at Solomon's Tower at the Slieve Mish. There are several at Bald Mountain, at Lake Ainslie on Cape Breton Island, who are being held captive. Donal O'Brien and Gabriel are there trying to rescue them from a dragon cave that is being guarded by werewolves. Eva was on her way back from leading Donal and Gabriel, each separately, to Lake Ainslie through the underground tunnel, when Moira and the dragons snatched her away and smashed her poor body on the rocks, killing her. Father Fiset felt that you should be sent for, as did Basil and Dillis. They have told Niamh about you. Please don't be upset. I'm sure you realize why this was necessary."

Maclear, at first, was a little upset that his secret had been exposed, but he quickly put his personal issues aside and focused on the grave situation at hand. Seeing several places where he was needed, he tried to determine which place he would be the most useful and the order in which to proceed. His first concern was for the safety of Old Sheniah, Dillis, and Basil, but his heart was broken to hear that Eva had been murdered. She was a dear, close friend, who he had always cared for.

"You three have risked your lives to come here," he said thoughtfully.

"Our lives would mean nothing if we lose anyone else. Losing Eva was horrible, not only for us but the Sea King as well, and for the Sea Kingdom," Dillis explained.

They all looked lovingly at sweet little Dillis and agreed. They all decided that their lives would be meaningless if they couldn't help the others.

"So where would you like to begin?" asked Basil boldly. "We don't have time to waste right now and need a fast plan."

"Well, Basil, I agree that we need a fast plan, and I think the first thing we should do is get you, Dillis, and Sheniah back to the church where you will be safe."

"We don't have time for all that right now," Basil told him confidently. "We need to get out there and save people. Should we go to Bald Mountain and get Gabriel to help us?"

"No, it would take too much time to climb the mountain, and you know that Gabriel can handle anything that is put in front of him. I have confidence that he will do what is needed. Right now, we need to make sure my father is safe. That, in my judgment, is the first course of action. I will go back with you three to the church, where you can watch over the others there, and I will go on my own to help my father. Let me just grab a few things here, and let's leave quickly! You can fill me in on the details on the way to the church. Do you know where Eva's body is?" he asked them.

"Not exactly," said Old Sheniah, "but we can send one of the whales to find out quickly."

Old Sheniah wasn't any happier than Basil about Maclear's decision to bring them back to the church first but decided to go along with it, for now. "Basil, we must listen to him," she said quietly, although Basil thought he saw her wink. Old Sheniah, Maclear, Basil, and Dillis headed off quickly to the church in Cheticamp with determination in their hearts that there would be no more casualties and everyone involved would be saved.

"Does Father Fiset know that you and Dillis came here?" Maclear asked.

"He doesn't know we aren't at the church," Basil said slyly.

"Did you two leave of your own accord, or did Father Fiset send you to fetch me?" he asked in another way, trying to find out the facts.

"He told us that we were to contact Old Sheniah to let her know to get you to help," Dillis admitted.

"So rather than staying in the safety and protection of the church, you took it upon yourselves to go to Old Sheniah in person and travel here with her?" he asked.

This was the first Old Sheniah had heard of exactly how the two came to get her, previously assuming that Father Fiset had sent them to her.

"We wanted to help and had that *feeling* that we should go in person," offered Dillis.

"I know that both of you realize that you could have just as easily contacted Old Sheniah telepathically, without leaving the church. Does my father know that you two have come here to get me?" he asked Dillis, since she gave the most direct answers.

"The Sea King believes that we are at the church with Father Fiset, and Father Fiset believes we are at the church too," she explained, "but we didn't want Old Sheniah to come here alone, and we wanted to be of help. Once we got to Old Sheniah's, she said we could come here with her."

"And Niamh is at the church?" he asked hopefully.

"Yes, when we left, she was there with her parents and the Gypsies and, of course, Father Fiset. She wants to help!"

"She is now aware of who she is, Maclear, and she is anxious to meet you and help wherever she is needed," Old Sheniah told him.

Chapter Twenty-Five
Rescues

By now, Alby and the Sea King had reached the small island where Eva's body was being guarded. Just as they were about to disembark the *Scuabtuinne*, dark, ominous clouds filled the sky and the Sea King knew this was a sign that Moira and at least one of her dragons were near. Alby took one look at the King and knew they had to change their plan quickly. Without a moment's hesitation, they quickly drove the *Scuabtuinne* to the other side of the island and on into the open waters heading toward Paroisse Saint-Pierre. As long as they were in the ship, Moira would be unable to attack, but had they gotten out and carried the body back, they might have snatched Eva's body away from them, never to be returned.

In the meantime, Maclear, Old Sheniah, Basil, and Dillis were heading for the church, hoping to leave Dillis and Basil in a safe place while the other two went on to help the King. Basil and Dillis were not happy about being dropped off but went along with it, for the time being, hoping to devise a plan to go on with Maclear and Old Sheniah, rather than be left behind. Being quite young and innocent, they believed they were immortal, which added to their bravery. They believed they needed to be of service to the Sea King, regardless of the danger to themselves, and felt that it would be better for all involved if they would be allowed to continue along with them, rather than go back to the church. It just didn't feel right to them that, just because they were little, their gifts should be disregarded. They knew that big people always liked to love and protect little ones, whether it be little people or little animals, but they felt so big that it was hard to see the reasons they had to be taken back to the church. Each of them felt confident that their services would be needed, so now they had to ensure they would be included in the journey, and hiding might be their only option.

The group that was at the church prayed earnestly for everyone's safety, while Father Fiset stayed in deep meditation, listening carefully for guidance. He realized that fate and destiny always had the final say, but this didn't hinder him from using his faith to trust for the best outcome for all involved. Being a priest for as long as he had, he realized that miracles were only a thought away, faith could move mountains, and focusing on the good would yield positive results. He had little in the way of material possessions yet had enough faith to fill a kingdom. He knew that his faith, along with the prayers of those at the church, would make a difference in the outcome, and he held fast to that belief.

The Elders of Iona climbed the long, winding stairs to the top of Solomon's Tower to gain a clear vision, spiritual as well as physical, along with guidance on what their next steps might be. They all agreed that they were to stay where they were until they received a message. Each contained the gift of sight and could see visions of whatever they chose to focus on. At this time, they saw Eva's body in the cave, guarded by seals, selkies, and mermaids, with Moira on her black dragon hovering overhead, screaming her banshee wails. They saw their beloved Sea King traveling with Alby, the white seal toward the church at Cheticamp; and they saw all those who were on Bald Mountain, in Cape Breton, waiting for the perfect time to escape. The final vision they had was something very shocking. They saw Basil, Dillis, and Old Sheniah, along with Maclear, heading toward the church. The shock of seeing Maclear caused all of them to look at one another in bewilderment. Knowing that the Sea King was also headed there and that they would arrive at approximately the same time caused them to realize that the time had come for reconciliation, and although a little vexed at this new vision, they felt very thankful that the Sea King's son had returned. They also knew that now that Maclear is back, if he took over the Kingdom and didn't leave again, there was a chance the Sea King would go to his watery grave and be no more, which saddened their hearts.

"I see the plan now," Artair spoke solemnly to the group, "Basil and Dillis have left the church and contacted Old Sheniah, then traveled with her to go to Maclear to convince him to come away from Vatersay and help the Sea King rescue the others. They are going to the church, first, to drop off Dillis and Basil, but they don't know that the Sea King is on his way there. The Sea King was unable to rescue Eva's body and is heading to the church, first. Those on Bald Mountain are making a plan of escape and waiting for the right timing to implement their plan. Those in the church are in prayer and meditation. Moira is hovering over the island with her black dragon and has caused dark clouds to surround the area."

"Yes, Son, this is what I know to be true as well," spoke Connall the Ancient. "Gabriel is with those on Bald Mountain and will lead them out, yet not without a fight with Moira and the dragons and the werewolves. Everything is in place for rescue, and on a brighter note, Moira can't be everywhere at once. I also see Dillis and Basil devising a plan to hide to continue with the others in their rescue attempts. Those two little ones are a powerful force to be reckoned with. When they get something into their hearts to help others, there seems to be no stopping them. They are young enough to maintain their courage and bravery, regardless of the consequences."

"I know that Moira would be more inclined to keep Gabriel from joining forces with the Sea King, so I believe she will head in that direction to try to get him in some way," said Conchobar, the Elder of Norse heritage.

"Yes, I believe you are right, Conchobar. Anytime Gabriel has worked with the Sea King, the battle was theirs for the taking. Moira knows their history and would keep this in mind. We must use our power of thought-travel to get this message to someone in the group, so that when they head out, they will go to Cheticamp first," suggested Connall the Ancient.

"I agree," said Artair, "we can focus this message on them."

As all the Elders began focusing, Dillis started to quietly meditate, feeling that she was about to receive an important message. Basil was still thinking about a way to get Old Sheniah and Maclear to allow them to stay on the mission and didn't notice that Dillis had gone deep into meditation. She had slowed her breathing down and cleared her mind, stilling every cell of her body, to receive the message.

Moira will not want Gabriel to join forces with the Sea King because that would ensure the battle would go in their favor. She will go there first. She will be on her way soon. Head to the island and pick up Eva's body while there is time.

Basil was the first to notice Dillis and nudged Old Sheniah to pay attention. She, in turn, alerted Maclear.

"She has a message," said Basil, very seriously.

"Yes, I see that she does," said Maclear.

"Dillis, dear, what is your message?" asked Old Sheniah.

"I received a message from the Elders of Iona. They said to go and pick up Eva's body. Moira is heading to Bald Mountain to stop Gabriel, so we have time to get her body and bring it back to the church."

"Then that is what we must do, but what about Gabriel?" Old Sheniah asked.

"Call upon the Sea Turtle to bring the message to the Sea King to go to Lake Ainslie," she told them. "May I?" she asked.

"Yes, of course, but wouldn't it be better if you stayed in your meditative state and let Basil call Sea Turtle?" Maclear asked.

"No, actually, I think you should do it instead," she said, looking straight into Maclear's eyes. She realized that he needed to reconnect to his heritage in preparation for taking his rightful position in his kingdom.

He looked at her as if he was going to say no, but then quickly faced the sea and called for Sea Turtle. The Sea Turtle is known throughout the

Kingdom to receive messages and deliver them quickly. When the giant Sea Turtle appeared, Maclear spoke, "I ASK YOU TO DELIVER A MESSAGE TO THE SEA KING THAT HE IS TO GO STRAIGHT TO LAKE AINSLIE, RATHER THAN THE CHURCH IN CHETICAMP. GABRIEL WILL NEED HIS ASSISTANCE. LET HIM KNOW THAT MOIRA HAS TARGETED GABRIEL AS HER NEXT VICTIM AS SHE DOES NOT WANT GABRIEL TO JOIN FORCES WITH THE KING. PLEASE LET HIM KNOW THAT BASIL AND DILLIS ARE SAFE. THANK YOU."

The Sea Turtle nodded and quickly took off to find the Sea King and Alby, while Maclear and his group headed to the island, through the thick fog and dark clouds, to rescue Eva's body. The closer they came to the island, the clearer the skies became, telling them that Moira and her dragons had left the area. They quickly met up with one of the selkies, who guided them to the cave where Eva's body was held. They had wrapped the body in a special type of red seaweed, called *agar,* to keep the body from rapid decay.

"Thank you for caring for her body," said Old Sheniah to those standing in attendance. "You have done a great job."

"It is so sad this happened. Do you think you could help bring her to life again, Maclear?" asked one of the mermaids. "I know that you have the power to help her. Please help her live. She is such a beautiful being, and our hearts are beyond sorrowful."

Everyone there, including Basil and Dillis, looked at Maclear to see what he would do. Maclear hadn't used his powers since he left the Kingdom and had nearly forgotten the ways of bringing sea creatures back to life. Without taking back his rightful position in the Sea Kingdom, his ability to resurrect her body wouldn't work. He had some hard decisions to make and knew that he must make them quickly, as time was running out before her body would begin the process of decay. The cave where they kept her was cold and damp, which allowed the *agar* to stay fresh and protect her cells, but once they took her out of the cave, it wouldn't take long before the *agar* would lose its strength.

"Let's bring her to the boat, and I will think about this request," he told them as he picked up the body wrapped in *agar* and carefully hoisted it on to the back of a waiting walrus to carry it to the boat. "We must hurry and get her to the boat. I cannot do anything right now, and first we must get her to the Sea Kingdom."

The walrus slid ahead of the rest of the group on the slippery rocks and waited at the boat while the rest of the party wound their way down the path. Once there, Gabriel picked up the body and gently laid it on the ship, while Basil, Dillis, and Old Sheniah boarded. It was a time of solemn reflection for

Maclear, and a time to realize that his decisions would change the future course of events forever. Old Sheniah wrapped her arms gently around Basil and Dillis, comforting them with love and soothing words of reassurance, while Maclear steered the boat toward the Sea Kingdom.

The Sea King and Alby were just pulling the *Scuabtuinne* into the dock at Cheticamp when the Sea Turtle appeared and gave them the message about Gabriel and how they needed to head off to Lake Ainslie. Hearing that Basil and Dillis were safe gave his heart much peace, and now that they were safe, he could continue forward without having to stop at the church. He could pick the others up after he got Gabriel and those at Bald Mountain into the *Scuabtuinne*. The Sea King didn't know that Maclear was with Old Sheniah, Basil, and Dillis and didn't realize that Eva's body had been retrieved.

Gabriel, Trini, John, Donal, Ocean Marie, and Faolan had devised a plan of escape but didn't know that Moira and her dragons were on their way back to Bald Mountain. Their plan included capturing one of the werewolf children and holding it hostage until they got down the mountain. To get to the young werewolf, whom they had been watching for a couple of hours, they would have to cause a ruckus in the opposite direction, which would cause their caretakers to look away long enough to race out and grab the little one. Gabriel and Faolan were the strongest, so Donal and John were going to catch the small one while Trini kept watch for the elk to give them signs. Her arm that was injured earlier in the day was beginning to turn red and become swollen with infection, so they decided that she should be the one to keep watch. Also, she was the one tuned into the elk's messages.

Each hid in their respective places, waiting for Trini to see the elk and give them the signal to go ahead with the plan. They were all silent and hopeful, knowing that they must move as quickly as possible, once they began. Trini suddenly motioned that the elk was near and for all to take their places. Suddenly, the elk's face appeared, peeking out from behind some pine boughs, and stared directly into her eyes. She felt mixed messages. She was confused about what the elk was showing her but gave the signal to the others, regardless.

Faolan threw a large branch and a rock at the same time in the opposite direction, which caused the caretaker werewolf to look away and go in the direction of the sound. Donal and John quickly jumped out and grabbed the little werewolf, holding on to him as tightly as they could without injuring him, while everyone started racing down the trail, followed by several large werewolves. Gabriel and Faolan stayed in the rear to fight off any of the adult werewolves, while Ocean helped Trini maintain her balance while running.

Within a moment of when they began running, the sky turned dark and they all heard Moira's recognizable banshee scream and saw the shadow of her riding through the skies on her black dragon. Their hearts sank, they could try to run but knew they would be running right in the direction where Moira would be able to see them.

"Keep running," Trini yelled out loudly, suddenly realizing that the message the elk was giving her was the impending danger of Moira's arrival. "Run and don't stop for anything!" The werewolves were following close behind and gaining in speed as they ran down the mountain path, following the group. Trini's arm was throbbing from exertion, and she was beginning to feel faint, but she ran as fast as she could, with Ocean Marie running beside her, helping her keep her balance. From out of the bushes came a loud shriek and a huge werewolf pounced out right in front of Trini. It stood staring into her eyes for a second, then ran past her toward the young werewolf hostage.

Moira and the black dragon flew maliciously overhead. As long as Gabriel and the others stayed close to the trees, the dragon couldn't get at them, though, and Moira would have to wait until they came into the clearing to grab Gabriel. The adult werewolf was now facing off with Donal and John, both had a tight grasp on the little werewolf. He wasn't allowing them to go any further but hadn't attacked yet. The other beasts were in the back, grabbing at Gabriel and Faolan. Gabriel reached down for a fallen branch and began fighting them off, while Faolan grabbed some rocks and began throwing at their heads.

The whole group was now in dire straits, with Moira hovering overhead on the black dragon and werewolves in the rear fighting, while the one in front looked ready to attack the two men to get the young werewolf back. The elk was watching from behind the trees. Suddenly, when it looked like all was lost, Maclear appeared out of nowhere. "Grab this line, Faolan," he yelled as he tossed one end of a rope toward him. Faolan quickly grabbed the rope and held it tightly while Maclear promptly circled the werewolves at the rear, rounding them into a circle tied tight by the rope, then quickly knotted it and ran to the front of the line, followed by Gabriel and Faolan.

"John, you and Ocean get Trini out of here," yelled Gabriel, which resulted in Donal being the only one holding the little werewolf. Gabriel quickly ran to help Donal, while John grabbed Trini and headed down toward the beginning of the trail. They had to pass into a clearing where Moira might have seized them, but Gabriel knew that he was the target and yelled for John to run with the women till they reached John and Trini's house.

Maclear, Gabriel, Faolan, and Donal were now facing the werewolf at the front. She was of a ferocious nature and would just as quickly kill and eat them as look at them, at this point. She would do whatever it took to get the baby werewolf back. Gabriel watched as the elk came out from behind the tree, distracting the werewolf long enough for them to make a run for it, but they still had to get past Moira.

"Take off your shirt, quickly," said Maclear to Gabriel as he started taking his shirt off while running. "Here, put this one on," he said as he threw him his shirt. "Moira can't see much from up there, and we have the same hair so she will think it is you in the clearing." He knew that Moira would capture him but let him go as soon as she found out it wasn't Gabriel. She didn't know Maclear and didn't know what a valuable capture he would be. This would give the others enough time to get to Trini and John's house.

"Okay, release the young werewolf...now!" he yelled as they were just reaching the clearing, and both men had the other's shirt on. Donal released the young one, and the adult went to it instantly, rather than following the group. "Run to the house, quickly, while I deal with Moira," Maclear said just as Moira's black dragon swooped down and picked him up with its sharp talons.

Trini, John, and Ocean had already made it safely to the house, and Trini and Ocean watched out the front window while John ran to the medicine cabinet for antiseptic for Trini's wound.

"John, hurry!" she yelled as she saw who she thought to be Gabriel snatched into the sky, being held by the dragon's talons. "It's Gabriel and he's been captured by Moira and the black dragon," she said as John rushed downstairs to her. He quickly looked out the window and saw three men running toward the house. "Let them in," he yelled while he went to the pantry for his gun, thinking he might shoot the dragon out of the sky.

Ocean opened the door and watched while they raced toward the house. She felt confused when she realized that Gabriel was dressed differently and was running with Donal and Faolan. She suddenly realized that the man who had appeared to help them had changed shirts with Gabriel.

"Hey there," yelled Maclear to Moira. "What are you capturing me for and letting Gabriel get away?"

At that, Moira looked down and realized she had captured the wrong man. She was so frustrated that she ordered the dragon to lower Maclear to the ground and let him go. Moira got off the dragon and stomped around the grounds, yelling and swearing, then picked up a stick and started beating the black dragon, calling him a stupid idiot and moron, unfit to live. While she continued her rampage, Maclear took advantage of the opportunity and ran to the house with the others as quickly as he could run. By the time Moira realized he was gone, she assumed it was too late to find him. She had no idea that they were all right across the street, hiding safely in Trini and John's house.

"Let me get something for you to drink," said John to the rest of the group while wrapping Trini's arm.

"No, we are going to have to get going. We will cut through those woods in the back of your house to the lake. We have to get to the Sea Kingdom," said Maclear, knowing there wasn't much time before Eva's body would decompose. "I'm Mannan Maclear, by the way. You are welcome to come with us. It might not be a bad idea since we know that Moira is in the vicinity."

"The son of the Sea King," Trini said in wonder.

"Yes, the Sea King is my father," he responded.

Trini and John didn't waste a second accepting the offer to go to the Sea Kingdom. It was a dream come true, something they thought only existed in legends and tales. "Of course, we would love to come with you, but is it possible? Will we be able to breathe there?" she asked.

"Yes, you will be able to breathe and will find it to be quite comfortable, but we must hurry. I have something essential that needs to be taken care of. Moira has murdered one of the mermaids, Eva, of the royal lineage of mermaids. We have just rescued her body from a cave where the seals, selkies, and mermaids have been watching over to protect it from Moira. I must return her body to the Kingdom as soon as I possibly can," Maclear told them.

John finished wrapping Trini's arm, and they all hurried out through the back door, carefully following an overgrown pathway through the trees to Lake Ainslie, where they found Old Sheniah, Basil, and Dillis waiting under some fir trees to keep from being seen by Moira. They were catching their breath after moving Eva's body to the *Scuabtuinne*, which was nearby under a low-hanging tree, which created a shadow on the water, keeping them out of sight.

"I'm Old Sheniah, and this is Basil and Dillis," Sheniah introduced them while extending her hand in friendship as they boarded the *Scuabtuinne*. "And this is Alby," she introduced the ancient white seal, and then finally, walking them toward the helm, said, "And this is the Sea King."

"I'm Trini, and this is my husband, John," she told them, "I feel like we've already met," she told Dillis and Basil while remembering her very vivid dream that she had on the plane on her first trip to Ireland, after her mother passed away. Suddenly, she remembered the whole dream, in detail. She remembered the sacred book with the golden glow and the messages Dillis had taught them outside, in the beautiful summer morning after she and John had been chased by the owl from the library in Dublin. *When any lesson or time comes up in your life, whether it is a hard lesson or a natural one, staying peaceful is the most important thing you can ever do.*

"My son," said the Sea King, tearfully, as he embraced Maclear. "My son, my son. How I have longed to see you again." Maclear and his father, after a warm and tearful embrace, set to the task at hand. They needed to get to Cheticamp, pick up the others, and then get Eva's body back to the kingdom.

Chapter Twenty-Six
Another Rescue

The Sea King and his son, Maclear, were finally together and content. Knowing that they could work together once again gave them both peace in their minds and hearts. The *Scuabtuinne,* guided by *Enbarr of the Flowing Mane,* traveled quickly through the underwater passageway from Lake Ainslie to Cheticamp and pulled into the marine dock. Gabriel said the magic words in Gaelic that halted the water long enough for the *Scuabtuinne* to enter the underwater port. Then, once inside, he lit a torch and they all walked quickly on the boardwalk to the basement of Paroisse Saint-Pierre and up the stairs to meet with the others. After many very quick but warm introductions and embraces, and a huge welcome from Ocean Marie's family, they hurriedly grabbed their things to leave the church. Father Fiset was offered the opportunity to come with them, yet he regretfully declined, saying that he had pressing matters to attend to. After everyone thanked the priest for his kindness and hospitality, they headed to the *Scuabtuinne* for another voyage to the Sea Kingdom. All left but one, Roger, who had been talking with the priest throughout his visit and had decided he wanted to stay on in the parish; perhaps at some point he might have the opportunity to become a priest himself, like Father Fiset. He had no family he would want to become part of again, after all.

The Clearys, the O'Briens, Gabriel, Faolan, Old Sheniah, Basil, Dillis, The Sea King, and his son, Maclear, all left for their voyage, racing against time to get Eva's body back to the Kingdom and restore her to life. Then, some would need to go and rescue the Elders of Iona. The *Scuabtuinne,* led by *Enbarr of the Flowing Mane,* practically flew through the water, moving so quickly that the beautiful crystalline waters and lush plant and sea life were a blur. As soon as the *Scuabtuinne* landed on the crystalline landing pad, everyone embarked, followed by Faolan and Gabriel, carrying the *agar*-wrapped body of precious Eva. The Sea King told his attendants to prepare the healing room, and have the *Scuabtuinne* ready for a small group to leave again, shortly.

"Son, you know that by bringing Eva back to life again, you would have to commit to staying on and taking your place within the kingdom?" the Sea King asked Maclear hopefully.

"I don't want you to die, Father. That is why I left. If I take over the kingdom, then you will die," Maclear said sorrowfully. "That is why Old Sheniah, my mother, left as well. Father, neither of us are capable of ruling this Kingdom with the compassion and love that you have shown in all these years. We aren't YOU. There is something so unique, special, and fair about you. You are always fair to everyone. I can't possibly walk in your shoes, and my mother feels the same way. If you can find a way to live and not die and allow us all to be together, then I can agree to this. Is there any way? Could it be possible? You seem to have an extra dose of wisdom and something special that neither my mother nor I possess."

"Son, there is a way. I only wish you and your mother would have talked to me before leaving the way you did, without a word. I realize now that you wanted to save me, and knowing this helps me overcome the pain of loss I experienced when you left. I feel healed from the sorrow and anguish, and my fondest wish would be to reunite with my wife and my son. You are home now, Son, and we can all be together if your mother agrees, but first, we have to restore Eva's life, if there is still time."

"Father, does Niamh know of her lineage and her powers? Is she aware that we are of the Tuatha de Danann, and possess special gifts? I saw that she has her scepter with her. She could help me to restore Eva, if she would. I think it will take the energy of few—myself, Brigid, and Niamh—if they agree. Had we been able to get back here sooner, I am sure I could have done this on my own, but after so much time has passed, I feel that any help I could get would be beneficial."

"Yes, she is aware but hasn't used her powers, yet. I will call her and Brigid now, and I must send someone to rescue the Elders. The *Scuabtuinne* should be ready to leave again shortly. I was hoping to send Niamh with Gabriel, Faolan, and Ocean Marie, but if you need her here, then I will ask her to stay. As you mentioned, she has the golden scepter, and we will need that for the process."

He then called for his attendants to bring Ocean Marie, Faolan, and Gabriel to his office and bring Brigid and Niamh to the healing room. He hurriedly spoke to Gabriel and told him to take the other two with him in the *Scuabtuinne* to Solomon's Tower and quickly asked Niamh and Brigid if they would assist Maclear. Everyone readily agreed, without hesitation, to the Sea King's requests, grateful for the opportunity to help the others in any way possible. He then requested that his attendants make everyone else comfortable and have the chefs prepare meals for everyone. He told them that he would be staying in his office for the time being, in quiet meditation. Suddenly, Basil and Dillis appeared, tapping quietly at his office door.

"Yes?" the Sea King asked them both, already knowing what they were going to ask.

"We want to go with them on the *Scuabtuinne*, may we please?" Dillis asked respectfully.

"Are you going to tell me you feel a NEED to go?" the Sea King asked.

"Not exactly, but we would like to go, and we could help them," Basil replied.

"Well, I'm afraid I'm going to have to say No to both of you, this time. I feel that you should both stay right here, in this office, with me, until the *Scuabtuinne* leaves. Just in case you two have devised any of your plans. So, sit right over there, on the couch, and when my attendant lets me know that the *Scuabtuinne* has left, you can go and join the others in the banquet hall."

"But, but we want to go with them. We can help them," Basil complained.

"You can be more helpful to me, right here. I sense a need for you two to be in my sights right now. Not having to worry about you two will give me peace. Do you understand, Dillis? Basil?"

Having said it like that, Basil and Dillis had no choice other than to accept his wishes and stay in his office until the ship left.

"Then can we help in the healing room?" Dillis asked sweetly.

"No, the door has been closed and cannot be opened until their work is done."

"Then what CAN we do to help?" Basil asked the kind old Sea King.

"I have a significant job for you both. Once everyone is back here, and we are all safe together in the banquet hall, I would like to have music and food for everyone. Dillis, I know you play the harp beautifully and sing. Basil, I know you love to sing as well. Would you two please prepare a song to honor our guests, and hopefully, to celebrate that Eva has been returned to life? That would mean everything to me, to hear you two sing together, and I'm sure it would be a big blessing to all of our guests. What do you think?"

The two, Basil and Dillis, looked a little disappointed at first because they had their hearts set on a big adventure on the *Scuabtuinne*, yet quickly determined that singing a blessing and thanksgiving song would be needed and also fun, so they agreed.

Just then, an attendant came in and told the Sea King that the ship was underway and they had closed the portal behind it.

"Please bring Dillis and Basil to the music room, so that they might practice. They will be blessing us with a song when everyone returns. Please show her the harp, and tell the music mistress, Madame Friset, that Dillis has my permission to use the royal harp, and that Basil will be practicing with her."

"Thank you," said the Sea King to Basil and Dillis.

"Can we please go on the next trip?" Dillis asked.

"I'm not sure if you can go on the next trip or not. That would depend entirely on what the next trip is. Now that Old Sheniah is here, depending on what her answer is when I ask her to stay, you may be living here permanently," he confided with a twinkle in his eyes.

They both looked at each other and smiled. They loved the Sea Kingdom above all places and thought they would love to live there.

"We have a lot of room here, so there will be invitations to other guests to live here permanently, as well. But, that is a secret I will ask you to keep, for now. We will have answers to those questions in due time," he told them. "Now, run along and practice your song. I am excited to hear it."

Chapter Twenty-Seven
The Healing Room

The healing room was at the far edge of the castle, far from any noise that might come from the banquet hall. There was a golden symbol embedded in the ancient wooden door; the same one that was on the leather satchel that showed up with Fintan, embroidered on Niamh's cloak, and on Solomon's Tower. It was similar to the one in the stained-glass window in Paraoisse St. Pierre, as well. It was also the symbol on the scepter that was given to Niamh. It was the symbol of the Tuatha de Danann, and the royal lineage. When the door opened, a sweet aroma of roses and balsam fir filled the senses.

Inside, hanging from the ceiling, there was a golden salmon, a symbol permanently linked to Maclear since ancient times, when Maclear had sealed a partnership with the salmon, promising to keep the Celtic culture and tradition alive. Within this partnership, the salmon became an ally to Maclear and promised to help to preserve the ancient truths; in exchange, Maclear awarded the salmon eternal life. If Maclear ever went back on his promise, the salmon would get all of Maclear's magic, which included all of his knowledge. This way, the magic of the Celts would be forever kept alive.

Under the salmon, there was a spring of water that came from one end of the room, went through the room, and came out an opening leading to the outside of the castle. It was contained by large labradorite stones, which were highly polished from the constant water flowing over them. The stones were known to impart strength to the chakras, raise consciousness, and increase intuitive abilities, and they changed color, depending on which angle they were viewed from. They might look deep violet, indigo, green, or golden, depending on where you were standing.

The room was softly lit with a warm, golden-yellow glow, and fresh breezes blew softly through the windows. There was a tall rectangular table made of very smooth wood, and on one table laid the body of Eva, now fully unwrapped from the red *agar* used to protect her body. Maclear, Brigid, and Niamh stood over her with their hands resting on her head, abdomen, and feet. They were very still, and when they spoke, it was in the Gaelic language. They looked entirely focused, concentrating on their hands resting on Eva's body. Whenever they spoke, a soft green light would emanate from Eva's body, softly at first and then stronger, seeming to light up parts of her body with the pale-green glow. This room was a sacred space, a place where solitude was expected and miracles occurred.

Although all three had hopes and anticipation of success, you wouldn't have known it by looking into their faces, which held a peaceful yet focused appearance. Niamh looked as if she had done this work all of her life. She didn't appear to be untrained in the least, but instead focused and confident. She pulled the Gaelic words from deep within her being and spoke them with authority. The Gaelic words were not spoken to each other, but to some distant world that held Eva's soul until it could be returned to her perfectly still body, which had not deteriorated at all—thanks to the wisdom and knowledge of the selkies who had wrapped it instantly. As soon as the soft green light began emanating from Eva, from her head to the tip of her tailfin, although faint, the three spoke in a more firm way and spoke more words, this time in unison.

"I'm going to use the elixir now," Brigid spoke quietly in Gaelic as she poured a few drops from the tiny amber glass vial she had been holding into the corner of Eva's mouth. As soon as she had opened the vial, a soft lavender-pink mist traveled from the vial and began swirling about the room, over Eva, until it formed the shape of an ancient angel that hovered over Eva, its soft pastel-white wings outstretched and its hands facing downward toward Eva's body.

Where each of Eva's chakras were within her body, on the outside, soft circles of color began pulsating and rotating clockwise until they were all rotating at the same speed, and the colors gained in intensity to match each other. Each of those present increased their focus as they saw light radiating from the angel's hands and into Eva's body. As this occurred, the soft green light became brighter and brighter, until her closed eyelids began to flutter gently and her fingertips began to stretch. Her body, which had been cold to the touch, began to feel warmer, meaning that her heart was pumping blood again, yet ever so faintly. Her head began to move a little, and her tailfin began to flutter gently. The chakra colors; red, orange, yellow, green, blue, purple, and white were twirling lights hovering only inches from Eva's body. Finally, when all the colors were 'settled,' they seemed to enter back into her body, and the ancient angel held both hands up toward the ceiling as if its work was finished.

Suddenly, her beautiful eyes opened, and she smiled softly, sweetly. *Welcome back to this world, beautiful Eva.*

Chapter Twenty-Eight
Return to Solomon's Tower

Ocean Marie, Faolan, and Gabriel arrived without incidence at the island where the Elders of Iona were in session at the top of Solomon's Tower. Although the Elders were well aware that they were being rescued, they had received inner guidance to stay in the tower until further notice and not travel to the beach to be picked up by their rescue party. Not knowing when or if Moira and her dragons would strike again kept everyone in a state of constant vigilance. Ocean was the first to disembark the *Scuabtuinne,* and the two men followed her onto the beach. Gabriel quickly told *Enbarr of the Flowing Mane* that if he saw or smelled any trouble, to lower the ship and stay underwater until they got back with the Elders.

The three quickly headed toward the well-hidden trail, careful to stay as quiet as possible, while the Elders, sensing their arrival, made their last-minute preparations to leave. After making their way to the tower, they climbed the long winding stairway to the top, where the Elders of Iona were waiting and ready. After warm hugs and greetings, they were about ready to descend and return to the *Scuabtuinne* when a white raven suddenly appeared on the worn gray stone of the western window ledge, causing the party to stop and pay attention to the western horizon. What seemed to be a small black dot on the horizon, upon closer inspection, was Moira and her black dragon, flying directly toward them.

"We need to get to the cave, quickly," said Gabriel while ushering everyone down the stairs as fast as possible and onto the back trail leading to the cave.

"What about *Enbarr* and the *Scuabtuinne?*" asked Artair. "Moira's dragon will surely need to quench its thirst and go to the water."

"I've instructed *Enbarr* to stay vigilant, and if he hears, smells, or sees anything, to lower the *Scuabtuinne* into the water. He will stay hidden. We can only hope that Moira will come here, think we have left, and head out. I don't believe she knows about the cave, and even if she does, she won't be able to enter it."

Just as the last of the party entered the cave, they heard Moira's screeching banshee call and loud flapping of the black dragon's wings as it lowered itself onto the ground next to Solomon's Tower. "Go and get your water, you old idiot, and I will go up the tower and get those fools. Hurry up, then get back here," she spoke cruelly to the dragon and headed up the stairs to the top of the tower.

"I know you fools are hiding in here somewhere. Come out so I can kill you, you know you can't hide from me for long. I'm all-powerful, and there is no place you can run, no place you can hide. I will find you idiots and kill you after I torture you!" she growled while climbing the stairs, and looking around each corner. "If you think I don't know you are here, hiding, you are dead wrong!" She was convinced that they were hiding in the stairwell, and even more convinced that she could destroy them on her own. Her plan, thinking they were in the stairwell, was to force them out into the open and call her dragon to help her mutilate then kill them, once and for all.

Moira had been awake for two nights, not eating or drinking, but designing her plan to kill off everyone who was in the way of her marrying Liam. She was tired and thirsty, but running on adrenaline, knowing in her mind that she was close to her goal. When she got to the top of the tower and didn't find her prey, she looked out of all four window openings. Not seeing anything, she sat down on the floor, hoping to rest for a moment. *This floor is warm. They were here, and not too long ago. They can't fool me.* Sitting on the floor, deep in thought, she happened to see something white fly past the east window. Then suddenly, she saw something white flutter past the west window opening. She decided to get up and look out to see what it was, and just as she did, the white raven flew up quietly behind her, out of view, and left a small package wrapped in a 'kerchief. As the white raven dropped the package, the 'kerchief opened, revealing a small bottle of what appeared to be wine and a piece of bread and cheese. The white raven then silently flew out of sight.

Moira, tired, thirsty, and hungry, couldn't see the source of the white fluttering, nor could she see any sign of the people she hoped to torture and murder, so decided to sit back down for a moment before descending the long winding steps out of the tower. It didn't take her very long before she saw the small present the white raven had left for her, and upon finding it, thought it was accidentally forgotten and left by the Elders. *Ah, see how all my needs are met! Those fools went without their food and drink. Look at this,* she thought to herself, *a bottle of wine, and a small meal. Those stupid idiots can't even remember to take their drink and food with them.* Moira quickly uncorked the bottle of 'wine' as she quickly stuffed large pieces of bread and cheese into her mouth. She was so thirsty that she hurriedly gulped down most of what was in the bottle.

In the meantime, Gabriel, Faolan, Ocean Marie, and the Elders of Iona were waiting patiently for inner guidance on their next steps, yet hoping that they wouldn't have to wait long, as they were very anxious to get to the Sea Kingdom to confer with the Sea King. Faolan was the first to receive guidance. "I'm going to go out and do some reconnaissance and find out where the dragon is. We may be able to make a run for it if the dragon is drinking on the other side of the island."

"That won't be necessary," said Ocean Marie. "We are free to leave now."

The Elders looked at her in disbelief, as if she, being a woman, would tell them what they could do. *If anyone was going to receive a message, why wouldn't it have been them?* they thought. *How might she, a mere Gypsy woman, know when it is time for US to leave? This is insulting...*

Gabriel and Faolan were not so quick to judge, as Gabriel knew she had special abilities and was of a royal Gypsy lineage and Faolan believed her because he had been overseeing her. The Elders, being of the traditional and bygone form of thinking, would eventually see that, although a woman, her powers were strong. "Yes, we can leave now," said Gabriel.

The Elders listened to Gabriel because he was a man. Gabriel was merely following guidance from Ocean Marie. Faolan looked at the expressions on the Elders' faces and wanted to smile, but chose not to, out of respect, and instead helped them pick up their backpacks and took some of their burden unto himself. Gabriel decided to head out first, with the Elders following him, then Ocean and Faolan, in the lead of the others. He knew Ocean well enough to know that she would not have spoken so boldly had she not received a clear message.

"Ocean," asked Faolan quietly as he walked next to her, "would you mind telling me what message you heard, letting you know that it was time to leave?" She looked at him, reading his eyes to see if he was merely curious or was doubting her. When she was satisfied that his question was simply out of curiosity and saw the respect and admiration radiating from his heart, she answered, "There was no message!"

Still trusting her, yet wondering what she could mean, he waited patiently for her next response. "I used some old Gypsy magic on Moira and the dragon. When we disembarked the *Scuabtuinne,* I left a bundle behind that old sycamore tree that we passed. Do you remember when the white raven showed up at the top of the tower when we were up there? I asked him telepathically to retrieve the bundle as soon as he knew that Moira was in the tower and leave it on the floor for her. On the ship, I poured some potion into the wine. I also threw some of the potions into the watering hole that was right next to the beach, hoping the dragon would choose that place to drink from. When we were in the cave, I heard the raven call and knew that Moira drank the potion, the dragon had used that particular watering hole, and both would be asleep for a long time."

Faolan was so impressed that his respect grew even stronger for Ocean until he felt his whole heart warm. "I hope you don't mind if I say that you are one special person," he said as he reached out for her hand to help her down a slippery rock. She looked up into his eyes and knew that he would be an eternal part of her life, in a big way. He felt like family to her, and she hoped they would become friends.

Once the Elders were safe aboard the *Scuabtuinne,* with *Enbarr of the Flowing Mane* guiding the ship, Gabriel quietly went to Ocean and thanked her, apologizing for the lack of belief and judgment coming from the Elders. "Please don't worry about that, Gabriel. It is just the way they are. I know that they don't mean anything personal against me. Their judgment is just because I'm not a man. Someday, they will see and know that we are all people. They are very wise, and I respect them immensely. I don't see any reason why we cannot work together. I wasn't trying to show them up, or cause them to feel inadequate, but was just trying to help. My parents taught me that, no matter who judges me for my gifts, not to take it personally or allow it to upset me. The important thing is that we are all safe, and now we can get to the Sea Kingdom, which I'm sure will make the Elders happy."

"Yes, I'm quite sure of that, and I am very thankful that you used the foresight that you did because it saved us all a lot of the aggravation that might have, and probably would have, occurred, had you not thought to leave that bundle. How long will Moira and the dragon be asleep?" he asked.

Ocean Marie smiled mischievously, and said, "Depending on how much of the potion she drank, anywhere from forty-eight hours to seventy-two hours. The dragon will probably be awake in a couple of hours and hopefully will fly off without her. The potion that he drank should help to ward off her control of him. Dragons are usually very nice and helpful. They only misbehave if they are being controlled, you know. I'm sure that black dragon, being the leader of the other dragons, will be able to help the others stay hidden from Moira. I'm not sure what will become of her on that island, without a way to get off."

"I'm sure she will figure out something, in due time. She won't be able to get into the cave, where there is plenty of food and water stored, so she will have to be very creative to survive," Gabriel told her. "I wonder what became of her daughter, Deliah. The last time anyone saw her was when Moira rescued her and they took off on the green dragon."

"I had a dream," Ocean told him, "she was in a cave with the green dragon, with the other dragon outside. I believe her mother planned on keeping her there for a bit, until she could get back to her. The dragons won't hurt her, and at least she is out of the way, for the time being. I'm sure she is concerned about her mother and wondering when she will be back to get her, but she is safe, for now."

"Do you know where the cave is?" Faolan asked.

"It seems to be on an island off the coast of Scotland. It may be Vatersay?" she told them. "But I am unsure. I'm not familiar with that area."

"Not to change the subject, Ocean, but do you know where you and your family will be going after this?" Gabriel asked.

"No, I'm not sure. Father said that we would know when the time came. We are travelers, you know. We stay wherever we are welcome, and leave when we receive guidance to go. It has always been our lifestyle. I just hope it is near the ocean! I couldn't imagine not living near the ocean. The ocean has my whole heart and soul. The Sea King is the luckiest of all, being able to live right in the ocean! I can hardly imagine any life better than this," Ocean said lovingly as the *Scuabtuinne* entered through the gates of the Sea Kingdom and landed on the crystalline landing space outside the castle.

Chapter Twenty-Nine
Lunar Eclipse

The moon and the sea are forever linked together. For the Sea King and his subjects, the lunar eclipse was a special occasion, one to be celebrated; a time of reflection on one's own life, and a time for new beginnings. On this night, the Sea Kingdom would have an overflowing of blessings to commemorate, not only the lunar eclipse but also Eva's restoration, along with the thwarting of Moira's evil schemes. Each of the guests was dressed in their most elegant clothing for this joyous occasion and held deep appreciation and excitement in their hearts and minds.

The giant Pacific octopuses stood up, proud and strong, holding their shiny abalone serving trays filled with sumptuous fare, fit for a Sea King and his guests, while guests continued to be seated. Everyone in the banquet hall was in good spirits, happy once again after hearing about Eva's restoration. The hall was decorated magnificently with vibrant green gossamer curtains and pale to deep aqua tablecloths, each having a silver border. Each place setting had an abalone shell dinner plate with pearl-handled silverware and hand-carved quartz crystal goblets for drinks. The centerpieces were highly polished larimar crystals surrounding pearlescent-white candles, all lit for this special occasion.

The crystal-clear river flowing through the hall toward the mermaid table was lit up with white floating candles and pink peonies floating on the top, while the waterfall was sparkling brightly, reflecting light from the many surrounding candles. The stage was decorated with every shade of aqua, green, and orchid, set off by uniquely designed silver candelabras holding large pearlescent-white candles, giving the stage a softly lit etheric ambiance, much to the Sea King's liking and taste. Beautifully colored blown and stained glass chandeliers hung over each table; each formed into the shape of a unique sea creature. Although the kingdom was underwater, the air was dry and very comfortable, giving little impression that this setting was under the sea.

After each guest was comfortably seated and given a sparkling beverage, a hush fell across the room as the Sea King entered the stage in front of the gossamer curtains. As he entered, one could hear slight scuffling in back of the curtains as Basil and Dillis, helped by Madame Friset, set up their music stands in preparation for their performance.

As the Sea King stood in front of his guests, Madame Friset left the stage as Dillis and Basil began their performance, playing the harp softly and singing quietly as a backdrop to the Sea King's announcement.

"My beloved friends and family, I am standing here today in front of all that I hold dear to my heart. All that I have dreamed of for many years has now finally come to pass. My long-awaited and greatest wishes have been fulfilled, and my deepest prayers have been answered. My family has now returned, and we are reunited. The restoration of my beautiful and dear friend Eva has brought great joy to my heart, in the place of the enormous pain and suffering I endured from her accident. As you all know, this time of the great lunar eclipse, which is sacred to us and our underwater kingdom, is now upon us. Great and intense change is upon us as we enter into this holy time."

As he continued his speech, the wispy gossamer curtains were pulled back to reveal Dillis playing the royal harp and Basil standing nearby, both sweetly singing *Dreams of Connemara* in Irish Gaelic. The guests were mesmerized by their angelic voices and the melodious notes emanating from the royal harp, as well as by the expressions on their dear little faces.

"Please enjoy your meal. I will be making some important announcements later in the evening." The Sea King gave a small wave and seated himself next to Old Sheniah, while the giant Pacific octopuses quickly brought everyone their first course, consisting of cream of pumpkin soup, spiced with nutmeg and cinnamon—a soup reserved for special occasions such as this.

Everyone enjoyed the beautiful meal and great conversations while they eagerly awaited the announcements soon to be made by the Sea King. Basil and Dillis, being the youngest of the guests, were so excited that they could barely eat, hoping and praying that Old Sheniah would agree to move back to the Sea Kingdom so they would be able to live there permanently.

"Dillis, aren't you going to eat more than two bites?" Basil asked her.

"I just can't eat yet. I'm too excited to know the news!" she told him quietly.

"Look at the Elders of Iona, eating without a care in the world. They must have been pretty hungry," he added.

"Let's go and talk to them after we eat," Dillis said.

"Yes, but first let's talk with Eva. I am so happy to see her alive and well," Basil said as he looked over lovingly at Eva, who waved to him when she saw him look her way.

"Do you think Old Sheniah will stay?" Dillis asked Basil, seriously.

"Yes, I think she will, but you just never know. She loves our house and loves being on the outside, helping everyone. We will just have to wait and see. The Sea King might announce it tonight. I hope he does because I don't think

I could stand to wait any longer. Our whole future rides on her decision, Dillis. And the Sea King wants her to stay, and I couldn't bear to see him be unhappy again."

"We have to remember to use the Golden Glows, Basil. Remember that if we stay positive, we will draw positive outcomes."

"Yes, Golden Glows number three, staying positive draws positive outcomes. I will put that in my thoughts right now!"

"Come on, let's wander around, and see everyone before the Sea King gets back on stage," Basil suggested as he grabbed for Dillis's hand to help her down from her seat.

The two little ones walked to each table, greeting everyone, exchanging pleasantries, until they got to Eva's table, where she sat with the other mermaids. When the mermaids saw them coming, they scooted in closer together to make room for the Dillis and Basil to sit with them.

"Basil, Dillis, how are you doing, my two small loves?" Eva asked.

"We are good," they both said in unison. "We wanted to tell you that we are so happy that you are back and sorry that you had such an awful accident," Dillis said lovingly.

"Well, thank you both. The Sea King told me how both of you wanted to be part of the healing team that restored me. Is that right?" she asked.

"Yes, we both did want to, but they had already closed the door and were not allowed to open it, once the process began," Basil explained.

"I have an important question to ask you," Dillis said as she looked straight into Eva's beautiful eyes. "Do you like living here or being on the outside more?"

After thinking for a moment, she told them that she liked living in the Sea Kingdom the best but felt good when she could go outside and help others.

"That's an excellent answer," Dillis told her.

"I'm wondering, Dillis, why do you ask?" Eva questioned.

"Well, I'm just curious, that's all. I love living at our house with Old Sheniah but think it must be so incredibly amazing to live here, in the Sea Kingdom," she told Eva.

"Where would you choose, if you had a choice?" one of the other mermaids asked Dillis.

"I would live here if everyone I loved could be here too!" she said without reservation.

"I would love for you both to live here with us. Your music is such a blessing. We all enjoyed it very much. It is so different than the music we are used to hearing. Did you write it?" Eva asked.

"Yes, Dillis and I wrote it together at Old Sheniah's house. We always write music together. We don't know how actually to write it down, though, so Old Sheniah does that part," Basil explained.

"I would love to learn how to write music and sing the way you both do. Maybe sometime you could teach me to sing like that?" Eva asked.

"Yes, if we have time before we have to go back, we would be happy to," Basil told her.

Eva smiled as she hugged them both and told them to hurry along if they were going to have time to talk with the Elders of Iona before the Sea King returned to the stage.

"Aren't they such beautiful souls?" one of the other mermaids asked the others.

"Oh, yes, I do hope they get to stay here permanently," Eva told them. She already knew the answer, from when she had her meeting with the Sea King, but he had sworn her to secrecy.

Basil and Dillis made their way across the vast banquet hall to the table where the Elders were just finishing their meal and greeted them warmly. The Elders were charming to the two little ones and told them they appreciated hearing their beautiful music. They each shook hands with Basil and Dillis and smiled warmly.

"Basil, look, the Sea King is going back to the stage. We should go and take our seats now," Dillis told him as she tugged on his arm, practically dragging him back to their seats at the table where their plates were still quite full of food.

"Let's eat fast," Basil told her as he grabbed some cheese and four strawberries and shoved them in his mouth all at once.

"Okay," Dillis said as she hurriedly poured honey on a roll and took a large bite. Both sat quietly with their mouths chomping away, trying to get a few bites in before the waiters removed their plates.

"Look!" Basil pointed to the stage, showing Dillis that several other people were lining up on the sides of the stage. "I know most of them, but who is that blond lady?"

"I have never seen her before. Where did she come from?" Dillis asked.

Just as Dillis asked, the blond woman was introduced as the guest speaker of the night, Miss Halley Torrington.

Chapter Thirty
Blessings

"I would like to thank the Sea King for bringing me here to his beautiful Sea Kingdom and thank you all for the opportunity to be your guest speaker for this evening's great lunar eclipse celebration. These are undoubtedly magical times that we are living in, and times of great blessings. Some of you know me, but most of you don't. I am a professor of botany and environmental science at the University of Wales. I have known John and Trini for a very long time and consider them to be dear friends."

"It has recently been brought to my attention by Greenpeace that the Irish Sea is the most radioactively contaminated sea in the entire world, due to eight million liters of nuclear waste being discharged into it daily from reprocessing plants—contaminating seawater, sediments, and marine life. I realize that here, in the Sea Kingdom, there is no pollution, but outside of here, the sea life is in dire condition. I am here to ask each of you for your help, that you focus your positive energy on this situation, for it to be resolved, and I'm also here to talk with you about the third lesson of the Golden Glows."

"In your sacred book, the Golden Glows, the third and most compelling teaching is that positive thinking attracts positive results. I can see that many of you have used these sacred lessons to attract the goodness that you hoped for, and in so doing, have resolved long-standing issues, as well as attained short-term goals. I have used the principles found in the Golden Glows and found them to be remarkably efficient, not only for accomplishing goals but also for peace of mind and general well-being. My overall health has improved, including my vision, since I began practicing the knowledge found within these teachings. It is truly fascinating how negative thoughts can create illnesses, while positive thoughts can create wellness."

"This brings me back to the pollution in our seas; not only in the Irish Sea but in all others, as well. By teaching the mindful practices found within the Golden Glows, I genuinely believe that together we can turn this dire situation around to the point where our oceans are no longer polluted. At the very least, we can stop polluting the waters any further. By all of us joining in agreement that negative feelings and the lack of regard for the oceans will cease and only good and positive feelings and thoughts will abide, we will still have time to save many of the species that are endangered."

"I know that many of you have worked tirelessly for the betterment of our planet, including our oceans and air. Many of you have cared for the sick whales and sea life that are affected by pollution and the entanglements of fishing nets. Many of you have studied endlessly to find answers to the world's problems, and that tells me that you have a heart that cares about others. This is why I am here tonight, to ask each of you to join me in a quest to clean up our polluted waters and to focus all your positive thoughts on creating positive change."

"Thank you again for this opportunity, and now, I will turn this stage over to the Sea King."

The Sea King could be seen wiping some tears from his cheeks as he walked back up the few stairs to the stage and thanked Halley for her informative talk.

"Let's have a round of applause for our new friend, Halley Torrington," he said to the guests as he shook her hand and led her to her seat.

"What a beautiful speech, Halley. Thank you for honoring us with your presence, and I'm sure that everyone here will agree to focus positive energy on the situation you spoke of. And now, I have a few significant announcements I would like to make. We will be adding some new residents to our Sea Kingdom."

Basil and Dillis held each other's hands so tightly that they nearly cut off circulation as they waited for the Sea King to make the announcements, in hopes that they would be included in his plan. They could barely breathe, as they were so excited.

"First of all, I am delighted to announce the engagement of Analine Cleary's daughter, Ocean Marie, to our beloved Donal O'Brien. I have invited them to stay on in the Sea Kingdom for as long as they like. I have also extended the invitation to Ocean Marie's family to live here."

As he made the announcement, he motioned for Ocean Marie and Donal to come to the stage and stand with him. He embraced each of them warmly as the guests clapped their hands in joy. Basil and Dillis were entirely thrilled by the news, but still held on to each other tightly, hoping that the Sea King would mention their names. After the applause died down, the Sea King continued, "Second, I'd like to announce that the entire family of Liam O'Brien will be moving here permanently."

The crowd was cheering so loudly that Basil and Dillis had to hold their ears. Everyone couldn't have been more thrilled to hear this news.

"Next, I have also invited Trini and John to live here, but they, unfortunately, have declined my offer and would prefer to stay on Cape

Breton Island. This way, they can help Halley and Greenpeace. I would like for them to know that they are always welcome to visit, whenever they want."

There was a low rumble of disappointment from the guests after hearing that announcement, as they were hoping that Trini and John would stay. Everyone knew that Trini and John would fit in nicely in their community, as they were like-minded and had similar goals.

"And now, for the last announcement, my wife Sheniah and my son Maclear have decided to move back here permanently and help me run the Sea Kingdom as a family. Basil and Dillis, will you please come up to the stage? I would like to ask each of you if you would be willing to live here in the Sea Kingdom with us. Basil, what do you think? Dillis, how would you like to live here permanently?"

Basil and Dillis, who had been standing on either side of the Sea King, grabbed hold of each other and started jumping up and down, saying, "Yes, yes...we will do it...yes!!!" Their eyes filled with tears and their hearts filled up with love as they realized how blessed they were to have this amazing opportunity and live with the people they loved so much. Of course, they would miss their cozy cottage where they lived with Old Sheniah, but change is good and they welcomed the new opportunity to have many more friends and experiences.

There was so much joy in the room that night that the walls could hardly contain the light that emanated from so much pleasure. The Sea King's life was now complete, having his entire family together for the first time. Basil and Dillis were happier than they had ever been in their whole lives and felt very proud that they were part of a fantastic underwater kingdom.

All the inhabitants of the Sea Kingdom were focused and determined to help to save the oceans from pollution, and all of them decided to focus all their efforts and energy on practicing the Golden Glows.

Gabriel was thrilled that he would be able to spend more time with the lovely Niamh and had grand hopes for an eventual future with her.